GIANT SPECIAL EDITION!
TWICE THE ACTION AND ADVENTURE ON AMERICA'S UNTAMED FRONTIER—IN ONE BIG VOLUME!

DEATH STRIKE

Nate spun to confront an enormous Blackfoot bearing down on him like a berserk buffalo bull. The brave swung his tomahawk at Nate's face. Ducking, Nate pointed his fintlock and fired.

Struck in his left shoulder, the Blackfoot jerked with the impact. Spurting blood like a fountain, he grimaced, but otherwise ignored the wound. Nothing would stop him from sending the hated white man into the spirit realm.

Crimson drops sprinkled Nate's cheeks and chin as he lunged to one side and tried to stab the Blackfoot in the ribs. Even though wounded, the brave was able to dodge nimbly out of harm's way. For a heartbeat they faced one another, the Blackfoot crouched, ready to strike.

Growling like an animal, the Blackfoot sprang forward, his tomahawk aimed straight for Nate's head....

The *Wilderness* Series Published by *Leisure Books:*

#1: KING OF THE MOUNTAIN
#2: LURE OF THE WILD
#3: SAVAGE RENDEZVOUS
#4: BLOOD FURY
#5: TOMAHAWK REVENGE
#6: BLACK POWDER JUSTICE
#7: VENGEANCE TRAIL
#8: DEATH HUNT
#9: MOUNTAIN DEVIL

WILDERNESS

HAWKEN FURY

David Thompson

LEISURE BOOKS NEW YORK CITY

Dedicated to
Judy, Joshua, and Shane,
and the memory of Albert Lawrence Robbins—
a boy never had a better father.

A LEISURE BOOK®

June 1992

Published by

Dorchester Publishing Co., Inc.
276 Fifth Avenue
New York, NY 10001

Printed in the United States of America.

HAWKEN FURY

Chapter One

The bear was near.

Nathaniel King halted at the base of the towering mountain and tilted his head back to survey the dense forest above. A big man who was broad of shoulder and narrow of hip, he wore the typical attire of those hardy breed of men who lived in the remote Rockies in the year 1836: buckskins. Moccasins covered his feet, while crowning his mane of long, dark hair was a buffalo-skin cap. Slanted across his muscular chest were a powder horn and a bullet pouch, both used when loading the powerful Hawken rifle clutched firmly in his brawny right hand. A butcher knife hung from a beaded sheath on his left hip, and wedged under his wide leather belt above his right hip was a tomahawk. Tucked under that same belt, one on either side of the big buckle, were two matching flintlock pistols.

Nate's green eyes turned to the ground at his feet and he studied the clear tracks left in the soil by the black bear he had spent the better part of the morning tracking. Only last night the bear had paid his cabin its third visit in as many days, badly frightening his horses. Worse, the bear had torn down a buck he had hung up to bleed the day before, and managed to rip off a haunch before Nate roused from a heavy sleep and rushed out to confront it. But in the dark the bear had fled before a shot could be fired.

Now Nate hefted his Hawken and started up the slope. He wished he had brought his dog, Samson, a brute of a canine able to hold its own against any wild animal in the mountains, but he'd left Samson at the cabin because he felt his wife and seven-year-old son were safer with the dog around.

It was rare that a black bear gave him any trouble. Quite often he had to contend with prowling grizzlies, marauding wolverines, or packs of hungry wolves. Black bears, though, were more timid than grizzlies and by and large left humans alone.

From the size of the tracks Nate knew he was after a large male, one weighing upwards of five hundred pounds. Since he'd never seen its spoor in the vicinity of his cabin before, he surmised the bear had recently moved into the area and established itself in a convenient cave or cavity in a large tree. All he had to do was find the lair and he wouldn't have to worry about any more nocturnal visits from this particular bruin.

The tracks skirted thickets and trees in a meandering course that gradually climbed higher and higher. As with most bears, this one had been following its nose to whatever interested it, which most of the time happened to be rotting logs it tore apart to get at beetles, crickets, and grubs. Standing trees also drew its interest; the bear peeled off the outer bark to get at the sweet layer underneath.

Nate knew the beast had not been in any great hurry. Obviously, it did not expect to be pursued. With luck, he would find it sleeping and dispatch the nuisance with a single shot to the head. While black bears were not as ferocious as grizzlies, they would fight when cornered and their teeth and claws could easily slice a man to ribbons in no time flat.

He heard the flapping of wings and paused to watch a pair of ink black ravens soar overhead. They regarded him with curiosity, then swerved and swooped out over the valley below, their twin shadows flowing over the terrain beneath. If they kept going the way they were, in another five miles they would fly over his cabin.

Ahead appeared a clearing. Nate slowed and examined the tracks. They angled to the right and he did the same. Minutes later he reached a section of the slope where massive boulders dotted the earth, and the tracks led into the very heart of the monoliths.

Frowning, he pressed on, holding the rifle close to his chest. The press of the boulders didn't allow much room for movement, and should the bear burst on him suddenly he must be ready to employ the gun instantly.

For over 50 yards he wended deeper into the maze. At times the boulders were so closely spaced that his shoulders brushed on each side and he marveled that the bear had squeezed through. Animals never ceased to amaze him. They were routinely capable of feats he would have considered improbable if not impossible. Mountain sheep could traverse sheer cliffs with ease. Panthers could cover 24 feet at a bound. Grizzlies could scoop out a hole in the earth large enough to contain a man in the span of seconds as they burrowed for rodents.

Nate walked into a circular gap ten feet in diameter and stopped to scan the boulders in front of him. No sooner had he done so than a harsh growl arose to his left. A tingle ran down his spine as he spun and leveled the Hawken, his thumb cocking the hammer before he completed the turn.

Barreling out of a space between two vertical slabs of rock was the black bear, a massive bundle of sinew and flesh capable of matching the speed of a galloping horse. Its dark eyes blazed fury and its mouth gaped wide, exposing its tapered teeth.

There was no chance to take deliberate aim. Nate could only point the rifle and fire. The Hawken belched flame and lead and the ball smashed into the black bear's head just above the left eye. But the bear had gained too much momentum to be stopped by the impact. Snarling, it closed.

Nate had a horrific vision of the bear's wide maw, and then the bear slammed into him with the force of a steam engine, catching him on its right shoulder. Teeth bit into his arm and he was lifted bodily from his feet and rammed into a boulder. Jarred to his core, Nate felt the breath whoosh out of his lungs and he lost his hold on the rifle.

The bear, snarling louder, drew back and opened wide to bite again.

Dazed though he was, Nate knew he must move or die. He frantically hurled himself to the right and heard the bear's teeth snap shut on empty air. Landing hard on his shoulder, he rolled and scrambled to get away, feeling a damp sensation where the bear had bit him.

He inadvertently bumped into the bottom of another boulder, and wound up flat on his back with the enraged bear padding slowly toward him. His hands closed on the smoothbore single-shot .55-caliber pistols, a matched set he had purchased years ago in St. Louis. Whipping both out, he extended his arms, cocked both hammers, and took hasty aim on the bear's head. It was no more than a yard off when the pistols boomed, the sound of their blasts magnified by the encircling boulders.

One of the balls struck the bear in the right eye. The other caught it in the nostrils. Staggered, the bear halted and tossed its head from side to side as if warding off annoying flies. Blood poured from both wounds. It growled and stepped back, then reared onto its hind legs

Nate dare not try to reload. He let go of the pistols and drew his knife in one hand, the tomahawk in the other. Rising, he sprang in close and buried the tomahawk in the black bear's chest. It swiped at him, its heavy paw striking him on the side of the face and knocking him to the ground.

The world swirled as if in the vortex of a tornado and Nate lay still, stunned and helpless. He heard the bear snort, heard its footsteps, and then something lightly touched the sole of his left foot. Dreading the worst, he braced for the sharp pain of the bear's teeth ripping into him, but nothing happened.

After what seemed to be an eternity but couldn't have been more than 30 seconds, the dizziness abruptly ceased. Nate rose on an elbow and stared at his bestial adversary. The bear's nose was less than an inch from his foot, its lifeblood already forming a puddle. It was dead.

Nate rose unsteadily, a pounding in his ears from the blood rushing in his veins. His limbs trembled slightly and he leaned against a boulder for support. That had been much too close for his liking. If the bear had been a shade quicker it would now be feasting on his entrails.

It often disturbed him how a man could lose his life in a twinkling if he wasn't supremely careful, especially in the vast mountains where beasts and hostile Indians alike conspired to make every day an exercise in self-preservation. A man had to always be alert, had to always be on watch for those little things that frequently meant the difference between continued life and death. A bent twig, a patch of crushed grass, or the smudged mark of a print in the dirt might be all the advance warning a man had that enemies lurked nearby. Thankfully, Nate's years in the Rockies had endowed him with razor-sharp reflexes, or he would long since have become food for worms.

He took a deep breath and straightened. With the bear disposed of, he should get back to his family. First, though, he must tend to the butchering. Since bringing a packhorse into the maze of boulders would be impossible, any meat he wanted to take out must be carried on his shoulders. He set to work skinning the beast, first by rolling it over and then slicing his keen knife into its thin summer coat. After removing the hide he placed it to one side, flat on the ground with the hair underneath. Next he fleeced off the fat, then carved off an estimated 90 pounds of prime meat, which was as much as he could comfortably carry over five rugged miles. He carefully wrapped the meat in the hide.

Before venturing out of the boulder field he took the necessary time to reload all three guns, wedged the pistols under his belt, and cradled the Hawken in the crook of his left arm. Then, with the bundle of meat held at waist height so he could see clearly in all directions, he retraced his path down the mountain.

After the close call he felt invigorated, imbued with an enhanced appreciation of life, a reaction he knew many of his fellow mountaineers likewise experienced after similar situations. Facing the Grim Reaper made a man realize how sweet and precious simply being alive was, and he gazed about him as if viewing creation for the very first time.

Chipmunks scampered on nearby rocks. A squirrel ran from limb to limb in a high tree. Perched on the limb of a pine was a mountain jay. And to the south a solitary eagle soared, seeking prey.

The sky was a striking sea of blue through which floated pillowy clouds. A refreshing breeze from the northwest rustled the leaves and tall grass.

He strode briskly along the valley floor. In the distance, situated past where his cabin was concealed in the trees, lay a large lake, its surface shimmering in the sunlight. He had planned to go fishing that afternoon for their supper, but now juicy bear steaks appealed to him more.

His thoughts strayed to the upcoming Rendezvous and he grinned in anticipation. The annual gathering of mountaineers, both the company men and the free trappers, was the big social event for every white man living west of the mighty Mississippi. According to the word he had received from his aged mentor, Shakespeare McNair, this year the Rendezvous was to be held at the mouth of Horse Creek on the Green River, in the vicinity of Fort Bonneville.

Nate had 312 beaver pelts he was anxious to sell. The money would buy much-needed supplies and finery for the cabin. He hadn't told Winona because he wanted to surprise her, but he'd ordered a pane of glass to be brought in with the supply train. For years they'd covered their window with a leather flap that barely kept out the blistering cold wind in the winter and did little to deter the flies and mosquitoes in the warmer months. The glass pane would be a rare treat, one of the few luxuries they permitted themselves.

When he'd initially arrived in the Rockies, he'd been amazed at how simply the Indians and mountaineers lived. If they ate regularly and had a shelter to protect them from the elements, they were satisfied. How different it was back in the States! Particularly in the East, where the people were so caught up in making as much money as they could and living in fancy homes with servants at their beck and call to handle those chores disdained as menial labor.

In New York City he'd seen all too much of that avarice and the attendant lust for luxury. His own family hadn't been rich by any means, but they'd associated with the powerful and the prominent and circulated in elevated social circles because of his father's business and personal contacts. It was through his father that he'd met the Van Buren family and the woman he had almost married.

It was odd, he reflected, that after so much time had elapsed he still thought of Adeline now and again. Not that he regretted having left her to seek his fortune on the frontier, but he often wondered what had become of her. Surely she had found another man and was happily married, probably with five or six children and a fine mansion in an exclusive section of the city.

In a rush of memories he recalled how his Uncle Zeke had written him from St. Louis, urging him to come west and share in a treasure Zeke had found. He remembered his secretive departure from New York, and the letters he had written his parents and Adeline explaining the reason for his leaving and detailing his promise to return one day a rich man.

In a sense, he owed Adeline a debt of gratitude. It was due to his desire to give her the kind of life to which she had grown accustomed, a life of wealth and ease, that he'd taken Zeke up on the offer. If not for Adeline, he would have stayed in New York and gone to work for her rich father. He never would have met Winona, never known true happiness.

Of course, he reflected wryly, if he had known that Zeke's so-called treasure was actually the gift of untrammeled freedom, he might not have been so eager to set forth into the strange and dangerous realm beyond the borders of civilization. He'd expected to share in a gold strike or become partner in a fur company. Never in his wildest imaginings would he have expected to become a free trapper with an Indian wife.

So he owed Zeke a debt too. A debt he could never repay. Which reminded him. He needed to put fresh flowers on Zeke's grave.

Suddenly he halted and stiffened, anxiety blossoming at the sound that came from the direction of the cabin, a sound that carried far in the clear mountain air.

The sound of a shot.

Chapter Two

He broke from the forest to the south of his cabin and raced around the corral containing his horses, the Hawken leveled for immediate use. Expecting to find his loved ones under attack by Utes or a marauding grizzly, he drew up in surprise on seeing the two visitors, a man and a woman, who stood chatting with his wife near the cabin door.

The grizzled man turned and beamed, his lake-blue eyes and lined features radiating genuine friendliness. Fringed buckskins covered his powerful frame. A brown beaver hat crowned his head of bushy gray hair, while a beard and mustache the same color as his hair adorned his face. Like Nate, he wore a powder horn and an ammunition pouch. On his right hip rested a butcher knife, under his belt a single flintlock.

He held a rifle in the bend of his left elbow.

"Hello there, Nate," the mountain man greeted him, his eyes twinkling. "You look right tuckered out. What have you been doing?"

"Running my fool head off, Shakespeare," Nate responded, lowering the Hawken and advancing. "I thought my family was in trouble."

"Why would you think a thing like that?"

"I heard a shot."

Shakespeare, the perfect picture of innocence, took his rifle in both hands and said, "Why, that must have been me. I shot a big duck for our supper," he said, and nodded at the west shore of the lake 40 feet away. "It never occurred to me that you would come on the run."

Winona took a step forward, her concerned brown eyes roving over Nate's clothes and fixing on the tear in his sleeve. "The bear?" she asked in her precise English.

"He won't bother us ever again," Nate informed her, and inadvertently winced when she reached out and touched the bite.

"It is not deep but you have bled a little," Winona said. She stepped to the doorway, her beaded buckskin dress clinging to her shapely body. "Come in. I will tend your wound."

"Don't tell me you've tangled with another grizzly?" Shakespeare inquired.

"A black bear this time," Nate revealed, motioning for them to precede him. Shakespeare's wife went first, a lovely Flathead woman named Blue Water Woman whose long raven hair was every bit as luxurious as Winona's and whose smooth, oval face might be that of a woman half her age. "Hello, Blue Water Woman," he said.

"Hello, Grizzly Killer," she replied. "It is good to see you again."

Nate let Shakespeare enter, then followed. "The same here. Why the visit, anyway? Did you just happen to be in this neck of the woods and decide to drop by?" he asked. Although Shakespeare was his nearest neighbor and only lived about 25 miles to the north, they often went weeks without seeing one another.

"Nope. I figured we'd head for the Rendezvous together," Shakespeare said. "There's safety in numbers, you know."

Nate nodded, thinking to himself that McNair had never been afraid of anything or anyone in his entire life. Shakespeare's newfound concern for safety had more to do with Blue Water Woman, Winona, and young Zach than his own protection. "Good idea. We can leave tomorrow or the next day if you want."

"There's no rush. We have plenty of time to get there before the supplies from St. Louis arrive."

They took seats around the table while Winona hung a pot of water over the small fire in the stone fireplace. Lying sound asleep on the bed against the south wall was seven-year-old Zach, his thin lips fluttering with every breath.

"Don't tell me your young'un is still taking naps at his age?" Shakespeare said.

"He was up most of the night after the bear paid us a visit," Nate explained. "Now he's catching up on his sleep."

"Too excited to sleep, eh?" Shakespeare said, and chuckled. "I recollect how it is when you're that young, even if I am pushing the century mark myself."

"You are not."

"Maybe I exaggerate," the mountain man admitted impishly, and then launched into a quote from one of the plays written by the English playwright he so admired. "But age, with his stealing steps, hath clawed me in his clutch and hath shipped me into the land, as if I had never been such."

"Meaning what exactly?" Nate inquired.

"Nothing much," Shakespeare said, shrugging. He gazed at the corner where Winona stored their food and kept their cooking utensils. "Say, you wouldn't happen to have any whiskey on hand, would you? The ride here parched my whistle."'

"No, we don't," Nate responded, surprised by the request. He rested his elbows on the table. "I never knew you were much a drinking man."

"I'm not, but a little now and again gets the sluggish blood in my veins flowing properly."

Blue Water Woman's brow creased in contemplation. "You have been doing more drinking lately than in all the years I've known you." She paused. "Too much drinking can put a man in his grave."

Shakespeare snorted. "By my troth, I care not. A man can die but once and we owe God a death."

Nate had never heard his friend speak in such a manner, and it disturbed him. There must be more to the drinking than Shakespeare was letting on, but what could it be? "Well," Nate commented, "there will be ample to drink at the Rendezvous. Half the trappers there spend most of their time drunk."

"My people will be there," Blue Water Woman mentioned. "I look forward to seeing my relatives and friends again."

Nate looked at Winona, who was checking the heat of the water. Her own people, the Shoshones, would also be at the gathering, as would the Bannocks and the Nez Percés and perhaps groups from one or two other tribes. Friendly Indians frequently journeyed hundreds of miles to participate in the ribald revelry and to trade for horses or guns or whatever else they wanted.

"This one promises to be the biggest and best Rendezvous of them all," Shakespeare said. "From what I've heard, the caravan will bring in enough goods to outfit an army."

"Just so they bring enough money to buy our peltries," Nate said.

"Don't worry on that score. Beaver hides are expected to fetch between four and five dollars apiece this year."

Nate whistled in appreciation of the sum, and hastily calculated he would receive between 12 and 15 hundred dollars for his haul, enough to tide his family over for quite a spell. The price the fur companies were willing to pay for prime pelts had gone up the past couple of years, which was a good thing considering there were fewer beaver around. He planned to save most of the proceeds for future use since he had no way of knowing what the next year would bring. The bottom might fall out of the market for all he knew.

"Such high amounts won't be paid forever," Shakespeare remarked as if he could read Nate's thoughts. "Sooner or later these mountains will be trapped out or folks back in the States will stop wearing clothes with beaver fur. All it will take is a change of fashion and every trapper in the mountains, both company men and free, will be looking for a new line of work."

"I hope the trade lasts another ten or twelve years," Nate said.

"If beaver trapping is still a moneymaking proposition in five years, I'll be surprised," Shakespeare said.

Winona interrupted their conversation by bringing a pan of steaming water and a tin containing an herbal mixture to the table and depositing both next to Nate. "Unless you want your arm to become infected, husband, kindly remove your shirt."

Nate glanced at his friend's wife.

"It is all right," Blue Water Woman said. "I am a Flathead, remember? The men and boys in my tribe often went around wearing nothing but breechclouts."

"I know," Nate said, but the idea of undressing in front of another woman, especially the wife of the man who had taught him everything he knew about life in the wilderness, still bothered him.

"Hurry up and get that wound dressed," Shakespeare said. "I left our horses tied to trees and I'd like to put them in your corral for the night."

"I'll gladly help," Nate responded. He stood and swung his chair around, then sat with his back to the table and peeled off his buckskin shirt. His arm ached like the dickens, causing him to wince. The bear's wicked teeth had torn an inch-long gash in his flesh.

Frowning, Winona obtained a cloth and began cleaning the jagged cut. "You must take better care of yourself," she commented.

"I try my best," Nate said, and tried to alleviate her concern by smiling, but she went on frowning as she continued with her doctoring.

"You're not doing too bad compared to all those who have come to the Rockies to live and wound up like poor Yorick," Shakespeare interjected.

"Yorick?"

"From old William S.," Shakespeare explained, and quoted the text he had in mind. "Alas, poor Yorick! I knew him, Horatio. A fellow of infinite jest, of most excellent fancy."

"Oh. That Yorick," Nate said.

"You would do well to broaden your cultural horizons by reading more," Shakespeare stated. "Buying that book on William S. was the best investment I've ever made. I couldn't begin to count the number of hours of enjoyment I've gotten from reading it."

"I'm partial to James Fenimore Cooper," Nate reminded him, thinking of the last book by Cooper he had read. Entitled *The Last of the Mohicans,* it dealt with the further adventures of Cooper's fictional hero Natty Bumpo, woodsman supreme. He wondered if Cooper had written another book since then, and made a mental note to find out should he ever venture to St. Louis again.

"That long-winded cuss can't hold a candle to William S.," Shakespeare said with a tinge of contempt. "William S. knew folks inside out and told all about their lives. Cooper writes about people as if they were puppets and he's the one pulling the strings."

"Your bias is showing," Nate said.

"Have you read *Hamlet*? *Macbeth*? *King Lear*? Read any one of them and you'll see right away that I'm right."

Nate knew better than to dispute the point. The aged mountaineer possessed an almost fanatical devotion to the bard who had given him his nickname, and many was the time the two of them had argued Shakespeare's merits and weaknesses long into the wee hours of a cold winter's night or while out setting a trap line in some distant valley. No matter what he might say, no matter how logically persuasive his arguments, McNair would never accept criticism of William S. "I just thought of something," Nate said to change the topic. "I left almost one hundred pounds of bear meat back up the trail. We'd better fetch it before some critter helps itself to a meal."

"While you are gone Blue Water Woman and I will prepare the meal," Winona offered. She was applying the herbal ointment. "Don't move yet," she directed, and went to a cupboard, from which she took an old blanket. Securing a knife from the counter in the corner, she cut off two wide strips and brought them over to Nate. Working expertly, she tightly bandaged the gash and nodded in satisfaction. "There. If it bleeds again you must let me know."

"I will," Nate promised, and hastily donned his shirt. He tucked the bottom under his belt, rose, and gazed fondly at his son, who slumbered on in blissful repose. How, he mused, could children be such devils when awake yet so angelic when asleep? He walked over, gave Zach a peck on the cheek, and stepped to the door. His Hawken was where he had left it, propped against the wall. In another stride he was outside with the rifle in hand and squinting in the brilliant sunlight.

Shakespeare emerged and stretched. "That sun sure does feel good."

What a strange remark, Nate thought. He spied Shakespeare's animals tied on the north side of the cabin and strolled over to help collect them. There were the two saddle mounts and three pack animals laden with beaver hides and supplies. He waited until they had all the animals stripped and in the corral before he brought up the matter that most interested him at the moment. "What is this about you doing a lot of drinking?"

Shakespeare glanced at the cabin door, then replied in a low tone. "Why don't we go get your bear meat and I'll fill you in on the way."

Nate didn't need to ask to know that McNair didn't want Blue Water Woman to overhear whatever was said. He led the way into the forest, the Hawken in his left hand, and waited until they had gone 20 yards before giving his friend a searching look. "Well?"

Rare worry lined Shakespeare's face and he averted his gaze and sighed. "This old body isn't what it used to be."

"Are you ill?"

"Worse. I'm wearing out."

"Are you kidding me? You're as tough and ornery as they come. You'll last forever."

"I wish," Shakespeare said softly. He walked several yards before speaking again. "Nate, even the best-made buckskin britches and shirts all wear out eventually. They usually fall apart at the seams and can't be stitched because the leather is too weak to hold a knot. The same thing is happening to me."

Nate forced a smile. "Your arms still look attached to me."

"I'm serious, damn you. About six months ago I started having problems, and it's getting worse as time goes on."

His mentor's solemn attitude made Nate realize Shakespeare must be gravely ill. Not once in all the years Nate had known him had Shakespeare ever complained of so much as a cold. The mountain man had never been fazed by the harshest adversity, never been affected by the severest weather. Shakespeare could hike for miles on end burdened with a pack weighing upwards of two hundred pounds; he could ride tirelessly for days through the worst country conceivable; and he could outwrestle and outshoot practically any man in the Rockies, Indian or white. Nate had come to regard Shakespeare as indestructible, and to suddenly have his friend's mortality borne home shocked him. "What are the symptoms?"

he inquired. "Can you be more specific?"

"Specific? Sure I can," Shakespeare said, and placed a hand on Nate's shoulder. "I'll give it to you as straight as I know how." He paused. "I'm dying."

Chapter Three

It can't be! Nate's mind shrieked. He walked for over ten yards without saying a word as he tried to cope with the staggering revelation. His fondness for Shakespeare went beyond simple friendship. In many respects—as a wise mentor, a dependable partner, and a caring companion—Shakespeare was more like a second father than a friend. He would be hard pressed to decide which man meant more to him, Shakespeare or his father.

His relationship with his domineering father, who had always been too busy with work to spend much time with their family, had been strained for years prior to his departure for St. Louis. The two had become virtual strangers. Except for a few polite words at meals and greetings every now and then, they had rarely spoken to one another.

How different things were with Shakespeare. McNair was someone he could talk to about anything. More importantly, Shakespeare accepted him as a man and never attempted to dictate how he should live his life.

"Care to fill me in?" Nate asked at length.

"If you insist," Shakespeare said, "but it galls me to discuss a personal problem with another gent, even if he is the best damn pard I ever had, and that includes your Uncle Zeke. God rest his soul."

A peculiar lump formed in Nate's throat and he coughed lightly.

"Six months or so ago was when it first began," Shakespeare reiterated. "I'd wake up in the morning all stiff in my joints and it would be hard to even lift my arms. And the condition kept getting worse and worse as the weeks passed. I tried everything I could think of. Used Indian medicine, used remedies I'd heard about from many different folks I'd met through the years, and even went off by myself and dug a sweat hole. Sat in it three days running and didn't feel a bit better when I rode back to my cabin."

Nate had seen such sweat holes before. They were frequently resorted to by mountaineers who had spine or muscle complaints and wanted a reliable cure.

The afflicted usually dug a round hole about three or four feet deep and three feet in diameter. Then a fire was made in the middle of the hole and kept blazing until the earth in the hole was hot to the touch. After the fire was extinguished, a seat or log was placed in the hole and the person stripped down as far as was necessary and put a container of water near the seat. The next to last step entailed covering the hole with blankets or heavy hides.

There the afflicted would sit, dashing water on the sides and bottom, while great waves of heat radiated from all sides and caused the sweat to run in rivers. The person stayed under the robes for as long as he could stand it, then emerged and took a dip in a cold stream or spring.

After repeated treatments of alternating hot and cold, most people recovered from their ailments. Few were ever so bothered again. Many trappers swore by sweat holes and would use no other cure.

"I knew I was in trouble when the sweat hole didn't work," Shakespeare was saying. "So I went to talk to a Flathead medicine man who is a good friend of mine and asked his advice. He supplied herbs even I didn't know of and I tried them too."

"No luck?"

"None. Then, one day, a few trappers I know stopped by my cabin. They had a bottle of whiskey along and offered to share a drink. Although I don't make it a habit to drink now like I did in my younger days, I obliged them."

"The whiskey made you feel better?"

Shakespeare nodded. "Damned if it didn't. When I woke up the next morning my body wasn't as sore as it usually became. They'd left the unfinished bottle with me, so that evening I drank more right before I turned in. And guess what? The next morning my joints hardly hurt at all."

"So you've been drinking regularly ever since," Nate said.

"Every night, leastwise. I bought a couple of bottles from old Pete Jaconetty. He always has a case of the stuff stored in his cabin. But now I'm running low and I need more."

"Which you plan to buy at the Rendezvous."

"Exactly," Shakespeare said, and scowled. "One other thing, though. As the weeks have gone by, the whiskey is helping less and less. I don't know why, but I'm starting to ache like the dickens again in the morning, and sometimes in the middle of the day."

They walked in silence for a spell. Nate put himself in Shakespeare's place and felt overwhelming sympathy. It must be extremely frustrating for the aged mountain man to be so impaired. Shakespeare had always been a robust man with boundless energy. This had to be affecting his spirit as much as his body. "Why don't you go to St. Louis and see a doctor there?"

"I thought about it. But to tell you the truth, I've never been fond of doctors of our race. They're always too ready to pour their drugs down your throat or cut into you with their little knives. Give me an Indian medicine man any day. They use natural remedies and they let a man keep his blood."

"What choice do you have? You might die if you don't go."

"Then I die."

"Just like that?"

"We all owe God a death," Shakespeare said, repeating the quote he'd used in the cabin.

"Maybe so, but I never took you for a quitter. If a man is still breathing, he has hope. Until they plant him in the ground and throw dirt on his face he should fight for his life with all the means at his disposal."

"That's easy for you to say. You're still a young man."

"What difference does that make?"

"Sometimes older folks see things differently. Sometimes they just grow tired of living."

"You're being ridiculous."

"Am I? Imagine a woman who has been married for forty or fifty years. Suddenly her husband dies and she's left all alone in this hard world. She lives on a while but the loneliness eats at her soul and she gets to thinking about joining her husband in death. So she walks off into the forest without food or water, picks a spot under a tree, and sits there until she's too weak to go anywhere and she slowly passes away."

"You knew a woman who did that?"

"My mother."

Again they hiked without speaking, Nate disturbed beyond measure. There must be something he could say or do to convince his friend to go to St. Louis.

"She's not the only one I know of," Shakespeare said after a while. "I've known whites and Indians who did the same thing or close to it. One old Sioux brave got so tired of hobbling around camp using a crutch to get by that he simply took off all his weapons and went out across the prairie until he encountered a grizzly bear."

Nate bowed his head. The old warrior must have been incredibly courageous to do such a thing. Could Shakespeare be right? Was he incapable of understanding? After all, he was young and healthy and vibrant with life. He had no true idea of what it must be like to be ill for months or years on end or to have his body betray him by becoming progressively weaker with age. And although there had been times when he had been alone, he'd never experienced the abject loneliness such as Shakespeare's mother had known.

"It's not that I want to die," the mountain man remarked wistfully. "I was looking forward to a long life with Blue Water Woman."

"Then go to St. Louis and be examined by a physician," Nate urged.

"I'd rather not."

"What harm can it do?"

"No."

"You're being stubborn," Nate said in exasperation.

"You're absolutely right. I've been a mule-headed cuss all of my born days and I'm too old to change now. So forget about St. Louis."

"You might find a cure."

"Drop the subject."

"But—"

"Drop it, I say!" Shakespeare snapped.

Startled, Nate faced forward. His friend had never spoken to him so sternly before and it shocked him. There had been a tinge of something else in Shakespeare's tone, an indefinable quality that if he didn't know better might have been a trace of fear. But such a notion was ridiculous. Shakespeare wasn't afraid of anything on God's green earth.

After a spell Shakespeare cleared his throat. "Sorry, Nate. There was no call for me to lash out at you like I did. I appreciate your concern."

Nate had a thought. Perhaps Shakespeare was leery of traveling such a great distance because he might perish along the way. The prospect of becoming too weak to travel and lying helpless on the prairie while hostiles or wild beasts closed in would dissuade any man. "I'd even go with you," he volunteered. "I'd like to see how much St. Louis has grown since I was there last."

"I'm not going and that's final."

"We could take our wives and Zach with us," Nate said, trying one last tack.

Shakespeare grunted in disapproval. "And you have the gall to call me stubborn! When you sink your teeth into something you don't let go come hell or high water." He chuckled. "You would have made a dandy wolverine."

For the next mile neither man spoke.

Nate's mind raced as he tried to think of a means to help his mentor. There must be something he could do. Some of Winona's people were well versed in the healing arts and might be able to help. So might medicine men from other friendly tribes such as the Crows or the Pawnees. Shakespeare was partial to the Flatheads but they weren't the only tribe who boasted skilled healers.

Nate ceased his contemplation to survey the ground ahead, recalling landmarks he'd passed during his mad run to the cabin. Instead of sticking to the trail he'd simply made a frantic beeline, and he recollected passing a certain boulder with a jagged upper rim shortly after stashing his makeshift pack. Once he located the boulder, finding the right tree would be child's play.

It took several minutes until the boulder appeared.

Nate lifted an arm and pointed, about to make mention of the fact to Shakespeare; when from up ahead there arose a series of feral growls and snarls. Instantly he crouched, the Hawken in both hands, and peered through the vegetation to try and glimpse the animals responsible.

"Wolves," Shakespeare whispered, down on one knee.

"They must have found the cache!" Nate exclaimed softly, and rose without thinking. After all the trouble he had gone to in obtaining the bear meat, he wasn't about to stand idly by and let a pack of wolves consume it. He dashed forward, treading as lightly as possible, angry but not foolhardy.

Wolves rarely attacked humans. Quite often they would gather in the darkness around a flickering camp fire and gaze in curious wonder at the men who had made it. Frequently they would sit there and howl as if they might be trying to converse in their eerie, primitive fashion. Only when they were rabid or starved were they dangerous, as Nate had found out some years ago when he'd nearly been slain by a small pack.

A thicket reared between him and the tree where the bear meat was cached. Stepping on the balls of his feet, he glided soundlessly to the right until he could view the tree and the snarling wolves.

There were seven, all told, five adults and two young ones. Their coats were gray, their sleek bodies rippling with muscles as they padded in circles around the trunk of the pine. The meat rested securely in a fork over eight feet above the ground, and now and again one of the adults would take a flying leap and try to snare the bear hide in its teeth. So far they had failed, but several times the largest of the pack came close enough to snip off fragments of bear hair.

Nate squatted and debated. Given time the wolves would drift elsewhere if they couldn't get the meat. But knowing their vaunted persistence, he realized hours might elapse before they admitted defeat, hours he was not willing to waste in waiting.

He could see what had attracted them. Blood had dripped out of the hide, trickled down the trunk, and formed a tiny puddle at the base of the tree. No doubt the wolves had caught the airborne scent of the blood and come to investigate. A wry grin curled his lips. At least he should be thankful a grizzly hadn't picked up the scent.

His thumb resting on the hammer, he held still and watched. The leader of the pack was a huge brute, about the same size as Samson, in the prime of its life. He didn't want to shoot it if he could avoid such an eventuality since he had an aversion to killing any game unless he needed food or a hide. He could always sew together a wolfskin cap from the pelt, but he already owned a few hats and had no desire for a new one, even if the wolfskin variety was quite the fashion rage among the trapping fraternity.

Perhaps he could scare them off. Wolves, like most wild creatures, possessed an instinctive wariness of humans. Even grizzlies, on occasion, would wheel and flee at the sight of a human, although such timidity was the exception rather than the rule.

Girding himself, Nate stood and advanced a few strides. Immediately the wolves froze in their tracks and glanced at him. Not one displayed the slightest fear. He waved the rifle at them and yelled, thinking the sound of his voice would rout them. "Go! Get lost! That's my meat and you're not going to have it!"

Instead of fleeing, the huge male snarled and sprang.

Chapter Four

Nate tried to bring the rifle to bear, but the wolf was on him before he could level the barrel. It crashed into the gun, its jaws ripping at his throat, its heavy weight staggering him backwards. Hot breath fanned his neck, and then he lashed out with the stock and clipped the beast a solid blow on the side of its skull.

The wolf fell and with uncanny coordination landed on all fours. In a twinkling it crouched, bracing its leg muscles for another jump.

From the right and left other wolves closed in.

Stepping back, Nate lifted the rifle to his shoulder. He'd get one with the Sharps and possibly another with a pistol. After that he must rely on his long butcher knife and count on Shakespeare to come to his aid. Where was McNair, anyway? He saw a bush to the south tremble and expected his friend to dart into the open with his rifle blasting.

Out of that bush came something, all right, but it wasn't the mountain man. A snarling black brute of a dog streaked into the midst of the wolves, its massive jaws tearing every which way in savage abandon. The ferocious momentum of its attack scattered the pack, all except for the leader. It spun to meet the dog and their shoulders collided. The wolf, which weighed 140 pounds or better, was bowled over by the impact but promptly scrambled erect.

And then a battle ensued such as few men had been privileged to witness. Nate stared in anxious fascination as the two beasts fought in a swirl of flashing limbs, white teeth, and throaty growls. They moved too fast for the human eye to follow, and he marked the progress of the clash with difficulty. He saw both animals tear chunks of fur and flesh from the other. Often they were pressed muzzle to muzzle, rolling over and over, back and forth. An instant later they would be upright, their mouths darting out with snakelike speed.

He glanced once at the other wolves. The rest of the pack had gathered under trees a dozen yards to the north, observing the conflict in typical stoic lupine silence. None made a move to interfere. This was a fight to the death between their leader and the black dog, a fight as primal, as elemental, as their existence itself. Nature had endowed them with a primitive code of conduct that prevented them from taking sides in personal disputes. And to them this was just such a dispute. In their eyes the leader had been challenged for leadership of the pack, and he must prove himself fit to hold that post or forfeit his life for his failure.

Several times Nate tried to help the dog, to snap off a shot, but the constant whirl of motion made a certain hit impossible and he wouldn't risk hitting the dog. So he impatiently waited for the outcome, which came so abruptly he was caught unawares.

The dog and wolf were spinning and biting in a dizzying display of speed and agility when there arose an agonized yelp and for a moment they were still, the wolf's broken front leg held in the iron grip of the big dog's teeth. Shifting, the dog let go of the leg and swept its mouth up and in. Those wicked teeth closed on the wolf's exposed throat and bit deep. Blood spurted. The wolf stiffened and vented a plaintive howl of despair, then desperately attempted to free itself. In so doing, it only tore its own throat wider still, spraying a crimson geyser onto the grass.

Rumbling like an enraged grizzly, the dog worried the throat back and forth in its jaws until the wolf sagged. For another minute it held on, its teeth grinding ever deeper. Finally, satisfied the wolf was dead, the dog released its hold and turned to face the pack.

The wolves waited expectantly.

Advancing a stride, with a harsh snarl the dog sent them running. They vanished into the undergrowth like shadowy ghosts from a goblin realm.

"Thanks, Samson," Nate said softly.

The dog turned and padded up to him. Blood from a score of wounds matted its sides and back. There was an especially nasty gash on its neck where the wolf had nearly succeeded in obtaining a death hold, and above one eye hung a flap of partially severed skin.

"You always know right when to show up, don't you?" Nate commented, squatting so he could examine the wounds carefully. None were life-threatening but there always existed the chance of infection. The gash and the torn skin should be tended as soon as possible.

"Remind me to never raise my voice at you in that dog's presence."

Nate looked back and saw Shakespeare nearby. Grinning, he stroked Samson, watching so he didn't accidentally touch a wound. "Samson knows you too well to harm you."

"So you say," Shakespeare responded. "But I'd rather not learn you're wrong the hard way."

The dog licked Nate, its slick tongue rasping over his right cheek. Gingerly, Nate gave it a hug and stood, his memory straying to the time years ago when he'd first encountered Samson in Crow territory. The dog had been a stray, and it had taken to him like a duck takes to water. Since then he had kept it as a pet and allowed it to sleep indoors whenever it was so inclined.

"I'll fetch the bear meat," Shakespeare offered. He walked to the pine and poked the pack with his rifle barrel until the bear hide slipped out of the fork and fell. With a deft snatch he caught it, his knees bending from the strain. "Lord! How much did you wrap in here?"

"Ninety pounds or so."

"The next time warn a man, will you? It about broke my back."

"Want me to carry it home?" Nate asked.

Shakespeare bristled at the innocent request. "No, thank you very much. I may be ill, but I can still do my share of the work here or anywhere else."

"For how long?" Nate inquired. "How long before Blue Water Woman discovers your condition?"

"She never will if I can help it."

"She will, though. One day you'll wake up and be too weak to move. How do you think she'll feel once she learns you didn't confide in her? She might think you don't love her as much as you claim."

Shakespeare glowered and took a step forward. "If any other man made such a remark to me, he'd be eating his teeth." Pivoting, he headed toward the cabin. "You would make me very happy if you would never bring the subject up again."

"But . . ." Nate protested, unwilling to let the matter rest when his friend's life was at stake. There had to be something they could do. There had to be!

The mountain man paused to glance at him. "Please. For me."

Sighing reluctantly, Nate merely nodded. He thought of the Rendezvous and the experienced mountaineers who would be there, men such as Jim Bridger and Joe Meek and others, wise men who knew all there was to know about the mountains and the various Indian tribes, who knew even more than he did. Perhaps one of them could offer advice that would save Shakespeare's hide. If not, he could always give Shakespeare a rap on the skull, tie him up, and head for St. Louis.

Samson limped slightly as they walked, and Nate stopped to examine the dog's right front leg. There were teeth marks in the skin but the underlying muscles and tendons appeared to be fine. Evidently the wolf had nipped the leg but had done no real damage.

He walked faster to catch up with Shakespeare. "So how about if we leave for the Rendezvous tomorrow? I can have everything we need packed and set to go by nightfall."

"What's your rush all of a sudden?"

"No rush. But why wait when our wives are looking forward to seeing their own people again and we both have prime peltries to sell?" Nate rejoined, deliberately maintaining a bland expression.

The mountain man shrugged. "Suit yourself. I suppose it would be better to get an early start so we can take our time. We can ride north along the foothills, then cross at South Pass and head for Fort Bonneville."

"Sounds good," Nate commented. The route would be easy on the horses and there would be plenty of game, principally buffalo, along the way. Should hostiles appear on the prairie, there would be adequate cover in the foothills.

They went half a mile without speaking. Then Shakespeare idly glanced at the bear hide in his hands and drew up short. "Damn. I almost forgot.

There's some news I figured you should know."

"News?"

Shakespeare nodded and resumed walking. "It's the talk of the country, from what I hear." He paused. "Niles Thompson and a few friends of his stopped at my cabin a while back. They were on their way into Crow country after paying a visit to St. Louis. Thompson needed a new rifle. Dropped his old one when he was scaling a cliff."

Nate heard loud chattering and looked around to see a large squirrel protesting their presence in no uncertain terms.

"Anyhow, he heard the news while he was there and he found a couple of old newspapers to bring back and show everyone. He left one with me and I have it in my possibles bag."

"Are you fixing to tell me or do I have to wait until I see this newspaper?" Nate asked impatiently. He gathered from Shakespeare's attitude that it must be something important. His friend seldom displayed any interest in news from the States unless it related to the trapping trade.

"Jim Bowie is dead."

"What?" Nate blurted out, and halted in amazement. Ever since his late teens he had followed the exploits of the knife-wielding firebrand with more than a casual interest. Thanks to the many tales of Bowie's exploits reported in every newspaper across the land, Bowie had become a genuine living legend in his own time.

Every schoolboy knew about the many fights Bowie reputedly engaged in. There was the famous "Sandbar fight" of 1827 in which Bowie had slain his bitter enemy Major Morris Wright despite having been severely wounded twice by gunshots. In 1829 Bowie bested Bloody John Sturdivant in a knife fight in which the two participants sat across one another at a table with their left hands lashed together. Sturdivant survived and later hired three assassins to ambush Bowie. They did, and were thus added to the long list of those who presumed to tackle the best knife-fighter ever known.

And there were other confrontations. Bowie once fought a duel while seated on a log facing his opponent, both with their buckskin breeches nailed to the log. On another occasion he fought a Mexican armed with a poniard. In New Orleans one night he entered an unlit room armed with his knife, while his Creole foe went in carrying a sword. When the door was opened, only Bowie was still alive.

"That's not all," Shakespeare said. "Davy Crockett is dead too."

Nate stared at his friend in disbelief. Crockett was another frontiersman who had attained prominent national status. He had fought in the Creek War under Andrew Jackson. Noted for his skill as a peerless hunter and his uncanny marksmanship, Crockett reportedly killed 105 black bears in seven months time, a prodigious feat by any standards. He later parlayed his likable personality and first-rate storytelling into a political career. Several books had been written about him, and a popular play that toured the country featured a lead character based on Crockett's exploits.

"Have you heard about the situation in Texas?" Shakespeare inquired.

"I recall hearing there was a push on for independence from Mexico," Nate said.

"Well, that push came to shove and the Texans have their independence. But it cost them. There was a battle back in March at an old mission called the Alamo and every last man was killed, including Bowie and Crockett."

"They were fighting together?"

"According to the newspaper and from what Thompson heard in New Orleans, Bowie went to Texas back in '28 and married the daughter of a wealthy Mexican. He obtained vast land holdings and was one of the richest men in that neck of the woods. Then his wife and two young sprouts died, killed by the plague. Some say he was never the same man again. Took to drinking heavy. But he was all for independence and proved it with his life."

"Crockett?"

Shakespeare chuckled. "There was a man. I've always been partial to that old he-coon. He was one of the few with grit enough to stand up to Old Hickory when Jackson proposed riding roughshod over the Indians. Cost Crockett an election. So he told his former constituents they could go to hell and he was going to Texas. Probably figured he could start over down there."

"This Alamo you mentioned. Where is it?"

"Down toward San Antonio, I think. The article tells it all."

Nate walked glumly on. In the back of his mind he had always entertained the notion he might meet Bowie one day and get to know the great man personally. Now that would never happen.

"In the reproof of chance lies the true proof of men," Shakespeare quoted. "Bowie and Crockett and all the rest at the Alamo certainly proved their mettle. I bet that folks will talk about the battle for years to come." He paused. "To tell you the truth, I always figured on going out the same way."

"Fighting?"

"Yep. I thought I'd go down under a heap of Blackfeet or with a cliff at my back and a grizzly in front of me. Such a death would be quick and easy. Now it looks as if I've got it to do the hard way."

Not if I can help it, Nate resolved. He owed Shakespeare more than he could ever repay, and somehow he was going to find a cure. No matter how far he must travel, no matter what it might take, he would see his friend healthy again or die in the attempt.

Chapter Five

"We're early," Shakespeare announced. "The caravan from St. Louis isn't here yet."

Nate nodded absently, his gaze roving over the extensive valley below the ridge on which they had stopped to rest their horses. While the trade goods and supplies had yet to arrive, scores of trappers and over a thousand Indians were already present. He saw four Indian encampments bustling with activity. The Bannock and Shoshoni Indians had set up their villages to the south of the fork while the Flatheads and Nez Percés were off to the north. The tribes had prudently positioned their camps in convenient bends of Horse Creek so the creek itself served as their first line of defense should they be attacked by the Blackfeet or any other enemy. No one could cross the stream without alerting the camp dogs and guards.

"There are more here than ever before," Blue Water Woman said.

"Let's go down!" Zach declared, gesturing excitedly. "I want to see everything."

The boy's enthusiasm made Nate smile. Zach had yet to visit a town or a city back in the States. The annual gathering of trappers and Indians was the biggest assemblage Zach knew of, and it never failed to bring out all of his boyish zest for life.

"Where will we set up our camp?" Winona asked.

"Let's have a look around before we decide," Nate responded, and took the lead going down the mountain. Their journey to the site had been remarkably peaceful and pleasant. Except for spying a grizzly in the distance once, they had not encountered any problems, had not even seen the smoke of another camp fire.

Wafting up from the valley floor came the sounds of boisterous laughter, loud voices commingled in a hubbub of conversation, the neighing of horses, the barking of dogs, and periodic gunfire.

"Think Campbell will be here this year?" Shakespeare mentioned with a grin.

"I hope not," Nate said. "Maybe fate has smiled on me and a bear ate him."

"It would give the bear indigestion."

Nate surveyed the area near where the Green River and Horse Creek met. Most of the trappers were congregated there, some busily erecting crude structures to serve as their homes for the next few weeks. A dozen or so men were busy building a larger building out of sturdy logs, and he wondered what it would be used for. There were eight or nine blue cloth caps in evidence. The distance prevented him from determining if Campbell was underneath one of them or not. The husky bastard usually wore such a cap adorned with a fine eagle feather.

They wound along a game trail until they reached the valley floor, then cut out across the lush flatland toward the center of activity.

"What do you make of that?" Shakespeare inquired.

Twisting, Nate spied a group of ten riders entering the valley from the east. They were a mixed group, Indians and whites, all talking and laughing in rowdy fashion. A tall figure in buckskins and a wolfskin cap broke away from the group and came straight toward Nate.

"That's old Niles," Shakespeare said.

Nate reined up to let the trapper overtake them. Niles Thompson had been in the mountains for over a decade and was widely respected by his peers and the Indians alike. He'd taken a Nez Percé wife a few years back, but she'd been taken by marauding Piegans. Since then he had accumulated the largest collection of Piegan scalps of anyone in the Rockies.

"Shakespeare! Nate! Good to see you again!" Niles shouted in greeting as he drew near. "And you've brought your lovely wives too." He looked at Zach. "But who's this man with you? He sure can't be a greenhorn from the way he sits that mare."

Zach laughed in delight. "It's me, Mr. Thompson. Stalking Coyote," he said, using his Shoshone name.

Niles halted, his rifle across his saddle, and shook his head in feigned astonishment. "I'll be damned. It is you, Zach. You're growing like a weed. Before I know it you'll be off wrestling grizzlies just like your pa."

"He doesn't wrestle them," Zach said. "He shoots and stabs them if they give him any trouble."

"Most folks have enough common sense to run when a grizzly is after them," Niles said good-naturedly. His shoulder-length hair and beard were both flecked with white, and there was a thin scar just below his left eye courtesy of a Piegan knife.

Shakespeare nodded at the group of riders. "What's the story?"

"We went out to meet the caravan," Niles explained. "Campbell figured we could have a little fun and put the fear of God into them."

"Campbell is here then?" Nate said.

"That he is, and eager for a rematch," Niles replied. "The boys are already placing their bets on the outcome. Campbell swears this is the year he beats you."

"He shouldn't count his chickens before they're hatched."

Shakespeare was watching the riders head for the fork. "You say you met the caravan?"

"Yep. We waited behind a hill and then charged the horse carts with our guns blasting, all the while whooping and hollering like a pack of bloodthirsty Blackfeet." Niles chuckled. "We had them pilgrims worried for a minute until one of their guides saw a white flag Campbell had tied to his rifle so they'd know we were friendly."

"It sounds like something that crazy Campbell would do," Nate commented.

"How far out is the caravan?" Shakespeare asked.

"Oh, they should get here in two days at the most. Wait until you see it. The line stretches out over a mile. There are nineteen horse carts, three wagons, about four hundred head of stock, mostly mules. Then there are the cows and calves."

"Cows?" Nate blurted out.

"Did you say wagons?" Shakespeare chimed in.

Niles sat back and grinned. "Oh, that's right. Neither of you have heard. I'm afraid we're getting a mite too civilized in these parts for my taste. Yes, I said wagons, and they belong to missionaries. So do the cows and calves."

For the first time ever, Nate saw shock on his mentor's face. He was flabbergasted himself. So far as he knew, no Bible-thumper had ever ventured west of Missouri. And *cows*! The last cow he'd seen had been way back in Indiana, and he couldn't even remember the last time he'd enjoyed a glass of milk.

"Dear God," Shakespeare mumbled. "Missionaries, you say?"

"There's three of them. Presbyterians. And listen to this," Niles said, leaning toward them, his expression indicating he had saved the best revelation for last. His voice lowered almost to a whisper. "Two of them have brought their wives."

Shakespeare stiffened as if struck by a bolt of lightning. "They didn't! Now I know you're telling a tall tale."

"May I be skinned alive if I'm lying," Niles responded indignantly. "I've seen the ladies with my own two eyes. One is a blonde but as stern as you please and the other is an invalid."

"I'm dreaming," Shakespeare said softly. "I must be. There's no other explanation. Wagons, cows, and white women, one of them an invalid?" He encompassed the surrounding mountains with an abrupt gesture. "The wilderness is dead, gentlemen, and you've lived to see it happen."

"Aren't you being overly dramatic, as usual?" Niles retorted.

Shakespeare shook his head. "Take my word for it. Nothing civilizes folks like religion. When those preachers take to telling us how sinful we all are there won't be a trapper in the Rockies who doesn't walk around with a burden of guilt on his shoulders. They'll have every man-jack among us thinking twice before we tip a bottle or shoot a Blackfoot."

"Oh, come on," Niles said with a grin. "They won't be saying anything that isn't already in the Bible, and there are plenty of men who tote the Good Book around with them."

"True, but when a man is done reading he can always put the Bible down and pay no mind to what he's read," Shakespeare countered. "But not so with preachers. They go around setting proper examples for others to follow. Before you know it half this country will be thinking and acting like prim, civilized citizens."

"Does this mean you don't believe in religion?" Nate asked. "You don't believe in a God?"

"I never said that," Shakespeare said sharply. "As it so happens, I do. But I know enough about history to read the changing times, and times they are a-changing."

Nate had never heard his friend speak on the subject before, and he was mildly surprised at Shakespeare's attitude. Certainly a visit to the Rendezvous by a few missionaries did not signify the dire end of the mountaineering way of life. Shakespeare, as he sometimes did, was exaggerating.

"I would like to meet these white women," Winona spoke up.

"So would I," Blue Water Woman said. "I have never met a white woman before."

And with good reason, Nate mused. No white man had ever brought a woman into the mountains simply because it had always been considered too dangerous. There were wild beasts to think of, not to mention hostile Indians, fierce weather, and the loneliness caused by being separated from relatives and friends by vast distances. White women, by and large, wanted a solid roof over their heads and a nice house in which to raise their children. They also liked to socialize with other women and share their hopes, dreams, and disappointments.

Indian women, by contrast, were accustomed to a life of always contending with Nature. They learned early how to survive in the wild. Many tribes followed the herds of buffalo, and their women accepted the constant travel. Unlike white women, Indian women expressed no interest in having a permanent dwelling. They made ideal wives for trappers because they shared the trapper's way of life.

Shakespeare, shaking his head sadly, rode toward the camp. and the rest of them fell in behind him. "Tell me, Niles. How did they get the wagons on this side of the mountains? Over South Pass?"

"Where else?" Niles rejoined. "It's the only place for hundreds of miles that a body could take a wagon over the Divide."

"Now that it's been done you can expect more to try it," Shakespeare said. "I expect people will flock out to Oregon before too long and this whole country will be crowded with settlers."

Nate laughed at the idea. "Why would anyone want to head for Oregon when there's more than enough land to go around back in the States?"

"You have a lot to learn about human nature and politics," was all Shakespeare would say.

They crossed the creek and sat and watched the men erecting the large log building. When completed, the structure would be about 18 feet long and an equal distance wide. No allowances were being made for doors and windows. Instead, a single opening that measured two feet wide and six feet long had been left four feet above the ground on one side.

A burly man in a mackinaw stepped back from his labors and wiped sweat from his brow. He glanced around and broke into a grin.

"Shakespeare, you old devil! How's your year been?"

"No complaints, Corbin," McNair replied. He jerked a thumb at the building. "Planning to set down roots?"

Corbin laughed. "Hell, no. This is going to be the fur company store. Tom sent orders ahead to have it ready when the caravan arrives."

"Tom? Tom Fitzpatrick?"

"The same. He's the new commander of the caravan."

"What happened to Lucien Fontenelle?"

Corbin lifted a hand and pretended to put an invisible bottle to his lips, then made as if drinking in great gulps. "Lucien couldn't lay off the hard stuff. Last winter he spent nine out of every ten days flat on his back. The company finally had its fill and discharged him."

"I saw it coming," Shakespeare said.

So had Nate. Lucien Fontenelle had been an important man in the American Fur Company, but Fontenelle had never been able to lay off the liquor. From all Nate had heard, the new man, Fitzpatrick, was steady and reliable and not likely to try and cheat any of the free trappers out of money due for pelts.

"Look me up once the Rendezvous is in full swing and we'll tip a few ourselves," Corbin said, and went back to work.

Nate looked at Shakespeare. "So what are we going to do? Stick together, or do you want to stay with the Flatheads? Winona, Zach, and I can always impose on the Shoshones."

"I'd like to camp together, but rightfully our wives should make the decision."

Winona and Blue Water Woman began discussing the issue, and Nate took the opportunity to survey the entire site. The sweetly bitter aroma of wood smoke tingled his nostrils, and somewhere someone was frying bacon. His stomach growled and he willed it to be quiet. Off to the south two Indians were engaged in a horse race and being cheered on by their respective supporters. Several Indian women were washing blankets in the river.

He hoped Shakespeare was wrong. The thought of such a gloriously independent way of life coming to an end disturbed him profoundly. Not until he'd left New York City, not until he had forsaken the false trappings of civilization for the real rigors of the wilderness, had he grown to appreciate the true meaning of the word *freedom*.

Out here all were truly free to do as they pleased. They worked when they wanted, ate when they wanted, and slept when they wanted. But they were also accountable for their actions to the person who stood to benefit or suffer the most from their decisions: themselves. If they didn't hunt, they didn't eat. If they slept too long, they didn't get their work done. The sole responsibility for their existence was in their hands and their hands alone, not in the hands of a vote-seeking politician or a penny-pinching storekeeper or a tyrannical boss. Every man who took to living in the

Rockies learned to appreciate genuine freedom and the responsibilities it entailed. "Out here we're free," he said softly to himself, cherishing the sound of the word, and then a tingle rippled down his spine as a harsh voice barked to his rear.

"As I live and breathe, Nate King himself! Are you ready to meet your Maker, Mouse Killer?"

Chapter Six

Nate glanced over his shoulder and adopted a stern expression as his nemesis approached. Robert Campbell wore the most lavishly beaded buckskins in the mountains and a blue cap in a style currently popular with the mountain men. The big eagle feather fluttered in the breeze. "I was hoping the Blackfeet had plucked out your black heart by now," Nate said.

"They only want specimens with hair," Campbell responded, and doffed his cap to display his nearly bald pate. Putting it back on, he stepped right up to Nate's horse and started to lift his hand. "Why don't we take care of business here and now," he said, and then froze when a rumbling growl issued from beside his left leg.

Samson stood menacingly, his lips curled up, his teeth glistening with saliva.

"Lord, Nate, call your mongrel off," Campbell said, easing his arm down again.

"Why should I?" Nate asked, and made as if to ride on.

"You'd let your dog do me in?" Campbell declared, and grinned. "Why, of course you would. You're too scared to face me man-to-man."

"Started having delusions, have you?" Nate quipped. "You're the one who should be scared to face me. After all, you've lost the past four bouts."

"That I did," Campbell agreed, then smirked. "But each year I practice, and each year I get better and better. This is the year I pin your ears back and I have a hundred pelts to back my words."

Nate hesitated. One hundred beaver hides was almost a third of his grand total. If he lost the match he'd also lose hundreds of dollars in income. It was all well and good for Campbell to boast and bet when the man didn't have a family to support.

"What's the matter, Mouse Killer?" Campbell taunted him. "Has someone painted a yellow stripe down your backbone since last we tangled?"

"I accept," Nate said, and out of the corner of his eye he saw Shakespeare roll both of his. "Name the time and the place and I'll be there."

"Let's wait until after the caravan arrives," Campbell suggested. "The more folks that see your defeat, the harder it will be for you to deny it later." Cackling, he spun on his heels and stalked off, whistling happily.

"That lunatic will break your neck one of these days," Niles Thompson remarked.

"He's not touched in the head," Nate said. "He's just determined."

"You wouldn't praise him so freely if you knew what I know," Niles stated.

"Which is?"

"When Campbell told you he's been practicing, he wasn't fooling. For the past four months he's spent every spare moment wrestling a bear."

If a grain of blowing dust had suddenly struck Nate, he would have toppled from his saddle. "A bear?"

"A big black bear. It belonged to that French Canadian, Chevalier. He raised the bear from a cub and taught it to wrestle, then he took it around offering twenty dollars to anyone who could beat it. No one ever could."

Nate had heard of the wrestling bear a few years back, but the last he knew the bear and its owner were up in Canada.

"After a while word about that bear spread and Chevalier couldn't find any takers, so he came south to visit Campbell. I hear they worked together as *voyageurs* once. Campbell bought the bear and has been tussling with it every darned day since."

No wonder Campbell had been so confident! Nate stared after the departing trapper, realizing he might have been duped. Campbell had put on a bit of weight and none of it appeared to be fat.

"There's a rumor going around that Campbell can now pin that bear four out of five tries," Niles went on. "The money will be on him this year, I reckon."

As well it should. Back in the States there were many traveling acts that toured the country and entertained for a modest price. Nate had seen men eat fire, women walk on high wires, and performers who worked with wild beasts in cages. And once, when only six or seven, his Uncle Zeke had taken him to see a man who wrestled a tame bear. The man had been big and strong but the bear had handled him as if he were a child. Afterward, the man had offered anyone in the audience a chance to wrestle the bear for a half dime, and five or six hardy souls had tried their best. The bear had pinned every last one.

Shakespeare chuckled. "Seems to me you'd better head into the mountains and rustle up a grizzly you can practice on."

"I bet everyone at the Rendezvous turns out for this match," Niles predicted. "Why, even the missionaries might like to see it."

Nate's shoulders slumped. The last thing he wanted was to be humiliated in front of every trapper in the Rockiest not to mention strangers he didn't even know. Stories about the match would spread by word of mouth until every white man and Indian between the Mississippi and the Pacific Ocean heard the tale.

"To wrestle, or not to wrestle. That is the question," Shakespeare declared impishly. "Whether 'tis nobler in the mind to suffer the sling and arrows of outrageous fortune, or to take arms against a sea of troubles, and by opposing end them."

"You are no help whatsoever," Nate told him.

"Excuse me, husband," Winona threw in. "Blue Water Woman and I have decided we should make our camp together. It will be nice to sit and talk and we can visit our own people any time we please."

"Fine," Nate said absently, and then perceived the women must have been discussing where to stay the whole time and had hardly paid attention to the talk about Robert Campbell. "Did you happen to hear about the wrestling bear?" he asked.

"I heard," Winona said.

"And you're not the least bit worried that Campbell might beat me?"

"No."

"Why not, may I ask?"

"No man can beat you."

Nate almost took her in his arms to give her a hug to end all hugs. Her unbounded confidence in him sometimes made him feel uncomfortable, especially since he had no idea what he had done to deserve it. Sure, he'd slain a few grizzlies and saved her from the Blackfeet and others, but many free trappers had done as much for their wives and his feats weren't remarkable in any respect. Yet she regarded him as a supremely capable man. At times he suspected she believed he was practically invincible, which disturbed him.

One of the lessons he'd learned since coming to the mountains was that no one knew when their time on this earth was up. Death claimed everyone sooner or later, and for trappers it often came suddenly and was totally unexpected. A man might be out checking his trap line and be attacked by hostile Indians, or a grizzly might pop up out of the brush and crush his skull with a single swipe. A rattlesnake might spook the man's horse, and the horse would throw him and break his neck. There were a thousand and one ways a man could die and the majority were unpleasant.

Winona's inspiring assurance in his ability filled Nate with pride, yet it troubled him at the same time. He was afraid a day would come when he would fail her, and his failure would occur when she needed him the most.

"I'd better be on my way," Niles commented, shattering Nate's contemplation. "I'm staying with a Nez Percé friend and he'll be expecting me." He turned his horse. "I'll look you up tomorrow." With a wave he was gone.

"We should set up our camp before it gets dark," Shakespeare proposed.

They rode north along the bank of the Green River until they found an isolated spot in a clearing among pines and a few quaking aspen. The horses were picketed, the saddles removed, and their supplies and pelts piled high to one side. Then Nate and Shakespeare constructed a serviceable lean-to for the women and Zach.

The sun hovered above the western horizon when Shakespeare went off to bag meat for their supper. Nate arranged their packs and parfleches next to the lean-to and took the horses to the river to drink. Gazing out over the serene encampment, he heard a man singing an old Scottish song. Dozens of columns of smoke drifted skyward from the four Indian camps. At the Flathead village, which was the closest, children ran and laughed accompanied by a frisky barking puppy.

The primitive scene etched itself indelibly in Nate's mind. He could smell the wood smoke and the aroma of roasting buffalo. Looking at the lean-to he saw Winona talking to Blue Water Woman while Zach played with Samson. For that idyllic moment, in that suspended moment of time and that tranquil, picturesque place, he was content and happy. He had a wife and son who loved him, good friends who cared for him as much as he cared for them, and all around them reared the majestic Rocky Mountains.

What more could any man want?

He had the horses picketed and was seated beside a growing fire when Shakespeare returned bearing three dead rabbits. The mountain man gave them to his wife, then joined Nate.

"After we eat I'm going to rustle up a bottle."

"Have you been in a lot of pain?" Nate asked, careful to speak in a low tone so the women couldn't overhear.

"In the mornings, mainly. Just like always," Shakespeare said. He stared blankly into the crackling flames, then sighed. "If my time does come, I want you to help Blue Water Woman the best you can."

"Quit talking that way. You'll be around for years."

"I'd like to. I surely would. There's so much I haven't done yet, so much I've always wanted to do. I've never been south of Santa Fe and I hear the country down there is worth seeing. I never found that gold I was looking for, and—"

"Gold?" Nate interrupted. "Since when have you been interested in gold?"

"Ever since I heard tell about the mining the Spaniards used to do in the Rockies. An old Ute once told me there was a mine not too far south of your cabin."

"He was wrong. The Spanish never came that far north."

"Yes, they did, but few know it. Old Badger Hair never told a lie in his life and he got the news straight from his own grandfather. Seems the Spaniards took a fortune in gold from those mountains before they were driven out."

Nate had heard tales too. Every trapper had. But few gave them much credence, and those who did had no idea where the Spanish mines were located, and weren't about to waste precious time that could be better spent trapping beaver in searching for the lost wealth.

"Will you?" Shakespeare asked, looking at him.

"Will I what?"

"Do whatever you can for Blue Water Woman. It would be better for her to go back to her people, but I expect she'll try and remain at our place. If I know you'll watch out for her, I'll go easier."

Nate disliked thinking about the possibility of his friend dying. He glumly wrapped his arms around his knees, and a hand fell on his arm.

"Please."

"You know I will," Nate said, and shifted uncomfortably under McNair's pleading eyes.

Shakespeare sat back and smiled in relief. "Thanks, son. I knew I could count on you."

Remembering his plan to find Jim Bridger or Joe Meek to ask their advice, Nate tried to come up with a plausible excuse for slipping away the next day. He certainly didn't want Shakespeare to tag along.

Footsteps crunched in the brush and four men suddenly appeared out of the dark, all trappers similarly attired in buckskins and toting rifles. Niles Thompson was in the lead.

"Hello, the fire. Mind some company?"

"Light and sit a spell," Nate replied, glad for the diversion. He wondered if Thompson might be able to help him. "I thought you were at the Nez Percé camp."

"I was," Niles replied, advancing with the others. "But two things came to my attention and I figured I'd best see you right away."

"What two things?"

"A Nez Percé hunter found Blackfoot sign north of their village. He estimated twenty warriors in the raiding party. They're all on foot, but knowing those bastards they won't be for long if they can get their hands on some stock."

Nate nodded. The Blackfeet often conducted their raids on foot. That way, if a brave wanted to save himself a lot of wear and tear on his feet and ride back to his village he had to steal a horse. Perhaps because of that, when it came to stealing horseflesh none were more skilled than the Blackfeet.

"Bridger thinks we should get together some men and scout around, see if we can find these Blackfeet before they attack. Since you're one of the best trackers I know of, I naturally thought of you."

"I'll go," Nate volunteered without hesitation. "Provided someone is handy to protect my family."

"Good," Niles said, and glanced at a lean trapper on his right. "There's one more thing, though. This here is Charley Gordon. He was in St. Louis about five weeks ago and ran into someone who knows you."

"Oh?" Nate said, and stared at Gordon, a young trapper who sported curly black hair.

"Yes, sir," Gordon responded. "I was at the Hawken shop stocking up on my ammunition and powder when Sam Hawken asked me if I was going to the Rendezvous. When I told him I was, he asked me to stop by the Chouteau House. There was this woman, he said, who was real anxious to get in touch with one of the mountaineers and he figured I could take a message for her."

"A woman?" Nate repeated, mystified. He knew no women in St. Louis.

"Yep. A real pretty lady, she is. Her name is Adeline Van Buren."

Chapter Seven

If the ground had suddenly opened and swallowed him whole, Nate would not have been more shocked. He sat in a daze, his mouth parted, only vaguely aware that Winona's head had snapped up at the mention of his former sweetheart and that Shakespeare had come alert at the news. He became conscious of the curious stares of Niles Thompson and the rest and forced his mind to work and his mouth to move. "I knew a woman by that name once, back in New York City."

"Well, she's in St. Louis now and she's hankering to see you," Gordon reported.

"Did she say why?" Nate inquired, struggling to compose his swirling thoughts. Adeline wasn't the sort to enjoy life on the frontier. She relished city living too much. She thrived on wealth, on the theater, on extravagant dances. He couldn't imagine anything that would induce her to forgo the comforts of New York City for the more primitive atmosphere of St. Louis.

"No, sir, she didn't," Gordon said. "But she practically begged me to look you up." He paused, noting Nate's expression. "I did gather she'd been hunting you for quite some time, and had about given up when someone suggested letting the Hawken brothers know. Pretty smart too, if you ask me. Every trapper in these mountains stops by the Hawken shop sooner or later."

Nate absently nodded. He deliberately avoided looking at Winona because he didn't want her to see the emotional turmoil undoubtedly reflected in his eyes. At the mention of Adeline's name all his old feelings for her had welled up inside of him. He had them under control again, but it bothered him that he could still feel affection for her after having been married to Winona for so many years.

"She's not alone," Gordon said.

"What?" Nate responded, listening with only half an ear as he stared at his moccasins. Should he go see her or not? Doing so might upset Winona tremendously.

"There's a gent with her," Gordon disclosed. "From New York, I reckon. Slim as a rail, and he has the face of a rattler. I wouldn't trust him as far as I could heave a bull buffalo."

Nate thoughtfully chewed on his lower lip. Who could this stranger be? A relative of Adeline's? Her husband, perhaps?

"He sat near us in the hotel lobby while we were

talking," Gordon said. "And he kept watching me like a panther about to pounce on its prey. I didn't take to him and I'm afraid it showed."

"You didn't get his name?"

"No, sir. She didn't mention it and I wasn't about to pry. I spotted a pair of pistols under his fancy jacket, and his hands were never far from them. If you run into him, you be careful. He's poison through and through."

"Thanks," Nate said.

Niles coughed and motioned for his companions to move off. "Be seeing you, Nate. Come to the Nez Percé camp at first light if you're still of a mind to help track down those infernal Blackfeet."

"I'll be there," Nate promised, although at that moment he didn't feel like venturing into the forest after the raiding party. He didn't feel like doing much of anything.

Shakespeare added a few branches to the fire and waited until the men were long gone before he spoke. "Isn't this an interesting development? I remember you telling me about sparking that Van Buren girl, but I'd never have guessed she's still interested in you."

"Don't be ridiculous," Nate snapped.

"Why else has she gone to so much trouble to find you?"

"How am I supposed to know? And I don't see where it's any of your business."

"True," McNair said softly, and sighed. "But I am your best friend, or so you've led me to believe."

Nate knew Shakespeare had been offended by

his brusque behavior, and he searched for the proper words to mend the rift.

"Perhaps you're right. She might have traveled across half a continent for another reason," Shakespeare said wryly, and then quoted the bard. "There are more things in heaven and earth, Horatio, than are dreamt of in your philosophy."

Not about to bandy words with a man who could talk rings around a tree, Nate looped his arms over his knees and marveled at the incredible turn of events. He'd never expected to see Adeline again. This surprising news filled him with conflicting currents of curiosity and reservation.

A figure materialized at his side.

"Do you plan to see this woman, husband?"

Nate glanced up. Winona's features were inscrutable but her tone had been strained. "I honestly don't know yet. My first reaction is shrug it off. Why should I, when Adeline and I mean nothing to each other anymore? But I can't help wonder. Maybe she's brought news of my family."

"Perhaps," Winona said with as little conviction as it was humanly possible to convey.

"Maybe she intends to marry that nasty gentleman Gordon was telling us about," Shakespeare commented. "Maybe she wants to invite you to the wedding."

Nate stared at him. "Has anyone ever told you that you have a deplorable sense of humor?"

"If you decide to go, I am going with you," Winona declared.

"What about Zach?"

"He is our son. He goes with us."

"The trip will take about three weeks and we'd have to cross Arapaho and Cheyenne territory. You would be safer staying at home."

"You do not want us to come?"

The hurt in her tone made Nate blink. "What a silly question. If you insist on going along, I won't object." He stood and took her hands in his. "I was only thinking of your safety. Your people aren't on friendly terms with the Arapahos and Cheyennes, and you know they wouldn't hesitate to take you captive."

"I would face any danger with you by my side."

Disregarding the presence of Shakespeare and Blue Water Woman, Nate tenderly embraced Winona and held her close. He could feel her trembling slightly as if she were cold even though the weather was warm. "You have nothing to worry about," he whispered in her ear. "I love you and only you. If I see Adeline it will not have any effect on us."

Winona nodded, then silently walked to the lean-to, where little Zach had curled up beside Samson and was sound asleep.

"You can't blame her for being upset," Shakespeare said quietly.

Nate sat down and poked a stick into the flames. "She should know better," he insisted.

"Think. Put yourself in her place. How many trappers have taken Indian wives and then gone off and left them? How many Shoshoni, Flathead, and Nez Percé women have been forced to rear half-breed children on their own after being abandoned?"

"I would never do that to Winona."

"You know it and I know it, and in her heart Winona knows it too. But her head right now is telling her she might lose you and she can't stand the thought."

"Then I'll go over and tell her to her face."

"Won't do any good," Shakespeare said. "Women only take a man's word when they're courting. After marriage they doubt everything a man says. He has to show them, to prove himself by his deeds."

"Winona believes everything I tell her," Nate stated flatly.

"Oh, she'll tell you she does. But deep down she won't accept that you don't love Adeline until she sees the two of you together and can judge with her own eyes," Shakespeare said. "If you don't take her to St. Louis she'll always have a nagging doubt gnawing at her mind. Were I you I'd take her and no doubt about it."

"That's easy for you to say," Nate responded. "You'll be safe at your cabin while I'm risking life and limb to get my family safely there. You know how far it is. You know how dangerous . . ." He suddenly stopped, struck by inspiration, and said quickly, "Come with us."

"What?"

Nate intentionally raised his voice. "I'd take it as a favor if you would come with us. Bring Blue Water Woman, if you want. She might like to see St. Louis herself."

"I have no desire to see a city again. They're filthy places, like rat nests. There's always garbage and worse in the gutters, the air reeks, and there are swarms of people scurrying about like chickens flapping around with their heads chopped off. No, thanks."

"I appreciate your feelings, but four guns are better than two. With four adults we can hold our own and keep the hostiles at bay."

"There is safety in numbers," Shakespeare admitted. "But I truly don't want—"

From near the lean-to Blue Water Woman spoke up. "I have always wanted to see one of your cities. And I would feel guilty if something were to happen to Nate and his family and we weren't there to help."

Frowning, Shakespeare gazed at her. "You have no idea what you're asking. The dregs of the earth gather in cities. It's where weaklings and cowards can breed in safety, where all types of human vultures congregate. Imagine the worst sort of people there can be, and you'll find them in cities. Thieves, murderers, scoundrels of every stripe are everywhere."

"There must be good people in the cities too," Blue Water Woman said.

"Some," Shakespeare reluctantly admitted.

"I would like to go. We are getting on in years, as you have many times said, and we should make the journey while we still can."

"I'd rather not."

"Please. For me."

"Damn it all, woman."

"Please."

"Why I married you, I'll never know," Shakespeare said gruffly, and gave Nate a quizzical look. "Satisfied?"

"I don't know what you mean."

"Like hell you don't," Shakespeare retorted, then sighed. "Very well. When a man's own wife and best friend turn against him, what else can he do? Blue Water Woman and I will go to St. Louis with you."

Nate nearly shouted with joy.

A pink tinge colored the eastern sky when Nate made his way alone toward the Nez Percé encampment. Samson had wanted to come but he'd left the dog behind as a playmate, and guard, for Zach.

He hummed softly and stepped with a happy stride, inwardly chuckling for the hundredth time at his good fortune. Thanks to Adeline's unforeseen arrival on the frontier, he would get Shakespeare to St. Louis. Once there, he would convince Shakespeare to visit a doctor or trick him into going.

And he was happy for another reason having nothing to do with Adeline Van Buren. It had been eight years since last he was in the States, eight long years since he'd enjoyed the dubious benefits of civilization such as sleeping in a down-filled bed or drinking tasty ale at a tavern. Although he now knew he could well do without such niceties, the prospect of indulging himself once more, perhaps for the very last time, tickled his fancy. He disliked admitting it to himself, but he was mildly excited over the trip.

Finally, there was Adeline. For three hours before he fell asleep he had reviewed every memory of her he had, and searched his soul for the answer to the all-important question: Did he still care for her? The answer was a resounding "No!" Not in the intimate sense that he cared for Winona. But he did feel friendship for her, and he figured seeing her again would be a pleasant experience if she had forgiven him for deserting her.

Deep in thought, he walked along the river until he spied the Nez Percé village. Already the women were up gathering wood for the morning fires. A few braves stood outside their lodges, observing the dawn. One tall warrior had just emerged and was stretching.

Nate had to go around a bend, and a stand of pines cut off his view. As he came to the curve he heard the soft clump of hoofs. A few strides later he saw a group of Nez Percé leading their horses directly toward him, no doubt heading for a flat stretch of shore a dozen yards away where they could water their mounts.

He recollected the annoyed looks Shakespeare had given him last night and laughed lightly. Shakespeare was no man's fool. The mountain man knew he had been duped, yet he hadn't pressed the issue. Nate speculated on whether Shakespeare might actually be glad they were going. Despite all that talk about owing God a death, no man in his right mind wanted to die. And a man like McNair, a natural-born fighter who had survived more years in the wild than any other trapper because he was a tough as rawhide and as feisty as a cantankerous mule, wasn't about to roll over and give up the ghost without a struggle. Tussling was as natural to Shakespeare as breathing, and it didn't matter whether the enemy was a hostile Indian, a bear, or the Grim Reaper.

Nate abruptly realized the Nez Percé had stopped and were staring at him in surprise. He gazed at them and felt immense surprise of his own commingled with fleeting panic.

Because they weren't Nez Percé.

They were Blackfeet.

Chapter Eight

Nate King divined what had happened in a flash of insight.

The raiding party—there were 19 in all—had crept to the Nez Percé village about half an hour before the first rays of sunlight painted the heavens and rounded up as many horses as they could without being detected. Now they were trying to get safely away by taking the stolen herd across the river and into the dense forest beyond where they could easily escape. They had almost succeeded too. If not for Nate's unexpected arrival on the scene, in another minute or two they would have vanished like ghosts.

The odds were overwhelming, but Nate didn't hesitate. All four Indian tribes attending the Rendezvous were friendly to the trappers. Mutual trust existed between them. The Nez Percé, Flatheads, Shoshonis, and to a lesser degree the Bannocks had done all in their power to welcome the whites to the mountains. Because of this, the trappers had sometimes helped their allies in the never-ending warfare against the Blackfeet and other hostiles. As a friend of the Nez Percé, Nate was obligated to do whatever he could to prevent the Blackfeet from stealing the horses.

In a blur of speed he swung the Hawken up and took a rapid bead on the foremost Blackfoot, a brawny warrior armed with a bow. His shot boomed out across the valley and the leader toppled.

A dozen arrows were trained on him the next instant.

Nate spun and dived, hitting the ground on his left shoulder. The angry buzz of speeding shafts went past his head and he heard one arrow smack into the earth within inches of his face. Desperately, he scurried around the bend and rose to his knees.

From the Nez Percé camp arose angry shouts attended by a general commotion.

He knew the early risers had heard the shot, seen the war party, and were now rallying their fellows to take up the pursuit. But it would be several minutes before the first Nez Percé got there. He must do something on his own to slow the Blackfeet up, to buy time until reinforcements came.

Rising, he drew his right flintlock and crept to the bend. He peeked past a tree trunk, and immediately had to snap his head back to avoid a slender shaft that thudded into the tree and quivered violently. His brief glimpse had sufficed to show him the Blackfeet were urging their stolen horses into the river. Four or five were watching the bend in case he popped out again.

So he didn't.

Nate went into the underbrush, staying bent at the waist, until he drew up behind a pine tree within 15 feet of the war party. Flattening and laying the Hawken beside him, he risked another look.

A third of the horses were in the water and splashing furiously for the opposite bank. Ten of the thieving Blackfeet were north of the herd, there to cover the retreat of their companions. With good reason. Swarming from the Nez Percé village was every man, boy, and woman capable of wielding a weapon.

Nate rested the flintlock on his left forearm and took careful aim at one of the braves nearest to him. Cocking the hammer, he held his breath to steady his arm, then squeezed off the shot. Flame and lead belched from the barrel, and the target clutched at his chest, spun, and dropped.

The cloud of gunsmoke gave away Nate's approximate position, and the slain warrior had barely touched the soil when three arrows cleaved the vegetation above his head. He rolled to the left and came to rest behind another trunk. Lying on his side, he jammed the expended pistol under his belt and pulled his last loaded gun.

Strident war whoops filled the air as the Nez Percé closed on the raiders. A fusee cracked, one of the inferior trade rifles frequently given to friendly Indians. A second later a man screeched in rage.

Nate rose into a crouch and ventured to stick his head out again. Half of the stolen horses were across the river, as were two of the Blackfeet. But the remainder of the animals, startled by the gunfire and the general bedlam, were milling about in confusion.

Already the fleetest Nez Percé were engaging the Blackfeet, exchanging shafts and lances as rapidly at they could shoot or throw. The few raiders who had been trying to slay him were hastening to the north to help hold off the Nez Percé. In moments the two forces joined and the fighting became hand-to-hand.

Nate left the Hawken lying on the grass and charged from concealment, drawing his knife as he did. The swirl of combatants and horseflesh had formed a shroud of fine dust over the battle, and he had to squint to see. Another fusee went off, and a lance came out of nowhere and narrowly missed his right shoulder.

Pausing to get his bearings and find a foe, he heard a whoop and spun to his left to confront an enormous Blackfoot bearing down on him like a berserk buffalo bull. The brave swung his tomahawk at Nate's face. Ducking, Nate thrust his knife to stop the Indian from getting any nearer, then pointed his flintlock and fired.

Struck in his left shoulder, the Blackfoot jerked with the impact. Spurting blood like a fountain, he grimaced, but otherwise ignored the wound. With maniacal vigor he renewed his assault. Nothing would stop him from sending the hated white man with him into the spirit realm.

Crimson drops sprinkled Nate's cheeks and

chin as he lunged to one side and tried to stab the Blackfoot in the ribs. Even though wounded, the brave was able to dodge nimbly out of harm's way. For a heartbeat they faced one another, the Blackfoot crouched, ready to strike, seemingly unaware of the heavy flow of life-giving blood that coated his body.

Growling like an animal, the Blackfoot sprang forward, his tomahawk aimed straight for Nate's head.

Nate raised the knife in time to block the blow, but the sheer force drove him backwards and he almost tripped over a rock. Recovering his balance, he waited for the next swing, which was not long in coming. This time he was ready.

Instead of the knife, he raised the pistol and deflected the tomahawk by striking the warrior's wrist with the gun barrel. At the same time he arced his other hand up and in, plunging the knife as far as it would go into the Blackfoot's muscular body.

The warrior stiffened and wrenched away, tearing the keen blade loose. More blood spurted, and he staggered. He blinked slowly, as if in astonishment, then snapped defiant words at Nate in the Blackfoot tongue. Finally he convulsed and fell on his face to lie stiff as a board.

Whirling, Nate sought other enemies. The dust still hung in the air, and he advanced until he could see what was happening. But there was little to see. The Blackfeet had received their due.

The tide of battle had been with the Nez Percé and their superior numbers had made short work of most of the raiders. Seventeen of the dreaded Blackféet lay sprawled in savage death, as did 14 of the Nez Percé.

"Well done, Nate. We saw that last scrape of yours."

Nate turned. Niles Thompson and 12 other trappers, the men he was to have joined to go hunt the Blackfeet, were a few yards behind him, having just arrived.

"Heard the ruckus but we couldn't get here in time to help," Niles said, stepping forward and surveying the carnage with satisfaction.

The Nez Percé were moving among the downed Blackfeet, verifying their hated enemies were indeed dead. Several were taking scalps.

"Those damned Blackfeet will think twice before they make a raid on a Rendezvous again," one of the other trappers remarked.

"Losing a few braves won't stop them none," another muttered.

Nate moved to the last warrior he'd slain, and knelt to wipe his knife clean on the man's leggings. His blood still pulsed from the excitement of the battle and he had to take deep breaths to calm himself down. As he stood and replaced the knife in its sheath the same tall Nez Percé he'd observed earlier walked over to him.

"Who are you, white man?" the Nez Percé asked in sign language.

Nate had to wedge the flintlock under his belt so he could employ his hands. "I am called Grizzly Killer," he replied.

"I have heard of you," the Nez Percé signed. "I am Otter Belt, war chief of my people." He gestured at the battleground. "Was it you who fired at them and stopped them from getting across the river?"

"I did what I could."

Otter Belt beamed and placed a huge hand on Nate's shoulder to give it a friendly squeeze. Then he stepped back and signed, "I thought as much. I had just spotted the Blackfeet when you shot at them, although I did not see you clearly." He nodded at the village. "You have done us a great service and we would be honored to have you share in our victory feast."

To refuse would be considered an insult, and Nate had no desire to offend the Nez Percé. He'd had few personal dealings with them, but he knew many trappers who lived among them and trapped their territory. Were he to decline, it might make life difficult for those men. "I would be happy to come," he said.

"Good," the Nez Percé responded.

"Is it all right if I bring my family and some friends?" Nate requested, thinking Shakespeare and Blue Water Woman might like to attend.

"You are welcome to bring all the friends you want," Otter Belt said, and glanced at the clustered trappers. "All of our white brothers may come if they wish."

Nate grinned. "Do you know what you are letting yourself in for?"

"Friends share with friends," the Nez Percé signed, and began to turn. He paused to add, "Join us when the shadows start to grow long. We will be ready by then."

"We will be there," Nate promised. A hand

clapped him on the back and Niles Thompson spoke almost in his ear.

"Wait until the boys hear about this! We'll raise hell clear to the moon and back!"

Nate saw a group of Nez Percé heading across the river to pursue the pair of Blackfeet who had escaped. Then he remembered his Hawken and went into the trees to retrieve it. Once on the bank again, he commenced reloading his guns.

The racket had drawn trappers and Indians from all directions. Bunches of mountaineers were hurrying in the direction of the Nez Percé village, as were bands of Flatheads, Shoshonis, and Bannocks. Jim Bridger, wearing his flat-brimmed black hat as always, showed up with over two dozen armed trappers and was approached by Otter Belt.

Involved in reloading, Nate paid little attention to the many conversations taking place all around him and the swarm of activity as the Nez Percé scalped and mutilated their foes. He had done his duty and now he could return to camp and let Winona know he was safe. She must have heard about the raid and might be worried about his safety.

"I'll be darned if you haven't done it again, Troilus."

About to shove his ramrod to the bottom of the rifle barrel to tamp down the powder and ball, Nate spoke without looking up. "I thought I was Horatio."

"Not today," Shakespeare said, stepping up to him and scanning the littered bodies. "I don't know how the dickens you do it, but you have a knack for being in the right place at the right time."

"What are you talking about?" Nate asked, looking at him.

"I met Niles a minute ago as he was running back to camp to tell everyone," Shakespeare said, and shook his head as if in amazement. "Seems you single-handedly stopped the Blackfeet from absconding with every horse the Nez Percé own.

"What nonsense. All I did was delay a raiding party until the Nez Percé could rally."

"Was that all? Well, by this evening the story will have been told and retold to the point where you could qualify for knighthood if noble King Arthur and his Round Table were still in business."

Nate smiled. "It won't be as bad as all that."

"Won't it? You should know by now that men love to tell stories, and the more exciting the tale, the better. Mankind has been doing it since before Homer, and we'll keep right on doing it because it's the best form of entertainment we have, better than the theater or the opera any day."

Off to one side stood two Nez Percé and three trappers who were regarding Nate with critical interest while speaking in hushed tones so as not to be overheard.

"See?" Shakespeare said, motioning toward them. "This incident has added tremendously to your reputation. Before long you'll have made a bigger name for yourself than Carson or Bridger ever will."

"Don't get carried away," Nate joked. "They're

known by every man in the Rockies."

"So are you."

"I doubt that very much."

"A man is known by the deeds he does, and the greater the deeds the more his name spreads. In the eights years you've lived in these mountains you've acquired more of a reputation than I have."

Nate slid the ramrod into its housing under the barrel and shrugged. "Even if you're right, which I don't think you are, what harm can having a reputation do?"

"You have a reputation for being able to lick grizzlies with one arm tied behind your back. They say you've killed Blackfeet in droves and won't back down for any man," Shakespeare disclosed. "You're the toughest, roughest man around, and when you go out you'll be lying in a heap of foes."

"What harm can such talk do?" Nate asked again.

Shakespeare nudged a dead Blackfoot with his toe. "Reputations have a way of catching up with a man. One of these days you might have to live up to yours."

Chapter Nine

The celebration was in full, rowdy swing when the trouble began.

Nearly every trapper was present, as were a good many of the Shoshonis, Flatheads, and Bannocks. Their Nez Percé hosts had prepared a lavish banquet fit for royalty. There were over a dozen tin pans measuring 18 inches in diameter heaped high with stewed buffalo and elk meat, boiled deer meat—or, as those in the States would call it, venison—and even some roasted mountain sheep. Huge containers of boiled flour pudding spiced with dried fruit were also offered for consumption, as were cakes and 20 quarts of a tart sauce made from sour berries and sugar. Plenty of coffee was available, as were ample "spirits" courtesy of the mountaineers.

When Nate's party got there the festivities had been under way for over an hour. Otter Belt immediately sought him out and gave him the seat of honor. Nate accepted, and only then perceived the feast was being thrown especially for his benefit, which was later confirmed when Otter Belt stood and gave a short speech in the Nez Percé tongue and sign language detailing Nate's part in saving the Nez Percé horses. When Otter Belt concluded, the trappers and some of the assembled Indians joined in a hearty cheer.

Seated cross-legged on Otter Belt's left, Nate smiled and tried to act nonchalant although he was extremely uncomfortable being the center of so much attention. He ignored Shakespeare who was grinning at him as if to say, "I told you so." Thankfully, after the cheer everyone settled down to eat in earnest and he devoted his attention to cramming as much succulent elk meat into his stomach as it would hold.

Twenty minutes later, after Nate had licked the grease from his fingers and was in the act of wiping his hands on his leggings, Otter Belt turned to him.

"My people would like to express our gratitude for what you did earlier," the war chief signed.

"This feast is gratitude enough," Nate replied, hoping they wouldn't embarrass him by making more of a fuss over him. Indians were like that, though. As generous as could be. If they believed a white man was their friend, there was nothing they wouldn't do for him. He knew of instances where Indians had gone hungry in order to share their last morsels of food with a visiting trapper.

"We would be happy if you would accept a gift," Otter Belt revealed.

"It is not necessary," Nate insisted.

"My people believe it is."

There was no getting around it. Nate put on his best face and inquired, "What kind of gift did you have in mind?"

Otter Belt glanced at a pair of warriors waiting nearby and clapped his hands. They promptly raced from sight around a lodge. Rising, the war chief gazed at the motley assemblage until nearly everyone had seen him and quieted down. Then his hands flew in sign and he spoke in his own language. "Friends of the Nez Percé. Never let it be said that my people do not know how to show our gratitude for those who do us a great service. Grizzly Killer honored us by coming to our aid when we needed it most. As a token of our friendship and the esteem in which we hold him, we are giving him a gift. When men see him on this gift, they will remember the fight by the Green River and how he risked his life on our behalf. And they will know that the Nez Percé do more than speak empty words when we say we are glad to share all that we have with our white brothers."

An expectant hush gripped the mountain men and Indians, and all eyes swiveled toward the lodge when the two warriors reappeared a few moments later leading the gift by its reins. Murmuring broke out, whispers of admiration and praise.

Nate felt his own breath catch in his throat. It was no secret the Nez Percé were the best horse breeders in the Rockies, and perhaps the very best of all Indian tribes everywhere, even better than the vaunted Comanches far to the south. Nez Percé horses had been renowned ever since the days of Lewis and Clark, and lucky was the trapper who managed to obtain one. Few did, because the Nez Percé were understandably reluctant to part with their carefully cultivated stock. But there, standing before him, was a Nez Percé horse all his very own. And it was, without any doubt, the single most magnificent animal he had ever laid eyes on.

A gelding, the horse was over 18 hands high and bore pied markings, distinctive white spots admixed with darker brown patches. Its very contours spoke of endurance and speed. A healthy, glowing coat added to the impression of vitality, and a long, full tail lent an extra element of beauty.

Otter Belt stepped to the horse and affectionately rubbed its neck. Then he beckoned for Nate to join him. "This is the best war horse in our village," he stated matter-of-factly. "it runs like the wind and does not know the meaning of fear. It has charged into a line of Bloods and never missed a step. It has run into a fleeing herd of buffalo without flinching." He smiled at Nate. "This is the kind of horse most men dream about owning, but never do. Any warrior in my tribe would give two hundred horses for this one."

Nate reached out a hand and the gelding rubbed its nose against his palm. He was tempted to tell the Nez Percé the gift was more than he deserved for the little he had done, but the sight and feel of the tremendous mount stilled his protest. Despite himself, he wanted that horse, wanted it more than he had ever wanted anything with the exception of Winona.

By the looks being directed his way, he was the envy of practically every man present. He walked around the horse once, noting its fine lines, then, on an impulse, gripped the reins and swung onto its bare back. Jabbing his heels into its flanks, he took off at a gallop and rode along the bank for hundreds of yards beaming like a kid who had just been granted his heart's desire.

He took his time returning, savoring the rhythm of the horse and its powerful stride. Stroking its neck, he spoke softly into its ear, letting the gelding become accustomed to the sound of his voice. "If this don't beat all. I'd be a fool to refuse you, and Mrs. King didn't raise her boys to be fools. So you and I are going to go everywhere together from now on. How would that be?" He stopped and ran his fingers through its mane. "You're going to need a name, something appropriate for a horse of your breeding."

They were almost to the village and a majority of the trappers had risen to meet them.

"I know," Nate said, recalling the many lessons on the ancient Greeks through which he had suffered while acquiring his education back in New York City, boring lessons imparted by a stern, prim teacher who always addressed the class in a dull monotone. "I read about a winged horse once that was supposed to be the best horse ever created. It's only fair that you have his name."

Holding his chin high, Nate stopped at the edge of the crowd to let them admire his new animal. "Gentlemen," he announced, "I'd like to introduce Pegasus."

"Pegasus?" a burly trapper said. "Now there's a fancy name if I do say so."

"I bet this animal would beat anything on four legs," another man remarked.

Nate chuckled. "I'd bet so too."

From the back of the mountaineers came a harsh challenge. "Then put your pelts where your mouth is. I'll gladly take you up on that bet right now. How about another hundred hides?"

There were mutterings of surprise among the trappers and they parted to allow the speaker to approach Pegasus. From the rear ranks swaggered Robert Campbell, his thumbs hooked in his belt, a cocky smile creasing his face. Three friends of his trailed behind, insolence written all over their features.

Otter Belt seemed puzzled by the confrontation. He glanced from Nate to Campbell, then stepped between them and used sign language. "This is a peaceful gathering, white brother. Grizzly Killer is our honored guest."

"Don't I know it," Campbell quipped in English before resorting to sign. "I mean no disrespect to your people. But the mighty Grizzly Killer believes the horse you have given him is the fastest around." He snorted contemptuously. "I say I have one that will run rings around that pied gelding of his."

The war chief nodded and addressed another Nez Percé. After a brief discussion, Otter Belt turned to Nate.

"Are you willing to race this man?"

As much as Nate would have liked to decline, he couldn't. Campbell, who had once been a *voyageur* or free trapper in Canada, had always been belligerent but crafty. He'd thrown down the gauntlet in public. Nate's honor, not to mention his reputation, was at stake. If he refused, he would be branded a man of big words but little deeds, a man of no account. He couldn't afford to let that happen. As much as he valued the money he would get after selling his beaver hides, he valued his self-respect and personal pride even more. "I will be more than happy to have Mister Campbell eat my dust," he declared.

Many of the trappers burst out laughing.

Campbell whispered to one of his friends, who ran off to the grassy area where those mountaineers who had ridden to the feast had tied their horses. "I've got you now, King," Campbell boasted. "You've put your foot in it for sure."

"The proof is in the pudding," Nate retorted for want of anything wittier. He saw Campbell's friend returning, and to his consternation the man was leading a superb black stallion every bit as big and powerful as Pegasus.

"I call him Jester," Campbell said proudly, "because he makes jokes out of every horse he races."

Nate could well believe it. The black had the lines of a well-bred racer but the prancing air of a half-wild Indian steed. If appearances counted for anything, then that horse would be as fleet as they came. He'd had no idea Campbell owned such a mount and remarked as much.

The *voyageur* chuckled. "Won him from a Crow who had stolen him from the Cheyennes. I never figured on using him to take my revenge on you, but a man learns to take advantage of opportunities as they arise, doesn't he?" He cackled with delight.

Nate noticed the black was saddled and looked down at the bare back of his new mount. Some Indian tribes used saddles on long trips and for special ceremonies, short leather affairs stuffed with buffalo hair and grass, saddles entirely different from the typical leather variety used by the mountaineers. Mostly Indians rode bareback, though. So if he transferred his own saddle to Pegasus, the gelding would probably object to the strange object by bucking or simply refusing to cooperate. And even if Pegasus accepted the saddle, the horse might be distracted enough not to run at its very best.

It appeared Nate had no choice but to take part in the race bareback. And that worried him. He hadn't ridden bareback in quite some time—he couldn't even remember the last such occasion. While doing so wasn't terribly difficult, it did require a bit more concentration on the part of the rider. And lacking a saddle meant the rider must cling harder with his legs and thighs. A single miscalculation, especially at a full gallop in a hotly contested race, could easily result in being spilled onto the ground.

"Is something wrong, husband?"

Winona, with Zach at her side, stood next to his right foot.

There's no fooling her, Nate reflected. Sometimes he was inclined to believe she could read his innermost thoughts. He gazed into her lovely eyes and said softly so no one else could hear, "I'd hate to lose all those peltries I worked so hard to collect."

"We will get by if you do."

"You must think I'm an idiot."

"I would not marry an idiot."

Nate grinned and reached down to affectionately stroke her cheek. "I love you, you crazy woman."

"And I love you."

Zach was gaping at Pegasus in wide-eyed wonder. "Is this horse really ours, Pa?"

"Ours and ours alone."

"How soon do I get to ride him?"

"A high-spirited animal like this?" Nate responded, amused by the request. His son was a skilled rider but there were limits to what a seven-year-old could handle. Indian boys, he knew, started on ponies and gradually worked their way up to full-grown war horses. "Oh, ask me again in nine or ten years."

Robert Campbell had swung onto his black stallion. He grinned at Nate and slowly walked his horse in a circle around Pegasus. "First I'm going to beat you at this, then at wrestling," he bragged. "In a few days everyone will be praising me to high heaven, not you."

Nate was sorry he'd ever agreed to wrestle Campbell for the first time five years ago. Such bouts were frequently conducted at Rendezvous for amusement, as were horse races, foot races, and hopping matches. Trappers were inveterate gamblers, and large wagers rested on every contest. He had wrestled Campbell to win a twenty-dollar bet and every year since, the *voyageur* had challenged him again in an attempt to erase the stigma of having lost. If nothing else, the man was persistent.

"Do you see that hill yonder?" Campbell now asked, pointing at a bald hillock about half a mile away.

"Yes," Nate said.

"Would you agree to race to the top and back for the extra one hundred pelts?"

Nate hesitated. The distance would be a mile all told, a mile riding bareback over rugged terrain.

"Well?" Campbell taunted him. "Is it agreed or are you afraid?"

"It's agreed," Nate said, and the words were no sooner out of his mouth than Campbell lashed the black stallion with a quirt and was off like a shot.

Chapter Ten

It took all of three seconds for Nate to react to being tricked and he promptly jabbed his heels into Pegasus. The gelding responded superbly, breaking into a full gallop in the span of two strides. But by then Robert Campbell already enjoyed a 15-yard lead and was racing to beat the wind.

Cheers and shouts of encouragement broke out among the trappers, as did a hasty round of betting. The spur-of-the-moment start had taken them by surprise; few had bothered to offer a wager on their favorite. Now they made up for the oversight in a flurry of yelled amounts and boisterous takers.

Nate held his body flush with the gelding's broad back, trying to make it easier on the horse. Pegasus flew, and there was no need to apply his heels again. Unlike Campbell and many Indians, he never used a quirt as a matter of personal choice. Smacking a mount to get it going had never struck him as being particularly humane or even smart when any horse that ever lived responded to human kindness with the same or better results. There were men who beat their mounts as a matter of course, liberally applying a quirt or whip. Such men, Nate believed, were essentially lazy. If they would take as much time to treat their animals with affectionate consideration as they did beating the poor creatures, their horses would do all that was demanded of them and more.

Nate had no idea of the number of races in which Pegasus had participated, but from the energetic manner in which the gelding galloped after Campbell's black stallion he gathered there had been plenty. Pegasus fairly flew. Head stretched, tail straight, the gelding flowed over the ground like greased lightning.

But it wasn't enough.

Campbell's black was more than equal to the occasion. Its lead fell to 12 yards and then it held steady, neither losing ground nor gaining. Campbell repeatedly glanced back and smirked, confident of victory.

Using his thighs as much as possible to grip the gelding instead of his lower legs, Nate urged it on with words of encouragement. "Go, boy, go! Faster, Pegasus! You can do it! Faster!"

The gelding couldn't possibly understand the words. It could and did respond to the tone, seeming to expend more effort than before.

Only vaguely was Nate aware of the frenzied uproar to his rear. The trappers and Indians were venting a collective roar that rose to the high heavens. He idly wondered if Winona and Shakespeare were cheering for him, then cleared his mind of all distracting thoughts and focused on the race. Paying attention to the terrain was paramount. Otherwise he'd surely lose.

Campbell skirted a thicket and was momentarily lost to view.

Just before doing the same, Nate glanced over his shoulder to gauge the distance already covered. A quarter of a mile, probably less, he guessed, and swept around the thicket with the gelding's hoofs pounding.

A large log lay directly in his path.

Nate's breath caught in his throat. He started to lift the rope reins, but was on the log in a flash. Appalled, he felt Pegasus leave the ground in a great, arcing jump, and he clung to the gelding's mane in desperation. The impact when they landed jarred him to his bone marrow. Despite his grip, his body slipped to the right, and for a terrifying instant he thought he was going to fall. Somehow, he clung tenaciously and righted himself.

Robert Campbell was laughing in devilish joy.

A suspicion hit Nate then, and his knuckles became white from the pressure he applied. What if that had been deliberate? What if Campbell knew this stretch of ground well and had tried to get him unhorsed? He wouldn't put such a ploy past the wily trapper. Perhaps

Campbell had planned to race others and had previously scouted routes that would give his black stallion an advantage. Perhaps, through a quirk of fate, Nate had played right into his hands.

Angry, he rode with renewed vigor, molding his form to the rhythm of Pegasus. Jumping the log had caused him to lose another three or four yards. Somehow he must make up the distance and pull even with the black.

To Robert Campbell's credit, the man rode with flair, an expert in the saddle. Obviously he had ridden the stallion so often that man and horse were essentially one, although he persisted in using the quirt when doing so wasn't really necessary. Every 20 or 30 feet he would lash the stallion a few times as if reminding it who was its master.

Their course so far had been across a flat stretch intermittently broken by thickets and small stands of trees. Now they entered a tract of virgin forest, which tested their horsemanship to its limits.

The trees were pines, tightly spaced. Nate used the reins adroitly, avoiding rough trunk after rough trunk, swinging wide around branches that threatened to snare him or injure the gelding. Again and again he had to duck low to save himself from a nasty rap on the skull.

Another log loomed directly ahead and he girded himself. True to form, Pegasus went over the obstacle as if endowed with the wings of his namesake. This time Nate was prepared and stayed aboard.

He broke from the forest only ten yards behind the black. Excited, he urged the gelding to go faster, then suddenly realized Campbell had intentionally slowed.

Why?

No sooner had the question come to mind than he saw the steep bank and the shallow creek below, a creek littered with flat, slick stones. The black went down the bank on its haunches, rose, and crossed the creek in short jumps.

The gelding was going far too fast when it reached the near bank. It was all Nate's fault and he knew it. He attempted to rein up, but Pegasus had too much momentum to do more than plunge down the steep bank at a lurching run, a run that carried them into the stream, where Pegasus's hoofs came down on the slick stones and the inevitable occurred.

Pegasus slipped and fell.

A blurred image of the ground rushing up to meet him prompted Nate to propel himself from the gelding. He hit hard on his right shoulder and rolled, inhaling water as he did. Pain speared through his right arm. In a heartbeat he was on his knees in the middle of the creek and staring in horror as Pegasus struggled to stand.

Ignoring the pain, Nate bounded to the gelding's side and grasped the bridle. He tugged, helping the horse to rise, afraid it might have sustained a broken leg.

Pegasus immediately headed for the opposite bank.

Swept off his feet, Nate frantically swung on top of the surging animal. If Pegasus had been harmed by the spill, there was no indication of it. Grinning, soaking wet, he clung to the reins as the gelding vaulted the rim of the bank and cut out after the black.

Campbell now held a 30 yard lead.

Nate was dismayed. Given the black's strength and speed, he didn't see how he could overtake the *voyageur* before the race ended. A ten-yard lead he could surmount, maybe. Certainly not a 30-yard gap. Nevertheless, he forged onward, refusing to acknowledge defeat. He would see the race through to the end. No one had ever accused him of being a quitter and no one ever would.

They were now crossing an area cut by gullies. Not deep gullies, nor very steep, but of sufficient number to render breakneck speed impossible.

Nate saw the trapper slow down and did likewise, not caring for a repeat of his narrow escape in the creek. Pegasus sensed the need for care and took the gullies one at a time, leaping each in a single mighty jump, then trotting on to the next. Negotiating the erosion-worn ditches was a slow, arduous process, but Nate was sorry when the dangerous stretch ended because he had reduced Campbell's lead by eight or nine yards. The black had balked at a few of the gullies until Campbell vigorously flailed away with the quirt, and the delays had proven costly.

Before them lay clear, flat land all the way to the top of the hill. Campbell lashed his mount in a frenzy, determined to regain lost ground.

Nate concentrated on staying calm and riding the best he knew how. His thighs were sore and his shoulder ached, but neither bothered him enough to ruin his concentration. As the seconds seemed to crawl by, he narrowed Campbell's lead. And the smaller it became, the more furious the trapper became. Campbell was belaboring his poor horse like a madman.

The gentle slope of the hill posed no problems for either man. Campbell reached the rim, whirled, and started back down. As he passed Nate he cackled and shouted, "Fool! Those hundred pelts are mine!"

Not bothering to banter words, Nate galloped to the crest, turned the gelding, and raced toward the flatland. Was it his imagination or was the black stallion running a shade slower than previously? Perhaps Campbell had pushed it too hard during the first leg of the race. If so, Nate stood a chance, a slim one, of saving those hides for the fur company buyer.

The second time across the gullies didn't take half as long. Pegasus knew what was required and took to the challenge like a frisky colt to its first run around a pasture. Those sturdy, powerful legs cleared each ditch with ease.

Much to Robert Campbell's evident distress, his black faltered at the last few gullies, and he only got it across them by pounding the quirt on the animal's head and neck.

Nate was elated to see the gap between them shrink to slightly over ten yards. He patted the gelding and spoke encouragement in its ear, as proud of it as if they had already won.

Campbell looked around, his features contorted in a mask of unbridled rage.

Neither animal experienced a problem at the creek, and then they were dashing through the pines. The black went to clear a log but its hind legs struck the top and it landed unsteadily, almost throwing Campbell. Cursing, the trapper resumed riding, his heels smacking into the black's flanks.

When they burst from the forest onto the final leg, Nate was only eight yards behind his nemesis. A great cry went up from the spectators. He thought about all the trappers and Indians who must have bet on him and hoped they wouldn't decide to get even if he lost. When drunk, trappers were highly unpredictable.

A low black shape suddenly materialized to the left of Pegasus, loping along beside the horse. Nate glanced down to find Samson shadowing him. In all the excitement he had completely forgotten about the huge dog that had lain so quietly at Zach's side during the feast. He had opened his mouth to shout at it to go away, afraid Pegasus would be spooked, when the gelding became aware of the dog's presence and responded in typical equine fashion.

Pegasus went faster.

Nate grinned and held on, deciding to let Samson tag along. The dog had to increase its speed to stay abreast, and when it did Pegasus compensated by increasing his speed.

Only six yards separated the two horses.

Campbell was beside himself. His quirt hit the black in a nonstop barrage of wicked swings that left welts and drew blood. He looked at the crowd in the Nez Percé village, then at Nate, and screamed at his mount, "Faster, damn you! Faster or I'll feed you to the wolves!"

The black stumbled, recovered, and gamely raced toward the finish.

But now Nate was only two yards away. Then one. Samson still raced at the gelding's side, which Pegasus didn't like at all. With only a hundred yards to go, Pegasus finally pulled even with the black stallion.

Robert Campbell looked at Nate and raised the quirt as if to strike him. Apparently thinking better of the idea, he lowered his bloody prod and hit the stallion instead.

Nate focused on Otter Belt, who stood by himself in a narrow strip of open grass between two long rows of trappers and Indians. He must reach the war chief first to win. Slapping his legs against Pegasus, he smiled when the gelding nosed ahead of the stallion. "You can do it!" he urged. "Just a little bit farther!"

"No!" Campbell screeched. "No!"

The black valiantly tried to overtake the gelding. In a flurry of hoofs it drew even, and they were running neck and neck for a dozen yards. But the wellspring of strength and endurance that had carried it so far was almost empty. Legs rapidly weakening, it abruptly fell to the rear.

Nate reached the lines of cheering mountaineers and Indians. The bedlam was deafening. He swore he felt Pegasus flinch in alarm, and then they were galloping up to Otter Belt and he glimpsed Winona beaming proudly at him and Zach clapping in childish abandon. There was a pounding in his ears as he thundered past the war chief and brought the gelding to a gradual stop.

From all sides swarmed trappers, Nez Percés, Flatheads, Shoshonis, and Bannocks, all offering hearty congratulations in their respective tongues or in sign language. Nate sat numbly in the saddle, inhaling deeply, and nodded in appreciation.

Only when Otter Belt forced his way up to Pegasus did the revelers quiet down.

"Grizzly Killer is the winner," Otter Belt announced, using his hands to translate the statement in sign. He had to pause as a mighty shout shook the clouds.

A hand fell on Nate's leg and he looked down into the loving face of his wife and son. He touched her chin and wished he could take her into his arms and kiss her passionately.

In the silence that followed the shouting, the weary plod of hoofs seemed oddly out of place.

Nate twisted and gazed into the hate-filled visage of Robert Campbell. The black stallion's neck and forehead were caked with blood and it favored a rear leg.

"You've won fair and square," Campbell declared so everyone could hear. "The hundred pelts I wagered will be brought to your camp." Then he leaned forward and spoke in a venomous whisper. "But don't think this is the end of it, King. We still have the wrestling issue to settle, and when the time comes I'll break your back!"

Chapter Eleven

The arrival of the caravan on July 6th sparked a whirlwind of activity.

On being informed that the caravan was near, the Nez Percés prepared to welcome the missionaries they had heard so much about. Both warriors and women adorned themselves in their finery, with the braves tying their normally wild manes of hair and adding eagle feathers to enhance their appearance while the women braided their hip-length black hair and tied the braids with brightly colored ribbons.

The warriors applied paint to themselves and their war horses, and upon hearing that the horse carts and wagons were in sight they rushed to their animals and cut out to receive the newcomers.

In a ragged line the mass of howling braves descended on the wagon train, many firing guns while others pounded on war drums. The fur company men smiled and waved, knowing the reception for what it was, but the startled missionaries at the rear of the column were convinced they were under attack by bloodthirsty hostiles. They started to gather in their stock and the women hustled into their wagons. Panic-stricken, they watched in horror as the Nez Percés swooped around them, and only then did one of the top men in the American Fur Company, Captain Wyeth, ride back to inform them there was no cause for alarm.

The trappers enjoyed a hearty laugh at the expense of the bewildered missionaries, and then the leaders of the Nez Percé were introduced. Otter Belt and others insisted that the men of the Great Spirit stay near their village, to which Dr. Marcus Whitman agreed.

Whitman, along with his pretty wife Narcissa, and the Reverend Henry Spaulding and his wife, as well as William Gray, composed the missionary party. They were enthusiastically devoted to converting the Indians to Christianity, and while quite ignorant of Indian customs and beliefs they were all keenly eager to learn.

After Whitman had set up his camp the Nez Percé lined up their entire village for a formal reception. Every man, woman, and child filed past, the warriors shaking hands as they had been instructed was the white custom and the Nez Percé women kissing Mrs. Whitman and Mrs. Spaulding on the cheek.

On the heels of the Nez Percé came some of the Shoshonis and Flatheads. Narcissa welcomed them all in sincere friendship, and at long last the majority of the Indians drifted away and she was temporarily left to her own devices. It was then, as she went to enter her tent, that she spied two women standing off to one side as if shy about approaching her. She wasn't knowledgeable enough about the various tribes to be able to determine to which tribe they belonged, although she suspected they hailed from different ones. Smiling, she beckoned for them to come near and said softly, "I won't hurt you, my dears. Please don't be afraid."

Narcissa didn't expect either to understand her words but she did feel they would respond in their hearts to her tone. So she was all the more surprised when the younger of the pair, a truly beautiful woman with the most gorgeous eyes Narcissa had ever beheld, answered in perfect English.

"Thank you, Mrs. Whitman. We did not know if we should impose on you or not."

"Wherever did you learn to speak my language so fluently?" Narcissa inquired.

"From my husband, Nathaniel King," the young woman replied. "I am Winona, a Shoshone." She nodded at her companion, a stunning older woman who carried herself with grace and dignity. "This is Blue Water Woman, a Flathead, and the wife of Shakespeare McNair."

"I have heard of Shakespeare," Narcissa said, recalling a conversation she'd had with Captain Wyeth concerning some of the more colorful characters inhabiting the Rockies. "They say he is a man to ride the river with," she added, delighted that she remembered that particular figure of speech as told to her by the same gentleman.

"We wanted to welcome you to the Rendezvous," Blue Water Woman said, and made no attempt to hide the intent scrutiny she gave the missionary. "You are very beautiful."

Narcissa blushed. "I thank you, my dear, for the compliment, but I'm afraid back in the States a man wouldn't give me a second look."

"White men can not be so foolish," Blue Water Woman said with a grin.

Narcissa noticed Winona was studying her too, but there was something in the younger woman's eyes, a hint of apprehension perhaps, for which Narcissa could not account. "Is anything wrong?" she bluntly asked.

Winona stared into the white woman's dazzling blue eyes and could barely find her voice. How could she tell about her fears? How could she reveal the terror lodged in her heart? She had became terrified by the very thought of Nate journeying to St. Louis to see Adeline Van Buren, and now she saw that her fears were justified. If Adeline was only half as beautiful as Narcissa Whitman, what chance did she have to retain Nate's affection?

"Is anything wrong?" Narcissa repeated, and placed a gentle hand on Winona's shoulder. "Forgive my manners, but you seem deeply troubled."

"You are very wise," Winona said. "I understand why you are close to the Great Mystery."

"The . . . ?" Narcissa began, and then caught on. "Oh. Yes. Actually, it is my husband who is the ordained minister. I simply help him in my own humble way."

Winona felt a wave of despair wash over her and she had to avert her eyes to hide her emotional strife. Deep down she had always wondered if Nate still cared for Adeline Van Buren, and now she was certain he must. If all white women were as kind and attractive as Narcissa Whitman, how could he not love her?

Blue Water Woman knew of her friend's feelings. Once, many years ago, she had entertained similar thoughts about Shakespeare. Now she came to Winona's aid by changing the subject. "We are leaving for St. Louis when the caravan returns. Will all white women treat us as graciously as you do?"

Taken by surprise by the query, Narcissa was about to answer in the affirmative when her instinctive honesty prevailed. "There will be some, I am sorry to say, who will look down at you. They will regard you as their inferiors. But don't let them spoil your stay. There are just as many white women who will be delighted to share your company."

Winona had regained her composure and faced the missionary squarely. "Tell me, Mrs. Whitman. Could your husband ever love an Indian woman?"

Narcissa blinked, even more surprised. "My husband loves me and I know he would never stray," she replied. She detected a fleeting flicker of fear on the Shoshone's lovely features and suddenly sensed there was much more to the question than casual curiosity. "I would imagine," she added slowly, choosing each word with care, "that my husband Marcus is very much like your Nathaniel. When a man takes a woman in marriage it usually means the man loves her to the depths of his soul and that he will do anything to make her life happier and easier." She paused. "A man has certain needs, just like a woman does, and one of those is to have a woman to cherish and protect. Oh, I know there are those who say women belittle themselves by looking to men for protection, but so long as there is evil and wickedness in the world and there are those who delight in hurting others, there will be a need for men to protect their families."

Having listened attentively, Winona nodded. "I know the truth of your words," she said softly.

From Winona's expression, Narcissa gathered that her words had done little to comfort the troubled young woman. She tried to fathom the underlying cause and ventured a personal question. "Has your husband given you reason to doubt his affection?"

"No," Winona said quickly. "Not at all."

"Has he been seeing another woman?"

"No," Winona responded, and bit her lower lip. She abruptly turned. "Thank you for talking with us, Mrs. Whitman. We are very grateful." With that she hurried off, Blue Water Woman at her side. Once she looked back to see Narcissa Whitman staring quizzically after her, so she smiled and waved. Then she walked toward their camp.

"You could have told her the truth."

Winona glanced at her friend. "She is a nice woman but I do not know her well enough to confide in her."

"So you will torture yourself all the way to St. Louis?"

"I have no choice. I must see for myself."

"Nate is not like most of the other trappers. He will never leave you, not even for a white woman."

"But so many trappers have done just that."

"Yes, but they usually leave their Indian wives after a winter or two. Few stay on as long as Nate has stayed with you," Blue Water Woman noted. She sighed and gestured at the fur company store where brisk trading was being conducted. "Were it any other white man but Nate, I might be worried for you. But Nate is different. He likes living in the mountains, and he has adopted many of our ways. In some respects he is more like an Indian than a white man." She nodded at peaks to the west. "Here is his home."

Winona reflected for a dozen yards before replying. "I have thought of all that. I have tried . . . ," she began, and left her sentence unfinished at the sight of Niles Thompson hurrying in their direction. Something about his posture told her he was extremely upset.

"Hello, Niles," Blue Water Woman greeted him.

The trapper nodded gravely. "Pleased to see you ladies again."

"Is something wrong?" Winona inquired.

Thompson shifted to verify no one had followed him or was paying any special attention to them. Moving closer, he spoke in a low tone. "Where's Nate?"

"At our camp so far as I know," Winona answered. "Why?"

"Warn him to keep a lookout for Campbell. That coon has been bragging around camp that he's going to stomp Nate into the dirt."

"My husband knows all this," Winona said. "He is being very careful."

"Does he know that Campbell intends to jump him when he least expects it? Does he know that Campbell has been hanging around with the Ruxton brothers?"

"No," Winona replied, alarmed. The Ruxton brothers had a reputation for being two of the nastiest trappers in the Rocky Mountains. No one knew much about their past except that they had left the States in a hurry after killing a man. They had become the scourge of the mountains, slaying several mountaineers in drunken brawls, at which they were masters. Decent trappers avoided them. And no Indian woman would marry either one or sleep with them because both invariably were filthy, their clothes grimy. Rumor had it they bathed once every two or three years.

"Why is Campbell spending time with those two?" Blue Water Woman asked.

"I don't know, but it worries me," Niles admitted. "Nate can take Campbell any day of the week, but if the Ruxtons butt into the affair there's no telling how it will turn out."

"I will inform my husband," Winona promised.

"There's one thing more," Niles said. "I was standing at the southeast corner of the company store filling my pipe when I heard men talking softly around the corner. It was Campbell and the Ruxtons and they didn't know I was there." He frowned. "I couldn't catch all their words, but I heard enough to guess that Campbell is betting heavily on the side and the Ruxtons have bet every hide they own on the outcome of the match."

"What do you mean by betting on the side?" Winona asked.

"Everyone at the Rendezvous knows Campbell has wagered a hundred prime pelts against a hundred of Nate's. But he's also bet other trappers. I'd say he'll lose his whole catch if he doesn't best Nate."

Blue Water Woman gazed at a group of trappers who were butchering four slain elk. "With so much at stake, Campbell can not afford to lose."

"Exactly. And with the Ruxtons involved, the wrestling match might well turn into a matter of life and death. Knowing the Ruxtons as I do, you can count on there being bloodshed. They might try to kill Nate."

"Wouldn't Campbell have to"—Winona sought the English word she had rarely used but heard Nate explain once—"forfeit any claim to the pelts?"

"Not if Campbell licks Nate fair and square first. I figure the Ruxtons will make their play then."

"Campbell will never beat my husband."

"What if they have some trick up their sleeve?" Niles said. "What if they provoke him somehow? Get any man mad enough and he becomes downright careless."

"How would they do such a thing?" Winona inquired, and insight speared through her like the razor tip of a lance. "I must get to our camp," she said, taking a step. But that was as far as she got when a gruff voice hailed her, sending a chill shivering down her spine.

"Well, if it ain't the wife of the mighty Grizzly Killer! Look at this, boys. Our prayers have been answered."

Robert Campbell swaggered toward them, his big hands swinging loosely. On either side was one of the wicked Ruxtons, tall, thin men who were as dark as the dirty clothes they wore.

"Hello, Campbell," Niles said, casually placing himself between the three men and the women. "What can we do for you?"

The *voyageur*'s features clouded. "*You* can do nothing, old man. I'm here to talk to Grizzly Killer's wife."

"I don't want you bothering these women," Niles said sternly. "The men at the Rendezvous won't stand for such behavior."

"Me? Bother these lovely ladies?" Campbell said in mock indignation, then leered at Winona. "Why, all I want is a little conversation."

Chapter Twelve

Winona struggled to retain her composure. Displaying fear in front of men like Campbell, men who delighted in intimidating others, only fed the flames of their exaggerated self-importance. They viewed themselves as models of manhood as they conceived manhood to be, as tough and hard and strong enough to best anyone else. When others cowered before them it reinforced their delusions and only made them behave even worse than they normally did. She had seen a few such men before—even Indian tribes had them on occasion. So now she held her chin high and said in a calm tone, "I have no desire to talk with you, Mr. Campbell."

The Ruxtons cackled, and one of them imitated her statement in a mincing tone.

"Why not?" Campbell demanded. "Ain't I good enough to talk to?"

Niles motioned for the trio to leave. "Let these women be, Bob. I'm warning you."

"*You're* warning *me*?" Campbell bellowed, and before any of them could guess his intention he hauled off and slugged Niles Thompson on the chin. His brawny hand, capped by rock-hard knuckles half the size of walnuts, had the same effect as a wooden club or a tomahawk.

Taken totally unawares, Niles buckled and sprawled in an unconscious heap, blood trickling from his mouth. Nearby trappers and a few Indians had witnessed the attack and were rapidly converging.

Appalled, Winona knelt to examine Thompson. But a rough hand seized her arm and she was wrenched to one side.

"Leave him be!" Campbell snapped. "He asked for it and he got it."

His warm breath touched Winona's face and she smelled the bitter scent of alcohol. Campbell wasn't drunk, but he had imbibed enough to aggravate his belligerent nature. "Please," she tried to placate him. "We do not want any trouble."

Campbell took a step and grabbed her wrist. "I want your husband, missy. Where is he?"

"Right here."

The *voyageur* and the Ruxtons whirled, their features betraying their surprise at beholding Nate not six yards away. Behind him, to the right, stood Shakespeare McNair. Both held Hawkens, and both practically radiated barely contained fury.

Over 15 mountaineers had gathered in a ring

and were gazing in disapproval at Campbell. More were hurrying over from all directions.

Nate took a step and suddenly pointed the Hawken at Campbell's face, the barrel almost touching his nose. "Let go of my wife," he growled.

Slowly, grinning maliciously all the while, Campbell released Winona's wrist. "Now, now, King. Don't be hasty. I'm not carrying a gun as anyone can plainly see. I'm not even toting a knife."

Nate glanced at Campbell's waist, where only a wide brown belt was in evidence. Without a word he extended his rifle back towards Shakespeare, who took the Hawken and then leveled the two he now held at the Ruxtons.

"Interfere and you'll both be sporting new navels," Shakespeare said.

"You have no call to be threatening us," one of the Ruxton brothers complained.

"I'm not threatening. I'm promising."

One of the bystanders knelt beside Niles Thompson, who was groaning as he slowly revived. "What is going on here? Why was Niles struck?"

"He butted into a personal matter," Campbell replied angrily. "He should have known better."

"So should you," Nate said.

"What?" Campbell responded, facing him.

Nate hit him. He didn't bother to announce his intention. He didn't threaten. He didn't bluster. His right fist swept up from beside his leg and hit the *voyageur* squarely on the chin, on the exact same spot where Thompson had been hit.

The force of the blow staggered Campbell. He tottered and started to sink to one knee, then recovered and shook his head vigorously. Rubbing his jaw, he grinned and said, "What will it be? Fists or wrestling or anything goes? I say we have our match right here and now."

"Fine by me," Nate said, removing his flintlocks and handing them to Winona. The sight of the *voyageur* mistreating his wife had been almost more than he could endure. He had come within a hair of shooting Campbell right on the spot, and now he couldn't wait to tear into the troublemaker and vent his fury.

A couple of men assisted Niles in rising and helped him move to one side. Others were shouting at the top of their lungs, "Fight! Fight! King and Campbell are going at it!" to draw the rest of the trappers.

Nate paid attention to none of them. He had eyes only for Robert Campbell until a tug on his leggings prompted him to look down. There stood his wide-eyed son, who had been trailing behind Shakespeare and him while playing with the ever-present Samson.

"Are you going to beat up this man, Pa?" Zach asked. "I thought you said we should be nice to everyone."

The question startled Nate. He realized Zach hadn't seen Campbell lay a hand on Winona, for which he was grateful. But now he had to explain to Zach's young, innocent mind why a grown man, his own father, was deliberately seeking a fight. "Yes, we are supposed to be nice to those who are nice to us. But not everyone you meet in life will be that way. Some, like this man, only know how to be mean and hurt others."

Zach looked at the *voyageur*. "He should be taught some manners."

"He will be," Nate said. "Now stand aside."

The boy moved over beside Winona.

Nate glanced at her. "Keep Samson under control. Don't let him interfere on my behalf."

"Be careful, husband."

Sarcastic laughter burst from Robert Campbell. "Ahhhh, how touching!" he declared. "I swear I'm about to start crying at any minute." He grinned at the Ruxtons. "I wonder if this squaw treats all her men the same way."

The dam broke. A tidal wave of rage swept over Nate and he sprang, driving his right fist deep into Campbell's midsection and doubling the man in half. A sweeping left clipped the *voyageur* on the chin, sending him tottering rearward.

Campbell regained his footing, touched his bruised chin, and chuckled. "Mad, are you, Grizzly Killer? Good. I want you mad, you son of a bitch."

Again Nate moved in to inflict punishment, but this time Campbell was braced and ready. Nate's right was blocked, his left swatted down, and then a pair of sledgehammers boxed him on the ears and the world exploded before his eyes. Dazed, he felt his knees strike the soil, and then another punch smashed into his jaw and he found himself on his side with everything and everyone swirling around and around and around. He heard mocking laugher and attempted to rise.

"Come on, Nate. At least put up a fight."

The taunting voice brought Nate's rage back and suddenly he could see clearly again. He lunged, his arms out, and tackled the unprepared Campbell around the knees. They both crashed down, with Nate on top, and then began grappling as each tried to get the other in an unbreakable hold.

As they wrestled one fact became disturbingly apparent to Nate. No matter how many times in the past he had defeated Campbell, no matter how inexperienced and rash Campbell had once been, all that had changed. The man had always been endowed with the strength of an ox, but now he was as coldly calculating as a wolf and as fierce as a wolverine.

Each of them applied and slipped holds a score of times. They tumbled end over end, their arms and legs intertwining as each attempted to pin the other. The trappers and Indians enthusiastically shouting encouragement were forced to back out of the way again and again as the combatants rolled almost into their midst.

Sweat caked Nate from head to toe. He got an arm looped around Campbell's head, but was instantly thrown onto his side. Iron fingers gouged into his neck as he tried to roll to his feet, so he gripped both of Campbell's wrists and heaved, flipping Campbell onto his back.

Nate surged upright and so did his foe. Campbell was grinning smugly, even more confident of victory now than he had been before the horse race.

"I'm going to rub your nose in the dirt," he

boasted savagely, and motioned for Nate to close with him. "Any time you're ready, bastard."

About to spring, Nate caught himself just in time. By allowing his anger to get the better of him he was playing right into Campbell's hands. He must be wary and call on all the skill at his command, skill honed in many a back lot in New York City during his childhood and teen years.

Next to boxing, wrestling was one of the most popular sports among boys of all ages throughout the States. Foot races came in a close third. Nate had participated in all three frequently, much to his father's distress. Neither of his parents had viewed such activities as fitting for a young gentleman, and every time Nate came home with torn clothes and bruises he was roundly chastised for his breach of discipline.

"Afraid, Mouse Killer?" Campbell taunted.

Nate adopted a boxing posture and circled, seeking an opening in the other's guard he could exploit. The *voyageur* imitated his example, all the while continuing to smile smugly.

"I think before I'm done I'll rip one of your ears off with my teeth," Campbell said, and laughed. "I did that once to a man up in Canada. You should have heard him howl."

Trying to concentrate on the fight, Nate had an inspiration. If Campbell could try to distract him with conversation, he could do the same. "Where were you born?" he asked.

Campbell paused, clearly puzzled. "Why should you care?"

"Just curious," Nate said, circling, ever circling.

"I was born in Vermont but I left home when I was fourteen and drifted up to Canada. Became a *voyageur* for ten years." Campbell stopped and studied him. "I don't see what difference it makes."

"You will," Nate said, and abruptly took a step backwards and closer to Campbell, who predictably stepped to the left and inadvertently set himself up for a wide, lightning-quick right. Nate flinched as his knuckles connected on Campbell's sturdy jaw.

Rocked on his heels by the blow, Campbell lashed out ineffectually with an uppercut. His punch was countered and a fist drove into his gut with the power of a battering ram. Doubling over, he gasped for air, and instead received another fist full on the mouth.

Unrelenting, Nate landed a jab on Campbell's left cheek, then lashed a left above the right eye. The skin split and blood trickled down over Campbell's eyebrow, making Campbell blink.

"Damn you!" he hissed.

Then the *voyageur* went berserk.

Nate barely firmed his footing before Campbell came at him like a whirlwind, fists flying. He blocked and ducked adroitly, but for every punch he avoided another hit home. In vain he tried to score, but Campbell thwarted every swing. His frustration mounting, he was forced steadily backward when without warning there came a frantic shout from Shakespeare.

"Nate! Look out! Behind you!"

Before Nate dared risk a glance something struck him below the left knee and he realized someone had kicked him. He fell, and while falling heard one of the Ruxtons whoop in triumph. The next instant Campbell delivered a devastating kick that bent Nate like a snapped twig, excruciating agony racking his chest. Stunned and weak he sputtered and tried to rise.

"Now I've got you!" Campbell gloated, drawing back his right foot to kick again.

DO SOMETHING! Nate's mind screeched, and he threw himself at Campbell's shins. The *voyageur* danced to one side but Nate's shoulder smashed into him before he was clear. Campbell went down, angling at Nate, and they clinched in mutual boiling wrath. Campbell's hate-distorted features were inches from Nate's face, his hot breath fanning Nate's cheeks, and it was more than Nate could endure.

Whipping his head back, then forward, Nate butted Campbell and heard a crunch as Campbell's nose shattered. Wet drops spattered his face. He butted again, and suddenly Campbell shoved free and scrambled to his feet.

Nate took longer to rise. His chest ached abominably and he wondered if he might not have a broken rib or two. His face pulsed with pain, and every breath was laborious. He barely heard Winona's cry.

"Nate! Be—"

But he did hear the sound of a thud and Shakespeare's statement.

"Don't worry. That Ruxton won't bother you again."

So the brothers had tried to turn the tide once more, but failed. He began circling Campbell, whose face was red, doubly so because it was caked with crimson. Nate's hands hurt when he balled his fists and his feet were leaden.

Campbell touched his crushed nose, his feral eyes narrowing. "I'll kill you for this!"

There had never been any doubt in Nate's mind that the *voyageur* had long since ceased to regard their bouts as friendly matches. And it was more than a matter of personal honor where Campbell was concerned. The man wanted to kill, to pound Nate to a pulp, to see Nate's lifeblood pumping onto the grass.

And now, with a harsh snarl more animal than human, Robert Campbell attacked.

Chapter Thirteen

Much, much later, when the assembled mountaineers were gathered around various evening camp fires and swapping tales, the overwhelming majority were to agree that never in all their born days had they witnessed such a starkly brutal fight, such a primitive display of sheer savagery.

Nate certainly wouldn't have objected to their collective opinion. Under the relenting barrage administered by Robert Campbell, he was compelled to give ground.

The *voyageur* punched, kicked, gouged, and clawed. When clinching he even resorted to biting. No tactic was too mean, too despicable. Uppermost in his mind was inflicting pain, and with single-minded purpose he applied himself to the chore as only a man who had been driven beyond the brink of human reason could do, with a ferocity only a man who had reverted to a bestial level could achieve.

Repeatedly bruised and battered and cut and scratched, Nate was pressed to his limits as he tried to counter and evade Campbell's blows. He never would have believed Campbell had it in him. With his forearm he blocked a punch that would have caved in his face, then swung a right, going for Campbell's jaw. But Campbell easily deflected the counterpunch and arced a fist into Nate's stomach.

For a second Nate thought he might be sick. His gut tossed and churned, bending him in half. A leg swept out of nowhere and a foot caught him flush on the cheek, catapulting him onto his back. He placed both palms on the grass, trying to rise, when another kick speared into his ribs. Everything spun. A ringing filled his ears. Only vaguely was he aware of being violently gripped by the front of his buckskin shirt and of being hauled upright.

"This time there's no escape!" Campbell gloated.

Mustering his strength, Nate attempted another head butt. A rough hand slapped his head aside.

"No you don't. I'm wise to your tricks," Campbell said, and began to slap Nate senseless.

Was there nothing he could do? In a fog of torment he felt his foot bump against Campbell's and instinctively he raised that foot and slammed it down on his adversary's instep, throwing all of his weight into the stomp.

Campbell yelped and limped backwards, his face distorted with anguish.

"Keep swinging, Nate! Don't give up now!"

Was that Shakespeare? In Nate's befuddled state he couldn't tell. Suddenly he saw a fist pound Campbell in the mouth. Then another. Grinning idiotically, he wanted to shout for joy and urge whoever had come to his aid to keep on going until, with a start that returned his clarity of mind, he realized he was the one giving Campbell a thrashing.

Robert Campbell retreated a few yards, dug in his heels, and wouldn't be moved come what may. He boxed with obstinate persistence, refusing to be budged or beaten.

All of Nate's previous experience now proved profitable. Elemental instinct seized control of every fiber of his being, and he battled without a sole conscious thought. Hit. Duck. Hit. Twist. It was almost as if his body had a mind of its very own and he was a casual spectator.

Granite-hard knuckles crashed into Nate's chin and he tottered. He saw Campbell swing again, and this time he gripped Campbell's wrist, whirled, and heaved. The *voyageur* shot over his shoulder as if out of a cannon and thudded to the hard ground.

Campbell took his time getting up. Every square inch of skin on his face was covered with blood. His lips were pulverized beyond recognition. One eye was swollen and his nose was a mess. But still he stood.

Nate met him with all the force of a hurtling bull, ramming a right and left combination to

Campbell's jaw that turned Campbell into a board and set him up for the punch to end all punches. Nate could feel his shoulder and back muscles rippling as he brought his fist from behind in a vicious half-circle and hit Campbell so hard that for a few seconds he believed he had broken his hand. But it was worth it.

Robert Campbell, arms extended and flapping wearily like the wings of a ungainly bird striving to become airborne, staggered, buckled, and toppled onto his back to lie completely still, out to the world.

Gasping for air, Nate shuffled next to his nemesis and waited for Campbell to rise. He was certain Campbell would. The man wasn't human; he was akin to a force of Nature, unstoppable as an avalanche. Nate tried to speak and found his throat strangely constricted. Coughing, he spoke in a strangled croak that hardly resembled his normal voice. "Get up, you bastard! Get up and finish it!"

Dimly he became aware of a tremendous din on all sides. A hand clapped him on the shoulder and he glanced around to see Shakespeare regarding him kindly. "What?" he blurted out. "Step back until it's over."

"It *is* over."

Shocked, Nate stared at Campbell and belatedly appreciated the truth. The man was a wreck, a demolished imitation of his former self. "I did that?" he asked in disbelief.

"You surely did," Shakespeare said.

A pervading weariness engulfed Nate like the black waters of a flash flood and he sagged, his knees giving out. A strong arm encircled him and he was held erect.

"Are you all right? Can you stand?"

Nate nodded, although he had no idea whether he could or not. Straightening his knees, he swayed, then held steady. A warm hand slipped into his and Winona was there, smiling proudly, Zach beside her, holding tight onto Samson, and equally happy.

"You taught him, Pa."

"I guess I did," Nate mumbled, amazed at how thick his lips seemed and how sluggish his mouth worked.

"We should leave, husband," Winona said. "You need much doctoring."

"I'm not the only one," Nate responded, thinking of McNair.

Winona, misunderstanding, gazed at Campbell. "True. But he is not much worse off than you are."

"I'm that bad?"

"Your own mother would not recognize you."

The statement brought unbidden memories of Nate's mother, fond memories because for all her stuffiness she had loved him dearly and treated him as best she knew how. Dimly, he felt someone else take hold of him on the other side and heard Niles Thompson's voice.

"Not to fret, Nate. Your friends are all around you. The Ruxtons won't dare try a thing."

"I'm sorry I didn't stop the one who kicked you," Shakespeare commented. "There were too many men all moving around at once. But I stopped him the second time."

Niles chuckled. "He gave that Ruxton a lump that will take a month to go down."

"Thanks," Nate muttered, and then he was moving, being propelled through the throng. He glimpsed Winona, Zach, Samson, and Blue Water Woman to one side, and other trappers, all men he knew well, had surrounded the entire party.

"Listen to me, Nate," Niles said. "The Ruxtons lost heavily. They won't take this lying down. You must be on your guard constantly. Do you understand?"

A numb nod was all Nate could manage. Raw fatigue ate at every nerve in his body. His eyelids felt as if they weighed a ton and he kept his eyes open only with the greatest effort.

"A bunch of us will take turns watching over the camp at night until you're on your feet again, and there will always be two or three of us handy in the daytime too," Shakespeare said, and hissed like a striking snake. "I wouldn't put it past those Ruxtons to try and sneak up on you after dark to slit your throat."

Niles nodded. "I'm afraid to say it, but sooner or later you and the Ruxtons will tangle. It's inevitable. Now that you've bested their champion and made them lose so heavy, they'll want to nail your hide to a tree."

"Let them try," Nate said, barely able to speak.

"That's the spirit," Niles responded, smiling.

Shakespeare laughed. "What else would you expect from the mighty Grizzly Killer?"

For three days nothing happened.

Nate spent the entire time in his camp, resting

to let his body heal and eating and drinking as much as he could to fortify his strength. His many bruises started to go down, his cuts started to heal. Only his ribs continued to bother him, and Shakespeare helped in that regard by binding his chest tightly with strips of cloth. It hurt to move, but not so badly he couldn't get around if he had to.

Winona hovered over him like a mother hen over one of its brood, supplying his every want. She rarely left his side. No matter when he opened his eyes she was right there, ready to comply with any request. Under her tender ministrations he mended swiftly.

Niles brought word that Robert Campbell was holed up in a dense stand of trees well south of the Rendezvous proper. Evidently Campbell had relocated his camp there after the fight. The Ruxtons and two other men were staying with him, and the rumor making the rounds was to the effect the Ruxtons had sworn to make Nate pay for their losses with his blood.

But Nate had many friends, and they proved their loyalty by showing their support in his time of need. Seldom did an hour pass that there weren't three or four trappers seated near his lean-to. At night two or three men would patrol in ceaseless circles. If the Ruxtons had intended to strike then, their plans were thwarted.

By the afternoon of the third day Nate had persuaded Winona to let him walk about. It felt good to use his legs again, to stretch his aching muscles. Niles and four more mountaineers were near the fire, drinking some of Winona's delicious coffee and listening to Shakespeare recite selected passages from the bard:

"Full many a glorious morning have I seen flatter the mountain-tops with sovereign eye, kissing with golden face the meadows green, gilding pale streams with heavenly alchemy. Anon permit the basest clouds to ride with ugly rack on his celestial face, and from the forlorn world his visage hide, stealing unseen to west with this disgrace. Even so my sun one early morn did shine with all-triumphant splendour on my brow. But, out, alack! He was but one hour mine, the region cloud hath masked him from me now. Yet him for this my love no whit disdaineth. Suns of the world may stain when heaven's sun staineth."

One of the trappers shifted his lean legs. "They sure were pretty words, McNair, but what do they mean? I confess I have a hard time following your trail sometimes."

Shakespeare grinned. "Let each man find the meaning in his own soul. My meanings are mine and might have no meaning for you."

The trapper laughed. "I swear you could talk a beaver out of his hide without ever having to set a single trap."

They all smiled.

Nate took the opportunity to speak up. "Niles, I appreciate all that you and the others have done. But I feel a mite guilty lying around while all of you are risking your lives on my account. So, since I think I'm well enough to protect my family if need be, there's no need for any of you to keep putting yourselves out on our behalf."

"Did he say something?" Niles asked Shakespeare.

"He's been mumbling a lot ever since he tangled with Campbell," McNair answered. "Don't pay any attention to him."

"You know darn well what I said," Nate said.

Shakespeare winked at him. "Good sir, why do you start, and seem to fear things that do sound so fair? I' the name of truth, are ye fantastical, or that indeed which outwardly ye show? My noble partner you greet with present grace and great prediction of noble having and of royal hope, that he seems rapt withal. To me you speak not. If you can look into the seeds of time and say which grain will grow and which will not, speak then to me, who neither beg nor fear your favours nor your hate."

"What does that nonsense have to do with anything?" Nate demanded, peeved he was being ignored. "Sometimes I suspect you make this stuff up as you go along."

"How dare you, sir. Old William S. is hardly *stuff*."

Knowing further argument would prove pointless, Nate stepped to the lean-to and sat down. In the corner Zach played with Samson, repeatedly offering a large stick to the huge dog, which it accepted and tugged on until the boy squealed with laughter and let go. "Having fun?"

"Samson is the most wonderful dog there is," Zach responded, and gave the beast an affectionate hug.

"Would you be upset if we were to leave him behind when we go to St. Louis?"

Zach's mouth dropped open. "Leave Samson? Never!"

"It was just a thought," Nate said. He had grave reservations about taking the dog to such a big city. Samson, after all, was still partially wild at heart and wild creatures seldom fared well in human jungles where the natural law of the survival of the fittest was modified—some would say perverted—by the laws of men.

"Which reminds me," Shakespeare said. "Winona tells me you're planning to go back with the caravan. If that's the case, you won't need me along to help ward off hostiles. I've changed my mind about going."

From a dozen yards away, where Winona and Blue Water Woman sat in conversation, came the stern voice of the Flathead woman.

"We are going to St. Louis, dearest, and that is final."

The mountaineers did their best to conceal their smirks.

"Women!" Shakespeare muttered. "If I ever figure out why the Good Lord created them, I'll die a happy man."

Blue Water Woman blew him a kiss.

Chapter Fourteen

The American Fur Company caravan started for the borders of distant civilization on July 18th. The horse carts and beasts of burden that had packed in supplies were now laden with the prime beaver furs collected by the fur company from their own mountaineers and purchased from the free trappers. As on the trip out, Tom Fitzpatrick served as commander of the caravan.

Instead of heading straight for St. Louis, the caravan leisurely followed a preplanned route that took them to Fort William on the mouth of the Yellowstone River. From there they made across the prairie toward Bellevue.

Nate rode with his family, Shakespeare, and Blue Water Woman near the head of the long column so they wouldn't be forced to breathe the dust swirled into a thick cloud in the caravan's wake by the passing of the cart wheels and the stock animals. Now that he was finally on his way, he was impatient to reach St. Louis. He kept asking himself the same questions over and over. What if Adeline had grown tired of waiting and returned to New York City? What could have brought her to St. Louis in the first place? Why had she sought him out after so many years?

The plodding progress of the carts ate at Nate's nerves. In his mind's eye he envisioned their location on the rolling plains, well northwest of St. Louis and heading roughly due east toward Bellevue, a frontier outpost approximately 450 miles from the city where Adeline waited. If he was to strike off on a beeline to St. Louis he would arrive there at least two weeks before the slow caravan.

That night, their tenth since leaving the vicinity of Green River, Nate cleared his throat and looked across the camp fire at his wife and best friends. "I have an idea," he announced.

"We're in trouble," Shakespeare said.

"What is it?" Winona asked.

"I'd like to shave some time off our trip by going straight to St. Louis instead of staying with the caravan."

No one said a word for over a minute. Shakespeare and Blue Water Woman shared knowing looks.

Winona looked down at the flames lapping at the wood she had gathered earlier and said softly, "We run a great risk if we leave the safety of the caravan."

"I've been talking to Fitzpatrick and some of the men driving the carts. They say no one has seen any sign of the Sioux or the Cheyenne in this region for a couple of months. The Sioux are supposed to be north of here, the Cheyenne hunting buffalo off to the south. We should be safe if we push hard and stay alert."

"Should be," Shakespeare said.

"You don't want to do it?" Nate asked, aware of the chilly reception his idea had received.

"I'm just thinking of your family and my wife," Shakespeare responded.

"And you think I'm not?" Nate bristled.

"I didn't say that," Shakespeare said. "I'll do it if you insist, but I have grave reservations."

"Winona?" Nate prompted.

She lifted her head and gazed at him with the strangest expression he had ever beheld on her face. Her mouth curved downward for a fleeting interval, and then she squared her shoulders, took a breath, and answered. "I will do whatever you wish, my husband. As always."

"Fine. Then I'll inform Tom Fitzpatrick," Nate said, rising. He hastened away.

Winona watched his broad shoulders disappear in the darkness. She rose, glanced at her sleeping son, and walked a few yards from the fire to be alone with her thoughts. She knew the reason Nate was in such a hurry and it upset her beyond measure. He was eager to see that woman from the great city! All of her fears formed into a single wave of panic that washed over her heart and made her tremble uncontrollably.

"Care to talk?"

"Thank you, no, Blue Water Woman," Winona replied, keeping her back to her friend so Blue

Water Woman wouldn't see the moisture rimming her eyes.

"It means nothing."

"Does it?"

"He was close to her once. His feelings are only natural. Just remember he loves you."

"Does he?"

"You know he does."

Winona kept quiet, struggling to maintain her composure. She heard Blue Water Woman move back to the fire and she stepped farther into the night, her arms folded across her chest, feeling chilly despite the warm temperature. She wished she could dig a hole, crawl into it, and pull the earth over her. For years she had dreaded losing Nate, and now her anxiety threatened to blossom into reality. For the life of her she didn't know what to do.

Should she go on as if nothing out of the ordinary were occurring? Should she behave as she always had on the assumption nothing was changed between Nate and her? Or should she confront him with her fears and see how he reacted? She could even demand they call off the trip and go back to their cabin. But what would he do if she gave him an ultimatum? Would he become angry? Would he leave her for this white woman?

She sighed, overcome with sadness, and rued the day she had ever been born.

The next morning at first light they rode off, bearing southeast. A few of the cart drivers and stock tenders waved.

"Good luck!" Tom Fitzpatrick called.

"The same to you!" Nate replied, and took the lead, his Hawken draped across his thighs for instant use. While he was glad to be striking off on his own, he was puzzled by his wife's sullen behavior. All last night and since awakening she had been unusually reticent, refusing to speak unless spoken to. With one exception. Around Zach she was her normal, cheerful self.

He tried putting himself in her place. What did she have to be upset about? Leaving the caravan? Or was she still disturbed over Adeline? He couldn't believe it was the latter. She must know by now that he loved her and her alone. The only logical conclusion left the caravan. She was mad because he was hazarding all of their lives to shave off a few weeks' travel time, an unreasonable attitude in his estimation. Being with the fur company caravan was no guarantee hostile Indians wouldn't bother them. Sometimes roving bands refused to permit the caravan to pass until the warriors received a certain amount of merchandise as a token of the whites' friendship. And there was always the danger of encountering a war party of Blackfeet, although those demons generally confined themselves to the mountains and the northern plains.

So he concluded he would say nothing to Winona. He knew her well enough to know it would intensify her anger, while if he let the storm pass she would be her old self before two or three days went by.

Or so he thought until six more days elapsed and she hadn't changed at all. Near him she invariably was morose. Where once he could get her to laugh with ease, now she wouldn't even smile. Neither Shakespeare nor Blue Water Woman offered any advice, although both were aware of the situation.

Late on the afternoon of the sixth day he was riding 20 feet in front of the others when Pegasus suddenly nickered and gazed off to the southwest. He looked in the same direction, his pulse racing upon discovering a large group of Indians riding over a low hill, heading westward. Instantly he reined up and raised the Hawken, fearing the worst, but the group disappeared moments later.

Shakespeare hurried up. "I saw them too, but I couldn't tell which tribe they belonged to."

"If they saw us and they're hostile, they'll try to get around behind us to attack," Nate said. "We'll play it safe and swing eastward for a while." By doing so they would put more distance and a few hills between the Indians and themselves.

"I could go check their tracks," Shakespeare suggested. "Might give us a clue."

"What if they're waiting for us to do just that?"

"They might be," Shakespeare said. "Indians can be tricky devils when they put their minds to it." He swung his white horse. "East it is then."

For the better part of an hour they pressed on, until Nate was satisfied they had nothing to fear from the band. He angled to the southeast once more, seeking a likely spot to make camp for the night, preferably somewhere sheltered from the constantly blowing wind and where their fire wouldn't be seen for miles around.

The sun sank ever lower.

Just when Nate had about resigned himself to making a cold camp on the open prairie, he spotted a line of trees indicating the presence of a creek. Rifle in hand, he rode closer. Other than a rabbit that bolted into the brush, there was no sign of life.

The creek was a thin ribbon of sluggish water that would probably dry up by September. A few pools of five or six inches in depth proved perfect for the watering of their mounts and their pack animals. Their camp was established under the trees on the east bank where a circle of undergrowth served to screen the camp fire from view.

"We were fortunate today," Blue Water Woman remarked as she helped Winona prepare the evening meal.

Nate didn't care to dwell on the subject since it would only fuel Winona's anger. "I wonder how much St. Louis has changed since last any of us were there," he remarked.

"Quite a bit, I'd imagine," Shakespeare said wryly. "But not enough."

"How so?"

"Once a city springs up, stopping its growth is about as easy as stopping a raging forest fire. So St. Louis must be bigger than either of us recollect. I'd also wager there are more footpads, pickpockets, and killers prowling the streets and alleys than there ever were before. Imagine it. Over fifteen thousand people crammed into that one area on the west bank of the Mississippi like so many sheep in a pen, just waiting to be fleeced by the wolves in their midst."

Nate saw a pensive expression on Winona and promptly responded, "I've been there, remember? It's not as bad as you would paint it."

"No. Worse."

Nate was all set to launch into an argument to soothe Winona's fears when a welcome interruption transpired.

"Pa, Samson hears something out there."

All eyes turned to the huge black dog, resting on its haunches next to Zachary. It was staring to the north, its ears pricked, its nose flaring as it loudly sniffed the air.

"Could be any kind of critter," Shakespeare said. "Nothing to fret over."

As if to prove the mountain man wrong, several of the horses whinnied nervously and stamped the ground.

Rising, Nate scooped up his Hawken and cautiously moved to the edge of the firelight. Shakespeare was at his side. He saw nothing, heard nothing. Which meant nothing. There were nocturnal creatures capable of moving soundlessly and unseen when the occasion required, fierce beasts such as panthers, wolves, and grizzlies. And there were always Indians, although they rarely raided at night.

"I have a bad feeling," Shakespeare said softly.

"A panther, you reckon?"

"Could be. Could be worse."

Nate placed a finger on the trigger and his thumb on the hammer. If it was a wild animal, he counted on the camp fire to discourage an attack. Few beasts, including grizzlies, would venture too near crackling flames, perhaps out of a primitive, instinctive fear developed ages ago by their bestial ancestors.

Shakespeare abruptly crouched and tucked his rifle to his shoulder. "Something *is* out there," he whispered.

"You saw it?"

"Yes. Low to the ground about a hundred yards out."

Straining his eyes, Nate failed to see whatever lurked in the dark. Long ago he had learned never to discount his mentor's exceptional sight and hearing. Time and again he had been amazed by Shakespeare's abilities. And here was another example. How in the world Shakespeare saw *anything* perplexed him. All Nate could see was a dozen yards or so of trees and grass, then a shroud of total blackness effectively blanketing the landscape in an impenetrable veil.

Pegasus neighed and tried to pull the picket stake loose.

"One of us will have to watch the horses while the other one protects our loved ones," Shakespeare said.

"I'll calm the horses," Nate offered, hastening to the stock. Deep down he would much rather have been closer to his family, but Shakespeare could protect them as well as if not better than he could. And with Shakespeare ill, it was only fair for Nate to tackle the more physically demanding chore.

All of the horses were upright, most bobbing their heads in their anxiety, some stomping their front hoofs. No two of them were looking in the same direction.

That fact worried Nate more than any other. The camp must be completely surrounded. But by *what*?

"Samson!" Zach suddenly cried as the dog rose and took several strides away from the fire, a growl budding in its barrel of a chest.

"Stay!" Nate directed, hoping for once the dog would obey. It was then he heard the chorus of howls that shattered the night, and identified the creatures he now saw swarming toward the horses in a snarling mass of exposed teeth and sleek bodies.

They were wolves.

Lots and lots of wolves.

Chapter Fifteen

It didn't matter that by all rights the wolves should be deathly afraid of the camp fire. It didn't matter that wolves rarely attacked humans. It also didn't matter that wolf attacks on the camps of Indians and trappers during the summer months, when game was most abundant, were practically unheard of. All that mattered to Nate King was that a large pack intended to deprive him of the horses he needed to get his family safely to St. Louis, and he wasn't about to stand idly by while the wolves crippled and killed his stock.

Rifle in hand, Nate ran to intercept the nearest wolves, a huge pair closing on Pegasus. He snapped the Hawken up, aimed hastily, and fired. The muzzle spat flame and smoke and one of the wolves stumbled and rolled headlong for a half-dozen yards, the ball lodged in its brain.

He heard Shakespeare's Hawken boom, then one of their wives got off a shot. But he didn't dare glance around to see if either had scored because the foremost wolves were on him and among the horses in a feral rush. In desperation he swung the Hawken like a club and knocked a hurtling beast aside. A frenzied whinny spun him around to see a wolf snapping at the legs of Winona's mare. His right hand was a blur as he drew a flintlock, cocking the piece even as his arm leveled. The pistol blasted, the wolf toppled, and already there was another there to take its place.

Nate dashed in swinging the pistol and the wolf fled. On all sides the horses were neighing and snorting and kicking their long legs at lupine adversaries. A few wolves were down, their skulls crushed or their ribs caved in. Pegasus, in particular, was giving a tremendous account of himself, his mighty hoofs flailing like sledgehammers.

Another shot cracked. Somewhere a wolf yipped in agony. Releasing the rifle, Nate drew his tomahawk and pounced on a wolf trying to rip open the belly of a lunging packhorse. The keen blade cleaved the wolf's neck as if the muscular flesh were mere wax and the beast staggered off, blood spurting from the cavity.

Whirling, Nate saw a wolf leave the ground in a magnificent leap, spearing at his face. He twisted, countered, and tore a nasty gash in the wolf's side. The nocturnal predator landed and turned for another try, but Nate was ready. In a single bound he planted the tomahawk in the top of the brute's cranium, then wrenched it free as the wolf fell.

Something struck Nate low down, below the knees, and he toppled over backwards, flailing his arms in a vain effort to stay erect. His shoulders hit and he rolled to his right, sweeping into a crouch just as a wolf rammed into his chest and razor teeth gnashed at his exposed throat. The impact bowled him over and he heaved, dislodging the wolf. In a flash it was on him again, going for his neck. He got an arm up and felt the wolf's jaws crunch down. Scrambling backwards, the wolf tenaciously clinging to him, he rose to his knees and swung the tomahawk. The blade sliced into the animal a few inches below the ear and the wolf let go and ran off into the swirling melee.

Nate felt his wounded arm become clammy with blood. He grimaced as he stood, and thought to glance toward the fire where his loved ones had been when the battle began. Winona and Blue Water Woman had Zach behind them and their backs to the fire. Both held knives, but neither, thankfully, was being attacked. The wolves were concentrating on the horses and displayed no interest in the women and the child.

"Look out!"

Shakespeare's bellow saved Nate's life. Instinctively, he pivoted, seeking the source of danger, and a wolf jumped past his face. His mentor raced up wielding a blazing firebrand and shoved it into the eyes of the startled wolf, which immediately turned and sped into the darkness.

Nate looked around, expecting to be charged again, but to his relief the fight was winding down. Seven or eight wolves lay still or convulsing on the ground. Several were limping off. The rest were in full flight.

"Damn, that was close!" Shakespeare muttered.

Their horses were still agitated, bobbing their heads and twitching their tails as they stamped the earth. Most had sustained injuries. A stock horse was down, its throat a gory mess, thrashing wildly as it tried to regain its footing. A few had pulled their picket stakes out but had not gone far. Pegasus stood untouched, his muscles quivering from excitement, his proud, aggressive posture showing he was prepared to fight again if need be.

"I never saw the like in all my born days," Shakespeare commented, lowering the firebrand. "Niles will never believe me when I tell him."

Nodding absently, Nate looked at the women and his son. "Are the three of you all right?"

"We are not hurt," Winona answered. "None of the wolves came near us."

"Where's Samson?" Zach asked in wide-eyed excitement, his features flushed. "I saw him go after a big wolf."

"We'll find him," Nate said, hoping he was telling the truth. If the dog had waded into the pack, outnumbered as it had been, it might be lying out on the prairie torn to ribbons.

"Your mongrel can take care of itself. We have to worry more about the horses," Shakespeare remarked, and stepped to the dying pack animal.

"This one is a goner, I'm afraid. We should put the poor thing out its misery."

"Give me a minute," Nate said. He quickly reloaded the spent pistol, then reclaimed the Hawken and reloaded it. Walking over to the feebly thrashing horse, he touched the tip of the rifle barrel to its forehead. "I hate killing a good horse," he mentioned, and did exactly that. The shot seemed to ripple off across the benighted plain.

"Do you think the wolves will return?" Blue Water Woman inquired.

Shakespeare shook his head. "Not likely, my dear. Critters have more sense than humans. They know enough to light out when they're licked."

Busy reloading again, Nate looked at his wife. "Stay close to the fire just in case. Zach, especially you, son."

"I want to find Samson," the boy protested.

"We will. Be patient." Nate walked to Pegasus and examined the gelding from its forelock to the end of its tail, from the mane to the fetlocks, but found no wounds, not so much as a nick. Two dead wolves attested to the gelding's courage when aroused.

"Most strange," Shakespeare said, prodding one of the bodies with a toe.

"What is?"

"This makes twice we've tangled with wolves since I came to your cabin. An Indian medicine man would be inclined to say it's an omen."

"Buffalo chips. It's bad luck, is all."

"Maybe," Shakespeare said, and grinned. "And maybe it's your guardian angel's way of letting you know you should forget all about going to St. Louis."

"My what?" Nate asked, scanning the black blanket of the prairie. Nothing moved. Not so much as a puff of breeze stirred the high grass.

"Your guardian angel. The angel that watches over you from the cradle to the grave. Didn't they teach you anything in Sunday school?"

"They taught me a lot. And you can forget about trying to scare me into changing my mind. You gave me your word and I'm holding you to it. We're going all the way to St. Louis."

"Has anyone ever told you that you can be an obstinate cuss at times?"

Ignoring the sarcastic comment, Nate set to work gathering the horses that had pulled their picket pins out, and used the blunt end of his tomahawk to pound the slender stakes back into the ground at appropriately spaced intervals. Then he went from animal to animal and examined all of the packhorses and their personal mounts. Other than Pegasus, all bore minor wounds.

He realized how fortunate they had been in losing only one of their original 13 horses. Not that they needed eight pack animals any longer. With their furs disposed off, two packhorses would suffice to tote all of their supplies to and from St. Louis. But there hadn't been time to take the extra packhorses back to their respective cabins, and rather than burden one of their many friends at the Rendezvous with looking after them, Shakespeare and Nate had decided to take all of their stock to St. Louis.

The fire was roaring at twice its original size when Nate finished ministering to the last of the horses and wearily sat down with his back to the flames so he could keep an eye on the surrounding prairie.

Winona brought over a steaming cup of coffee. "I thought you might like this."

"Thank you," Nate said, gratefully taking a swallow. He saw Zach sleeping and smiled. "This has been a night he'll remember the rest of his life."

"He is very worried about Samson. I'm surprised he fell asleep."

"I'll search for the dog come first light," Nate said, bending his neck to relieve a slight cramp. He took a deep breath and inhaled the pungent odor of the burning dried buffalo droppings Winona and Blue Water Woman had utilized for fuel. The women had gathered a substantial supply shortly before they halted for the night. He found the scent oddly pleasant.

It was strange, he mused, how the years changed a person. Back in New York City he would have laughed at the primitive notion of using buffalo chips to feed a fire. New York, after all, relied on wood, coal, and to an ever-growing degree, natural gas.

One city in his home state, Fredonia, had already set the trend for the rest of the country by converting all of the street lamps to natural gas and announcing plans for private homes to be likewise fueled. Natural gas was being touted by the press and the scientific community as the discovery of the ages, an economical means of one day providing all the lighting and cooking needs of the entire populace. And here he was relying on buffalo manure.

Nate smiled and stretched. He saw Shakespeare and Blue Water Woman had spread their blankets off to one side, near the horses, and were already snuggled close. Earlier he had agreed to take the initial watch, and he wondered if he could keep his leaden eyelids open long enough.

"Husband," Winona said softly.

He glanced at her.

"You should not discount Shakespeare's idea about the Great Medicine giving you an omen."

"Now don't *you* start."

"Hear me out, please. You know my people are very religious. We all believe in the Great Spirit, as your people call the source of all that is. And like some of your people, we believe that every man and woman has a guardian spirit who can guide them in all their actions."

Nate listened patiently. He was intimately familiar with Shoshone beliefs, as his wife well knew, and he was curious to see where the discussion was leading.

"To us, the spirit world is more important than this world in which we live because the spirit world controls us and everything around us. Few things take place by accident. When we see or hear something, it is for a reason. If someone sees an owl, that owl was sent to let the person know they would have good fortune. If a snake crosses your path, it means there are hard times ahead."

"Winona," Nate said, trying to forestall a detailed recital of the significance of sighting every animal known to her tribe.

"Allow me to finish. Twice now you have encountered wolves. You say it means nothing. But a medicine man in my tribe would not agree. And while I am not gifted as a prophet, I can make a guess as to why you have encountered them."

"I'd like to hear your explanation."

Winona stared at their horses. "The wolves were sent to warn you that you face great danger in St. Louis. Wolves are crafty creatures who prey on the weak, the young, and the sick. They never attack healthy animals or men unless they are running in a large pack."

"So you're saying I'll run into a pack of human wolves in St. Louis?"

"Something like that, yes."

Nate almost laughed. Doing so would arouse her indignation, so he wisely refrained. Years back he had learned how superstitious her people were, and all Indians for that matter. It was true they were religious, but many of their beliefs were based on childish fears of the supernatural, in his estimation. He had always been perplexed by the vision quests the young braves went on, and downright amazed by the peculiar torture endured by the warriors during the annual Sun Dance ceremony. Deliberately submitting to intense pain in order to achieve a spiritual vision had always struck him as highly illogical.

But maybe, he admitted to himself, his own prejudices were showing. Since he'd never submitted to the Sun Dance ceremony or gone on a vision quest, he had no right to judge those who did. Perhaps, one day, he would try one or the other simply to see for himself.

Omens were another story. Never in a million years would he believe that seeing an owl or a snake or even a white buffalo held any special significance. Such incidents were routine consequences of living in the wild, nothing more.

"I appreciate your warning," Nate said, putting a hand on her shoulder. "But wolves or no wolves, we are traveling to St. Louis so I can find out why Adeline Van Buren came so far to see me."

Winona bowed her head. "As you wish, husband." She then reached out to gently touch his wounded arm. "Is this blood? Why didn't you tell me you were hurt?"

"It's just a scratch. I forgot all about it."

"I will wash it anyway before it becomes infected," Winona said, rising. She walked to where their gear was stacked and picked up one of their water bags.

Her thoughtfulness touched Nate deeply, and as he smiled affectionately up at her he hoped he wasn't making the biggest mistake of his entire life. If anything happened to her or Zach he would never forgive himself.

Never.

Chapter Sixteen

Now where the heck was that dog?

Nate reined up on a low rise and surveyed the sea of limitless prairie stretching before his narrowed eyes. Overhead the sun blazed down, reminding him that he had been searching for almost two hours in ever-widening circles and the camp now lay miles to the northeast. Several times he had nearly turned around and gone back, but each time he remembered the anxiety in young Zach's eyes when he rode off at dawn. He must find Samson for his son if for no other reason, but for all he knew the dog might well be dead.

He hoped not.

Since acquiring the burly brute he had grown quite fond of it, and not only because Samson had occasionally saved his life. The dog displayed loyalty of the highest order and was incredibly gentle and affectionate with Zachary. Samson had become one of the family and deserved treatment accordingly, no matter what the risk entailed. Some would laugh at the notion, but they were the ones who had never owned a truly superb dog. Next to a fine horse, the best animal a man could have was a dependable, brave canine.

Sighing, Nate jabbed his heels into Pegasus and cantered down the rise, continuing in a generally southwestward direction. His mind turned over various possibilities. Samson might have been slain, the body consumed by the wolves. Or the dog could have gone too far and become lost, although he discounted that likelihood as extremely remote. Samson possessed an unerring instinct for always finding his way back to them.

Then what? Had Samson encountered another animal such as a grizzly? Even that great dog was no match for the lords of the Plains and the Rockies. Grizzlies were the undisputed masters of their wilderness domain. Wolves, panthers, even wolverines all gave grizzlies wide berths, although a wolverine might tackle one now and again.

Suddenly Nate spotted dark specks high in the sky and halted. Those specks were buzzards, slowly spiraling lower and lower. Where there were buzzards, there was death. The black birds with their featherless red heads might be descending to feast on Samson.

Again he goaded the gelding forward, into a

gallop, and went almost a mile before he saw a cluster of birds perched on a carcass at the base of a hill. From the size of the kill it was immediately apparent the dead animal wasn't Samson; it was too large. As he drew closer he distinguished the distinctive hump and massive contours of a bull buffalo.

He stopped well short of the carcass to avoid disturbing the vultures. They had a right to their meal because they served an important purpose in the natural order. Without them, carcasses would be left to rot. They were Nature's way of disposing of carrion quickly and efficiently. Regarded as repulsive by many of the mountaineers, they had always been viewed by Nate as essential elements in the intricate, outworking of the scheme of things.

What had killed the bull? He debated trying to get near enough to ascertain the cause. Maybe the wolves had done the deed. From the tracks he'd found, he knew the pack had scattered in all directions after the frustrated attack. Some might have come on this buffalo, perhaps an older animal or one weakened by disease, and brought it down. A gaping cavity where the bull's chest had once been indicated that a predator or two had eaten well of prime meat.

Pegasus raised his head, his ears alert.

Absently Nate looked up and his breath caught in his throat. He berated himself for becoming distracted by the dead buffalo when he should have been supremely alert. For there, on top of the hill, sat six Indians. The painted markings on their war horses and leather shields as well as their style of dress indicated they were Cheyenne braves.

None of them moved. They studied him intently, every so often surveying the prairie.

Nate knew what that meant. They were surprised to find a lone white man in this region, and they were sure there must be other whites nearby. Once convinced he was alone, they might try to take his scalp.

Keeping his emotions in check, Nate offered a friendly smile and used sign language to convey his sentiments. "Greetings. I come in peace. I have no quarrel with the Cheyenne."

The warriors exchanged glances. Finally the tallest of the group descended and drew rein ten yards away. "I am Two Hatchets," he signed. "You know we are Cheyennes. You must also know this is Cheyenne hunting ground."

"So I have been told," Nate signed, being careful not to raise his hands too far above his Hawken.

"We do not like whites hunting here," Two Hatchets, said, scowling.

"I am not hunting," Nate explained.

"Then why are you in Cheyenne territory?"

Nate decided not to reveal he was with others. Should these warriors get the better of him they would then backtrack him to the camp. And it was apparent this band intended to slay him. Five of the six held bows, arrows already notched to the strong strings made from buffalo sinew. Two Hatchets had a bow slung over his back, a lance in his right hand. Nate well knew how swiftly Indian men could bring such lances to bear. "I am on my way to the land of my people."

"And you are by yourself?"

Exercising infinite care, Nate lowered his left hand to the rifle. He needed only his right hand to answer, which he did while smiling to dupe them into believing they had him fooled. "Yes," he signed, and instantly grasped the reins, wheeled the gelding, and fled.

He bent low over the saddle horn and heard a swishing noise as the wicked lance cleaved the air above his head. Loud whoops broke out. Looking back, he saw the band in hot pursuit. Two Hatchets had unslung his bow and was nocking a shaft.

"Fly, Pegasus, fly!" he urged, trying to put more distance behind him before the first flight of arrows reached him. The gelding responded magnificently, galloping as if on air, rapidly gaining a considerable lead. But was it enough?

Nate glanced over his shoulder again and saw three of the warriors loose arrows. Sunlight glittered off the barbed points as the shafts rose in a sweeping arc and swooped down at him. He yanked on the reins, cutting to the right, and was gratified to see the three arrows thud into the earth instead of his body.

Now he had a dilemma. He didn't dare lead the Cheyennes back to his family and friends. Nor did he desire to spend the next several hours in headlong flight, going farther and farther from the camp, which just might happen if these Cheyennes were typically persistent.

He wished he had used his head when conversing with Two Hatchets. It had been a noted Cheyenne named White Eagle, after all, who had given him the Indian name of Grizzly Killer years ago after he had slain his first grizzly. Had he thought to mention he knew White Eagle, Two Hatchets and the others might have been less disposed to try and count coup at his expense. Even if this band came from a different village, the odds were they had met White Eagle or had heard of him.

Now it was too late.

Another arrow whizzed past, almost taking off an ear. He held the Hawken in his right hand, feeling the wind whip his hair. Pegasus was now 40 yards in front of the braves and increasing the distance with every stride. Unfortunately, there was no way to take advantage of his steed's superior speed because there was nowhere to hide, nowhere he could lose the Cheyennes, not so much as a single ravine or dry wash into which he could duck to shake them.

He resigned himself to a lengthy chase and adjusted his body to the rhythm of the racing horse. The Cheyennes whooped and hollered but were falling ever farther behind. He was tempted to stop and fire a shot to discourage them, but doing so would enable them to make up lost distance and might give one an opportunity to put an arrow in his chest. So he kept on riding.

Intent on spying any break in the flat countryside he could use to his advantage, Nate almost missed the danger under his mount's driving hoofs. A flash of bare earth drew his attention to the ground where he was startled to discover a small earthen mound. Gazing around he saw many more, and with a start he realized he was in the midst of a prairie dog colony.

Damn!

Not again!

Once before he had blundered into a prairie dog town and nearly lost a fine horse as a consequence. Not that the prairie dogs themselves were in any respect dangerous. Their dens, however, could cripple or kill a running horse unwary enough to let a leg slip into one of their many burrows. And since there were countless colonies scattered all over the prairie, a horseman had to always be on the alert for their familiar dirt dens.

He promptly hauled on the reins to slow Pegasus down, and glanced around to see the Cheyennes swinging westward in order to skirt the scores upon scores of dark holes that dotted an area roughly ten acres square. Taking a risk, he changed direction, angling to the northeast. If the band didn't want to lose him they would have to come directly through the center of the colony.

The Cheyennes did just that, changing course to gallop after him.

Nate held his trepidation in check and skillfully weaved Pegasus among the mounds. Sweat caked his brow and trickled down his back. He could hear the Cheyennes narrowing the gap but he refused to urge the gelding to go any faster. An arrow flashed past his left shoulder. One of the warriors was whooping like crazy. Then, after an eternity of anxious expectation, he spied the edge of the town.

Smiling, he hunched low. Forty feet more would see him in the clear. Thirty feet. Twenty. Suddenly a searing pain lanced his left arm and he knew he'd been hit. Looking down, he saw a tear in the sleeve of his buckskin shirt and a nasty gash in his upper arm. The arrow had ripped a superficial wound but had not imbedded in his flesh.

Nate twisted as he came to the last of the holes. The Cheyennes were more than halfway across the colony, wending through the mounds with a consummate expertise born of a lifetime spent astride a horse. He finally prodded Pegasus into a gallop again.

One of the Cheyenne's mounts abruptly whinnied in terror and crashed to the ground in a whirl of limbs and tail. The warrior was thrown a half-dozen yards to tumble end over end and ultimately lie still on his back.

Seconds later another onrushing warrior went down, his horse shrieking in torment as its foreleg broke with an audible snap.

Three of the remaining braves drew rein to aid their companions. Only one Cheyenne continued to give chase.

Nate recognized Two Hatchets and from the fierce determination on the warrior's face he knew Two Hatchets wasn't about to give up until Nate's hair was clutched in his bloody hand. Acting on impulse, Nate brought the gelding to a dust-swirling halt, wheeled, and snapped the Hawken to his right shoulder. He aimed carefully and grinned when he saw Two Hatchets swing onto the off side of his horse, maintaining a grip with just one hand and a heel. It was a common Indian trick to minimize the target presented and get the rider within slaying range.

He let the Cheyenne draw ten yards nearer, then fired. The warrior's stallion pitched headlong into a roll, throwing Two Hatchets into the air. Nate was in motion again before either came to a stop. He regretted killing the horse, but it was the only way he could think of to avoid having to kill Two Hatchets. And after the friendship White Eagle had shown, he wasn't about to slay a member of White Eagle's tribe if he could possibly do otherwise.

When next he glanced back, Two Hatchets stood beside the dead horse, shaking his fist in sheer rage and bellowing invectives in the Cheyenne tongue. Nate beamed and gave a polite wave that only infuriated the warrior further.

He faced to the northeast, eager to rejoin the others. Where there was one Indian band there might be more. Large parties hunting buffalo frequently separated into smaller groups in search of herds, and he guessed such had been the purpose of Two Hatchets's group since none of them had been wearing war paint as they would have were they a raiding party.

A black dot materialized in the far distance, a dot that grew slowly larger and became the trotting form of a weary dog.

Nate straightened in amazement, then rode swiftly up to the grimy, blood-spattered beast that had stopped and sat on its haunches with its big red tongue lolling out of its drooling mouth. "So here you are! Where have you been?"

Samson gazed up placidly. His fur was criss-crossed with slash marks left by tearing fangs and claws. His muzzle was caked crimson, and part of his right ear had been torn off.

"You look a mess," Nate commented. "I trust it was worth it."

The dog made a smacking noise with its lips, then turned and headed northeast.

"Sometimes I swear you can read my thoughts," Nate muttered, pacing Pegasus to the dog's speed. Since leaving the Rendezvous the gelding had become accustomed to Samson's presence and seldom objected to traveling side-by-side.

Waves of heat came off the dry plain. Overhead burned a relentless, blazing yellow sun. Other than an occasional hawk no wildlife showed itself.

Nate mopped the back of his sleeve across his brow several times each mile. Both the arrow wound and the wound inflicted by the wolf ached terribly. He was greatly relieved when at long last he spied the line of trees rimming the creek. "Wait until Zach sees you," he told the dog. "He'll hug you to death."

Hurrying, he gazed along the creek seeking the camp site. Oddly, it was nowhere to be seen. He began to think he had misjudged and the camp must be a bit farther north, but then he saw a sight that made him wrench on the reins as a chill seized his soul. Lying not ten yards off were the charred remains of their camp fire.

He had the right spot.

His family and friends were gone!

Chapter Seventeen

Bewildered, Nate slid to the ground and touched a hand to the blackened bits of wood. They were moderately warm to the touch, leading him to conclude the fire had gone out or been extinguished less than an hour ago.

Rising, he studied the ground, reading the tracks. He saw where Shakespeare had gathered the horses, where Winona, Zach, and Blue Water Woman had mounted, and where the quartet had ridden off to the southeast at a rapid clip. Moving in an ever-widening circle outward from the camp fire, he searched for some sign of why they had left. But he found nothing that would provide a clue.

Mystified, he peered into the distance and idly scratched his head. There must be a logical explanation, but for the life of him he couldn't imagine what it might be. Returning to Pegasus, he swung up and glanced at Samson. "Here's your chance to earn your keep, you flea-ridden rascal. Find Zachary."

The black dog stood but made no attempt to move.

"Come on," Nate prompted. "Don't act dumb. Find Zach and I'll go out and shoot a ten-point buck just for you." He motioned at the tracks to no avail, and unwilling to delay another second he rode out, too annoyed to care if Samson tagged along or not. The dog could have saved him a lot of time, tracking by scent instead of forcing him to rely on spotting tracks, which wouldn't be all that numerous because the carpet of high grass would yield few clear hoofprints. And the majority of resilient stems, where the passage of the mounts and the pack animals had bent the grass, had long since straightened. He would have to proceed carefully if he didn't want to lose the trail.

Thankfully, Shakespeare was still heading southeast toward St. Louis. After traveling over a mile and confirming his mentor hadn't deviated from their original course, he poked his heels into the gelding's flanks and rode at a canter. If he pushed it he might overtake them before noon.

Stretching to the horizon in all directions was a shimmering sea of prairie grass that swayed in the slight northwesterly breeze, the sea of grass that kept the immense buffalo herds well fed and thus indirectly kept the various Indian tribes alive. The grass swished against Pegasus's legs and rustled under the gelding's driving hoofs.

Nate looked down to find Samson on his right, easily keeping up with him. "Fat lot of good you're doing," he remarked, and surveyed the plain for signs of life. He must stay alert for Indians. Earlier he'd been exceptionally lucky. The next time he encountered a band might be a totally different story. Lone white men were usually easy prey for warriors bent on counting coup.

A half hour went by. An hour. He found distinct tracks here and there that confirmed he was still on their trail. A ridge appeared a mile ahead, a mere wrinkle in the limitless flat expanse, not over two hundred feet in height at the highest spot and perhaps half a mile long. Since it would afford an excellent view of the countryside he rode right to the top, then drew rein in dismay. "No!" he blurted out.

For as far as the eye could see there existed a virtual ocean of great shaggy bulks, wicked horns, and pronounced humps. A gigantic buffalo herd was ambling south, grazing as it went, composed of thousands upon thousands of the huge brutes.

Nate leaned forward and saw several hoofprints in a patch of bare soil. The trail led straight down to the edge of the herd. In sheer exasperation he smacked his right fist into his left palm. The herd had obviously arrived on the scene after Shakespeare and the others went by, wiping out every last vestige of the tracks he had been following. Hopefully, he would be able to find the trail again on the far side of the massed beasts. But how was he to get there?

At the moment the buffaloes were placidly eating, wallowing, or resting. Given their rate of travel it would take the better part of 12 hours for the last of them to file past the ridge.

He couldn't afford to wait that long. Nor could he afford to swing all the way around. He would lose too much precious time. An insane notion occurred to him and he absently bit his lower lip as he contemplated the odds of success. He knew that buffaloes weren't afraid of humans. Quite the contrary. Bulls and cows alike seemed to regard men and women as inferior creatures hardly deserving of notice, much as they did deer and coyotes. Which was why Indian warriors could creep right up to a small herd and slay two or three before the rest realized what was happening. And since many buffaloes were accustomed to grazing in close proximity to wild horses, a herd might allow a rider to mingle with them unmolested if the rider didn't use a gun or bow to bring one down. He'd heard tales of braves who had tested their courage by riding unarmed into a herd and deliberately patting the biggest bulls in passing. In his opinion such recklessness was unwarranted.

Usually. He dare not stampede them, or they might head southeast and erase the tracker he was following.

He glanced at Samson. "Try not to get gored. Zach would never forgive me." So saying, he rode down the slope and directly into the herd.

Most of the buffaloes simply moved aside, hardly paying any attention. A few looked at the horse and rider almost quizzically, as if trying to fathom the identity of this bizarre creature. One old bull loudly sniffed the air and pawed the ground but mercifully didn't charge.

Nate's skin crawled. Hundreds of caterpillars seemed to be walking all over his body. A tremor rippled through his body and he had to firm his grip on the reins. The pungent odor of the brutes clogged his nostrils. He smelled their urine and their droppings. He heard them belching and grunting and listened to their short tails flick from side to side. Waves of heat rolled off their massed bodies and sweat caked him from head to toe.

He felt his mouth go dry and nervously licked his lips. Shifting imperceptibly, he saw Samson padding along a yard behind Pegasus. Smart dog. The horse would screen Samson from the buffaloes in front, and unless they picked up the mongrel's scent it should walk through them without any problem.

He wished he could say the same for himself. Again and again a bull would eye him warily, stamp a hoof, and perhaps take an aggressive step or two toward the gelding. Always the bull stopped, pacified by the lack of hostility. But what if one didn't?

Up close a buffalo was an imposing brute, standing roughly six feet high at the shoulder and weighing close to one ton. With its great hump, shaggy beard, and deadly horns it was like a creature out of someone's worst nightmare. And when aroused, it transformed into a living engine of destruction formidable and nearly unstoppable.

And here he was, riding through an enormous herd of the smelly beasts with death on every hand. The slightest accidental provocation, from a toss of Pegasus's mane at the wrong instant to a bull getting a good, clear whiff of his scent, would instigate an attack. And once one bull charged, others might join in. Bulls could be marvelously protective of the cows and calves when the need arose.

He kept his eyes on the ground in front of the gelding, ready to whip the horse aside should they be attacked, and tried not to dwell on the distance he must cover before he would be through the herd. Take it one buffalo at a time, he told himself, and he would make it in one piece.

Repeatedly his feet and legs brushed against grazing buffaloes. Except for a cow that swatted her head at his foot and missed, none of the hairy monsters paid him any mind.

The sun climbed steadily.

Beads of sweat dripped from Nate's chin. He dearly wanted a drink but dared not make any unwarranted moves. Nor did he turn to check on Samson again. The dog was on its own until they reached the edge of the herd.

Despite his best efforts his thoughts strayed. He envisioned Adeline as he remembered her and wondered if she had changed very much. Knowing her, he doubted it. She had always been a beauty, one of those women with the kind of features every man hungered after and every woman envied. And she was aware of the reaction her mere presence provoked. She knew her charms and used them to her best advantage.

He recalled the first time he saw her, at a dance. It had been a wonder he'd seen her at all for the ring of potential suitors beseeching her to favor them. He'd watched and admired those young men for so boldly importuning such a virtual goddess, and then received the shock of his own young life when his father had taken him over to introduce him to Adeline and her father.

She had beamed, taken his arm, and whisked him onto the dance floor before he could gather his wits. The eyes of her many suitors had shot bolts of lightning, but he'd hardly noticed in his preoccupation with dancing with the loveliest woman in existence and hearing her laugh gaily at his awkward attempts at humor. Why, she had even laughed when he clumsily trod on her foot!

How he had loved her! Or believed he had. Only much later had he learned the meaning of genuine love. It involved a sharing of two souls in intimate companionship, not worshipping a woman for the perfection she supposedly personified.

A mammoth bull grunted and shook its hairy head.

Nate blinked, his reflection shattered. He stared at the bull in question, bracing for the sudden rush that would bowl Pegasus over if the horse wasn't nimble enough. Sweat trickled into his eyes and made him blink, blurring his vision, and when it cleared a second later the buffalo was shuffling toward him with its head lowered.

He gulped and rode on. Submitting to fear

would get him killed. If he could bluff the bull into believing he was harmless, he would make it. As the beast stepped ever nearer he held his breath, his palm slick on the Hawken. The rifle was next to useless since a single shot might not kill the bull. He knew of times when men put ten balls or more into a buffalo and it walked off as if it didn't have a care in the world.

The bull approached from the left to within two yards of the gelding, then halted.

Nate could practically feel those suspicious dark eyes boring into him, and he held himself rigid, his facial muscles locked. He was afraid to so much as blink. Pegasus walked on undisturbed, and for a count of five his fate hung in a precarious balance. Suddenly the bull snorted, turned, and walked back to rub against a cow.

Five more times a similar incident transpired before at long last he glimpsed the edge of the herd ahead. His nerves were frayed, his buckskins damp, by the time he rode between a pair of dust-bathing bulls and saw open prairie. In his happiness he threw back his head to whoop with joy, but prudently stayed silent. Scouring the plain for some sign of his family and friends, he saw several sleek animals not far from the buffaloes and tensed on recognizing them.

More damn wolves.

He scowled, observing the pack of five as they trotted from south to north. They were only 20 yards from the herd, probably scouting for calves or aged adults they could cull and slay. He hoped he was wrong. Should the pack pick a likely prospect and attack, they might spook the herd and start a stampede and he still had 40 yards to go before he would be in the clear.

With fewer brutes on either side he felt confident enough to ride a bit faster, going around a young bull and past a pair of cows contentedly chewing their cuds. The wolves still moved north, and he was sure he would soon be able to take a deep breath and relax. Unexpectedly, the pack proved him wrong by darting in concert at a frisky calf prancing near its mother. Both buffaloes were alert, and at a bawl from the mother they whirled and raced deeper into the herd.

That was all it took. As if a silent signal had coursed through the entire multitude in the blink of an eye, every last bull, cow, and calf spun and sped off to the southeast.

Nate put his heels to the gelding's flanks and swung around a rushing bull, then narrowly avoided a fleeing cow. Behind him thundered the din of a million heavy hoofs, and beneath him the ground shook and shuddered as if from an earthquake. He had to wrench on the reins to evade another bull, and then he was in the open and galloping away from the herd.

After going 30 yards he halted to catch his wind and look back. A billowing cloud of dust swirled above the fleeing horde, obscuring most of them. He could see scores of bounding humps and rumps and bobbing tails, and the air vibrated to the beat of invisible hammers. He could barely hear himself think. In all the confusion the wolves had disappeared.

"Good riddance," he said aloud, and remembered Samson. Had the dog escaped unscathed?

He twisted and saw the object of his concern sitting quietly nearby. "Doesn't anything ruffle your feathers?" he quipped, and let go of the Hawken to stretch. His shoulder and neck muscles ached from the prolonged tension.

He was glad to be alive. Never again would he go through such a harrowing experience, not for all the gold reputed to be in the Rockies. As he lowered his arms he saw the wolves appear out of the dust cloud and regard him intently. Grinning, he raised the rifle. "Come closer," he coaxed. "I could use a new hat."

The largest of the pack took a few steps forward. Tilting its head to test the air, it wheeled and led its fellows to the northwest, and they were all soon lost in the dust again.

Nate lowered the Hawken and clucked in frustration. "I swear. If I see another wolf I'm going to—" he began, and stopped abruptly on hearing a sound behind him.

It was the crunch of a footstep.

Chapter Eighteen

In a blur Nate twisted and leveled the Hawken, his thumb on the hammer. He was surprised Samson hadn't growled to warn him until he saw the smirking frontiersman a few feet away.

"Jumpy cuss, aren't you?" Shakespeare joked.

"Don't you know any better than to go around sneaking up on folks?" Nate snapped, while inwardly a wave of relief washed through him. "You could get yourself shot."

"Who snuck up?" Shakespeare responded. "You would have heard me if not for all the noise those critters were making." He gazed after the departing herd. "Pity you didn't think to shoot one before they ran off. We could all enjoy a nice, fresh steak for supper tonight."

"Why didn't *you* shoot one?" Nate retorted, gazing past his mentor.

"What? And spook them while you were smack in the middle of the bunch?"

"Point taken. Where's my wife and son?"

"Waiting for you," Shakespeare said, turning. "Come on. I'll show you."

Nate slid from the saddle and led the gelding by the reins. Samson fell in beside him. "I was beginning to think I'd never catch up," he commented.

"So were we. Your son will be happy you found the dog. I think he's been more worried about it than you," Shakespeare said, and chuckled. "What the dickens kept you anyway? We figured you'd rejoin us an hour or two ago."

"I had a run-in with some unfriendly Cheyennes."

"Oh?" Shakespeare said, and nodded. "Might have been the same band we saw about half an hour after you rode out this morning. They were a ways west of our camp, riding from north to south, and I didn't think they saw us, but I didn't want to take the chance either. Not with the women and your boy along. So we packed up and lit out. I knew you'd find our trail with no problem."

"I thought for sure I'd lose it when I came on those buffalo."

Again Shakespeare nodded. "I thought you might too, which is why we stopped to wait."

They walked 25 yards through the gently waving grass. Nate looked right and left but saw no sign of his family, and he was just about to ask his friend where they were when the grass abruptly ended at the brink of a narrow but deep gully. There were the packhorses, picketed where they could graze, and seated on an earthen shelf were his loved ones and Blue Water Woman.

Zachary glanced up, beamed, and leaped to his feet with his arms outstretched. "Samson! You came back!"

The dog sailed over the rim in a graceful bound, landed halfway down, leaped again, and came to rest in front of the boy. Zach immediately embraced it affectionately and bestowed kisses on its head while giggling in childish delight.

"Nice to be loved, isn't it?" Shakespeare asked Nate, and stepped to a gap in the gully wall created some time ago when that particular section collapsed. He walked to the bottom. "Here he is, ladies," he announced in grand fashion as the two women stood. "He would have been here sooner but he was busy picking ticks off of buffaloes."

Winona's features were composed when she came forward to greet her husband, but in the depths of her eyes lurked lingering anxiety. "I was worried," she said simply.

"You weren't the only one," Nate said, giving her a hug. He smelled the aromatic scent of her hair and swore he could feel her heart beating through her buckskin dress. "I won't go off like that again if I can help it."

"Where did you find Samson?" Winona asked.

"He found me."

"If you have no objections, we should push on," Shakespeare interjected. "It's a far piece to St. Louis and we're not getting any younger standing around here."

"Let's go, then," Nate said.

It took them five minutes to collect their stock animals, mount up, and head out. Nate let Shakespeare take the lead so he could ride with Winona and Zach. The sun beat down unmercifully and the breeze became sluggish at best.

Lulled into complacency because he was safe and sound, Nate dozed in the saddle. Each time his eyes closed and he began to sag he would snap awake with a start and gaze all around to verify the prairie was still empty. He wasn't worried about the Cheyennes following him. If he hadn't lost them before the buffalo stampede, he certainly had afterward. The thundering herd would have erased every vestige of his passing.

Gradually the afternoon sun traversed its heavenly circuit and sank toward the western horizon. Nate saw his shadow lengthen until it attained gargantuan proportions, as did the shadows of all the others.

"I know this stretch of prairie," Shakespeare remarked. "We won't strike water until tomorrow afternoon."

"Any places to camp?" Nate inquire.

"Not where we can lay low, if that's what you mean. Trees are few and far between, and if there's another gully handy I don't know of it."

"Then we stay in the open tonight," Nate said, wishing they'd stumble on a safer spot. They would need a fire, and no matter how small they kept it the light would be visible for miles. But search as he would, he saw no likely spot.

The sun had dipped partially from sight before they decided to halt. First the horses were picketed, then a fire was started. Winona and Blue Water Women prepared delicious biscuits and a savory stew using jerked venison and a handful of wild onions they had found. The five of them formed a ring around the fire when they ate, not so much for the warmth as to block off some of the light.

Nate ate stew until he was ready to burst. He leaned back on his saddle, patted his stomach, and gazed at the stars now dominating the sky. Out in the wilderness the nights were always clearer than they had ever been back in New York City, and once the sun relinquished its fiery perch a myriad of sparkling stars unfolded into infinity. The sight always inspired him. He would stare at the celestial spectacle in awe, convinced he was seeing the raiment of the Great Spirit in all its majestic glory.

Across the fire Shakespeare also looked on the heavens, his features downcast.

"Are you sad, my love?" Blue Water Woman inquired.

The mountain man blinked, then put a smile on his face. "Me?" he said, and began quoting the bard. "I have neither the scholar's melancholy, which is emulation, nor the musician's, which is fantastical, nor the courtier's, which is proud, nor the soldier's, which is ambitious, nor the lawyer's, which is politic, nor the lady's, which is nice, nor the lover's, which is all these. But it is a melancholy of mine own, compounded of many simples, extracted from many objects, and indeed the sundry contemplation of my travels, in which my often ruminations wraps me in a most humorous sadness."

Blue Water Woman glanced at Nate. "Did he say yes?"

"You're asking me?"

"If anything is bothering you, tell me," Blue Water Woman told her husband. "You have been behaving strangely for weeks now and I would like to know the reason."

"It's your imagination," Shakespeare said.

"You have never kept secrets from me before."

"And you wrongly accuse me of doing so now," Shakespeare replied. He quoted again. "If I be false, or swerve a hair from truth, when time is old and hath forgot itself, when waterdrops have worn the stones of Troy, and blind oblivion swallow'd cities up, and mighty states characterless are grated to dusty nothing, yet let memory, from false to false, among false maids, in love, upbraid my falsehood."

"Are you saying my love is false?"

"Never, dear heart," Shakespeare answered, tenderly taking her hand in his. "Your love is my anchor and as true as life itself." He paused, his brow creasing. "But to be frank, and give it thee again. And yet I wish but for the thing I have. My bounty is as boundless as the sea, my love as deep. The more I give to thee, the more I have." He paused once more and, lowered his head.

Alone among those present, Nate knew the reason for his friend's uncharacteristic sorrow and introspection, and he was annoyed with himself for not giving more thought to Shakespeare's illness. Once they arrived in St. Louis he would escort Shakespeare to a doctor without delay.

Adeline would have to wait.

The rest of the evening passed peacefully. Winona prevailed on McNair to quote a few sonnets. Zach was the first to fall asleep, and the women soon did the same. Nate and Shakespeare took turns on guard, dividing the night between them, and it was Nate who sat by the smoldering embers when the pink fingers of dawn started to push the night aside.

Day after day passed in a similar manner. Once they saw a smaller herd of buffalo, and three times they came on Indian sign but no hostiles. One day Nate shot a deer. Another time Shakespeare bagged an antelope.

The closer they drew to St. Louis, the quieter Winona became. Blue Water Woman too was less talkative than usual, and stayed by her husband's side. Only Zach laughed and played in innocent ignorance, Samson his constant companion.

Nate grew more excited every day but never showed it. Winona, he figured, would only become moodier. He went out of his way to avoid upsetting her, and did everything in his power to reassure her that all would go well in St. Louis. All his attention seemed to do little good.

By Nate's estimation they were a week out of St. Louis when they stopped to rest at midday in a stand of trees bordering a shallow creek. "I'll water the horses," he volunteered, and took the gelding and the rest of their mounts over to the edge of the rippling water. He would do the pack animals next.

South of the creek lay scattered trees and a

knoll. To the west and east pristine prairie. A hawk soared on the high currents and a rabbit nibbled on a plant 50 yards distant.

He leaned the Hawken against a tree and knelt to splash cool water onto his face. Reflected back at him was the face of a man badly needing a shave and a haircut. He looked down at his buckskins and noticed the grease and dirt stains he had come to take for granted. Good Lord! Before he could pay Adeline a visit he must make himself presentable. A bath and a shave were definitely in order, and new clothes wouldn't hurt either. It had been years since he wore store-bought garb, and he wondered if the styles had changed much.

Pegasus nickered loudly and Nate looked up, his hands immersed in the creek. Since so many days had elapsed without mishap, he wasn't expecting trouble and had permitted his attention to lapse. But trouble was what he found in the form of a huge panther slinking toward the horses, apparently coming from behind the knoll. Already the creeping cat was within a couple of yards of the creek.

Surprise caused Nate to hesitate for a second. Then he came to life and swept upright, clawing for both flintlocks. The Hawken was behind him and useless. If he turned his back the panther might well leap on him. His fingers closed on the pistols and they swept out from under his wide leather belt. But he realized with a sinking sensation in the pit of his stomach that he was too slow by far.

The sudden movement had caused the panther

to pick new prey. Rather than the motionless horses, it leaped at the figure it saw rising and cleared the creek in a terrific spring.

Nate was leveling the flintlocks when the big cat crashed into him, knocking him backwards. Razor claws bit into his shoulder and chest and the panther's tapered teeth were inches from his face. He went down, the panther on top, and fired both pistols without thinking. Whether he scored or the booming sound scared the cat, he didn't know. But the panther bounded off him and he rolled onto one knee, releasing the right flintlock to grab for his butcher knife. Again he was too slow.

A hurtling tawny battering ram struck him in the shoulder, smashing him onto his side. Pain seared his ribs and he twisted to see the panther bite into his upper arm.

Someone nearby was shouting.

He instinctively swung the left flintlock, bashing the panther on the nose. The cat jumped back, giving him an opening, and he surged into a crouch and swept his knife out of its sheath. Vaguely he was aware of Shakespeare yelling for him to move, that Shakespeare didn't have a clear shot. There was no time, though. The panther was on him in a rush, a rush he met head-on, grappling as he plunged his knife to the hilt in the cat's belly again and again and again.

The world spun as they rolled and thrashed. He knew he was being ripped and torn. He knew he should push back and give Shakespeare that shot. But he was afraid in so doing he would give the panther an opportunity to employ those wicked claws to even better effect. As long as they were body to body the cat couldn't make the most of its powerful legs. So he stabbed, stabbed, stabbed, pumping his arm without cease.

Water splashed all over him and he realized they had rolled into the creek. He swallowed some and sputtered. An intense stinging sensation seared his forehead and blood promptly flowed over his eyes. He couldn't see! In desperation he shoved away from the savage beast and wiped a sleeve across his face.

Somewhere a rifle blasted.

His vision cleared and he expected to find the panther dead. Yet the cat was attacking once more, reaching him in a single mighty vault. He thrust a hand up to prevent the panther from tearing into his throat and wound up flat on his back in the creek. Something sliced into the side of his neck. His senses swam and he couldn't concentrate. Dimly, he suspected he must be dying. A shapeless inky cloud engulfed his mind, and the last thing he remembered before emptiness claimed him was the shattering sound of thunder that eclipsed any thunder ever known.

Chapter Nineteen

The doctor sighed and raised his hand from Nate's hot forehead. He thoughtfully chewed on his lower lip for a minute, then pivoted and regarded his audience somberly. "I'm afraid there's nothing more I can do. His life is in the hands of a higher power than mine."

Winona, seated in a chair between Shakespeare and Blue Water Woman, with Zachary rigid on her lap, averted her eyes and swallowed hard. A peculiar lump obstructed her throat and she experienced difficulty breathing.

"We appreciate all you've done, Doc Sawyer," Shakespeare responded, rising.

"I just wish it could have been more," Sawyer said, and frowned. "He's lost more blood than any person can dare afford to lose."

The mountain man nodded, then stepped over to the bed. "We did the best we could. Rode day and night to get here."

Sawyer looked at Winona and Blue Water Woman. "The dressings these ladies applied did a world of good. Probably kept him alive until you arrived." He ran a finger over his drooping black mustache. "Perhaps they would be willing to share their secret sometime. I'm always open to Indian remedies. I've found they often work better than the cures touted by my learned colleagues back East."

"We will write the herbal ingredients down for you and give them to you the next time you visit," Blue Water Woman said.

"Thank you," Doctor Sawyer said, and stooped to pick up his large black bag. He stared one last time at Nate King's terribly lacerated features, grimaced, and walked to the doorway. "If he does by some miracle pull through," he told Winona, "he'll be scarred for life. I'm sorry."

"I don't care about scars," Winona said softly. "I only want him to live."

The physician mustered a wan smile and departed.

For a while no one else uttered a word. It was little Zach who finally broke the silence.

"Is Pa going to die, Ma?"

Tears filled the corners of Winona's eyes and she pretended to be extraordinarily interested in her moccasins.

"Will he, Ma?"

Blue Water Woman stood. "No one can say, young one." She leaned down and lifted Zach in her arms, grinning bravely. "Why don't you come with me and I'll let you have more of the pudding I made last night?"

"Could I?" Zach asked eagerly.

"Your mother won't mind," Blue Water Woman said, moving off.

"Thanks."

"Thank my husband. He was the one who taught me how to prepare it. Dried-fruit pudding is one of his favorites."

They were almost out the door when Zachary glanced at the grizzled frontiersman. "Shakespeare can *cook?*"

Then they were gone.

"Nice kid," Shakespeare muttered. "Takes after his old man."

Winona fought to prevent the tears from flowing. The women of her tribe prided themselves on their courage in the face of adversity and their ability to stoically endure any hardship. No warrior in his right mind wanted a wife who was weak in that respect, who whined and cried like a pampered child, and every Shoshone maiden worked hard at cultivating the proper emotional maturity. She had been reared to believe there was a proper time and place to express sorrow, and this was most certainly not it. Not with Nate needing her and Zach depending on her. She must be strong now, stronger than she had ever had occasion to be.

Shakespeare came over. "I'm going shopping with Tricky Dick and his wife. Care to tag along?"

"I will stay here."

"Suit yourself," Shakespeare said. "Is there anything you need?"

"No."

"Anything for the boy?"

"No," Winona said, but remembered something as Shakespeare walked away. "Wait. Yes. Nate promised to buy him some candy. Would you—?"

"Consider it done," Shakespeare said, and glanced at the prone figure of his friend covered to the neck by a thick quilt. "Tell you what. If you want, I'll take Blue Water Woman and Zach along. Give you some time alone with him. What do you say?"

She looked at him, her face reflecting her gratitude.

"I figured as much," Shakespeare said. He hurried from the bedroom.

Standing, Winona stepped lightly to the side of the bed and gently sat next to her husband. She reached out and tenderly touched his cheek, appalled at how his skin burned to the touch. The white bandage on his neck and the bandages on his arm, shoulder, and side were clean and fresh, changed by Sawyer ten minutes ago. She stared at the five deep gashes on Nate's forehead, at the stitches holding the severed skin together, and vented a low groan of despair.

If she lost him, what would she do? She couldn't conceive of life without him. Until she met Nate her life had been pleasant enough but empty. She had done her best to be a dutiful daughter and to make her parents proud of her accomplishments in the womanly arts. She had learned to sew and weave and cook and prepare animal skins, to find medicinal herbs and forage for edible plants. She had excelled in everything a Shoshone woman needed to know. But deep down she had always felt a certain emptiness, as if part of her were missing.

The many braves who had courted her had not interested her in the least. Not even the son of a prominent chief who had offered her father 60 horses for her hand. She had stood under a blanket with many and let them talk on of their deeds and possessions, but none had stirred her heart, none had touched the core of her being where every woman desired to be touched by the man she would marry.

And then along came Nathaniel King, a white man no less. She still vividly recalled the very first time she saw him, when he charged to her rescue during a Blackfoot attack. How brave he had been! How magnificent! The moment she had locked her eyes on his would always be etched in her mind. At that instant it had been as if her heart tried to fly from her body and stick to his. Her blood had raced, and she had felt a strange warm flush all over.

She touched a finger to his lips and felt his warm breath. If he died she didn't want to live. If not for Zach she would be inclined to put an end to her life as other Shoshone women who had lost their husbands had done, by venturing off unarmed and without food or water into the wilderness until hostile Indians or wild beasts put an end to their misery. But she had her son to think of. Nate would expect her to carry on, to rear Zach as they had planned. She must not fail him.

The Harrington cabin was quiet and she wondered if everyone else had already gone. Pulling a chair up to the bed, she sat down and took Nate's limp hand in hers. Fatigue tugged at her senses and her eyelids fluttered. For three days she had seldom left the comfortably furnished bedroom and eaten scarcely enough to fill a raven. She needed rest but she didn't want to give in, not yet, not until she knew Nate was going to recover.

Minutes dragged past.

Winona heard Nate's breathing and watched the quilt over his chest rise and fall. She closed her eyes to rest for just a little while. A few minutes, at most. That was all. A few peaceful minutes. A few . . .

Her intuition flared as her eyes snapped wide and she knew something was wrong. She sat up, blinking, annoyed that she had fallen asleep. In front of her Nate still slumbered. A glance at the window showed the sun shining brilliantly so she couldn't have slept for very long. Suddenly she sensed they were no longer alone, and she twisted in the chair to gasp in surprise as a shiver ran down her back.

Framed in the doorway was a beautiful blond woman dressed in the finest clothes money could buy. Sunlight from the window struck her golden hair in such a manner that it ringed her head in a shimmering halo. Her striking blue dress perfectly matched the hue of her eyes. She advanced without saying a word, her lovely face betraying no emotion whatsoever, and studied Nate intently before turning. "I came as soon as I heard."

Winona couldn't seem to find her voice. She stared in astonishment at this vision, icy fingers freezing her soul, and nervously licked her lips. "Who are you?" she finally inquired, knowing the answer before she asked.

"Adeline Van Buren. And you?"

"I am Winona," Winona responded, then thought to quickly add, "Mrs. Nate King."

The woman smiled but the smile didn't light her eyes. Her features were totally devoid of human warmth. "So. Yes, I had heard. Pity."

"I beg your pardon?" Winona said, struggling to control the turmoil in her breast. She placed both hands on the arms of the chair and rose slowly.

"That man Gordon and my other informants told me he had married . . ." Adeline said, and paused, then finished her statement distastefully. "An Indian woman."

"Informants?" Winona said, puzzled. "I don't understand."

"It doesn't matter," the woman responded, and rested her hand on Nate's shoulder. "All that matters is he's here and everything will be wonderful again. Everything will be just as it was."

Winona felt the first jealousy she had ever known, a bitter surge of raw resentment that made her yank the white woman's hand off her husband. "What do you think you are doing? Why are you here?"

Adeline Van Buren stiffened and rubbed her wrist. "To claim what is rightfully mine," she said coldly.

"Nate is *my* husband."

"Of course he is, dear," Adeline said with the condescending air of an adult addressing a vexed youngster. "And who can blame him for marrying you? He'd been off in those dreadful mountains for so long. He needed companionship on those cold winter nights."

Winona couldn't believe the woman was talking to her like this. She had heard there were many whites who despised Indians, but she had never met anyone like this woman who wore her hatred on her sleeve, as it were. She keenly resented Van Buren's attitude, and it was all she could do not to slug the white bitch in the mouth. "I want you to leave," she declared.

"We will shortly."

"We?"

Adeline Van Buren took a seat on the edge of the bed. "You must try to comprehend my position. I've expended a great deal of money and time in tracking Nate King down. I've come all the way from New York City to this wretched city that doesn't know the first thing about culture, and where it isn't safe for a woman to walk the streets alone after dark. And I have no intention of returning empty-handed."

Winona stepped between the woman and the door. "Nate is in no condition to go anywhere, and he would not go with you even if he were."

The woman laughed. "So you would like to believe. But given a choice between the two of us, which one do you think he would prefer?"

There it was. The very question Winona had worried over for weeks. For years. Would Nate pick her or this other? Did Nate truly love her? She gazed at him, thinking of all the happy times they had shared, thinking of their joy-filled life at their cabin high in the Rockies, of all he had done for her during their marriage, and of the love she saw frankly reflected in his eyes every time he looked at her. "He loves me," she said. "Not you."

"Perhaps he thinks he does. But all that will change with time."

"How dare you," Winona bristled, clenching her fists. "I want you out of this house this instant."

"I'm leaving, but I'm taking Nate with me."

"I will kill you first."

Adeline Van Buren smiled again, this time with real pleasure. "I came prepared for such a contingency." She gazed past Winona. "We dare not waste more time, Rhey. Yancy won't be able to delay McNair and Harrington forever."

Shifting, Winona saw a man enter the room, a thin man with angular features and dark eyes. From head to toe he wore black: black jacket, black shirt, black trousers, black boots, and a black hat. He was clean shaven, his skin unusually pale as if he rarely was abroad during the daytime. "What is the meaning of this?" she demanded, suppressing a flutter of fear.

"I think you know, dear," Adeline said, moving to one side. "And don't expect help from your friends."

The man in black halted and brushed the right flap of his jacket aside, exposing a pistol stuck under his black sash. But instead of grabbing it he reached into an inside pocket.

Winona saw him draw a small gun, smaller than any she had ever seen, and point it at her. She tensed, dreading what would happen next and wishing she had a weapon. "Why?" she asked, stalling while she racked her brain for a way out of the fix she was in.

"That you will never know," Adeline said harshly, then seemed to soften. "Actually, I can't blame you, can I? I hear that any Indian woman would give her eyeteeth to hook a white man. You were only doing what comes naturally to your kind." She glanced at Nate. "He'll get over you eventually. And he'll get over your half-breed brat as well."

"Don't you lay a finger on our son!" Winona cried, taking a step toward the woman and raising her right fist to strike. She heard the crack of the small gun, her legs gave way, and she fell. The last sight she saw before a dark cloud enveloped her mind was the smirking face of Adeline Van Buren.

Chapter Twenty

Was that a shot?

The thought startled Nate and he tried to open his eyes. His consciousness seemed to be adrift in a black sea, bobbing on invisible waves. The last thing he could recall was tangling with the panther. How long had he been out? How badly was he hurt? Gritting his teeth, his blood pounding in his temples, he struggled to rouse himself. Dimly he heard voices. And then the surface of the black sea transformed into a gigantic tidal wave that swept down upon his flickering awareness and drowned him in a whirlpool of vertigo and confusion.

Later he experienced a sensation of movement and had the impression he was being carried.

Much later he thought his eyes opened briefly and before him stood a vision of radiant loveliness. But again he passed out, lost in limbo.

The merry chirping of sparrows brought him around once more and he lay still, listening and gathering his feeble strength. He felt weak and disoriented. His mouth was abominably dry, his body warm. He carefully organized his thoughts, remembering the fight with the big cat and the wounds he had sustained. The images he had seen and the impressions he had had since the fight might be the product of his imagination. For all he knew just a few minutes had gone by and he was lying on the ground near the panther. If he moved the cat might pounce.

So he held himself still, recuperating, and realized a soft object had been draped from his toes to his neck. By the smooth feel of the fabric on the tops of his hands, which rested on his thighs, he guessed it was a blanket. So he must be lying in camp somewhere, but if so why didn't he hear the crackling of a fire or the voices of his family and friends?

After an interminable period he mustered the energy to open his eyes. Immediately he suspected he must be dreaming for he was in a large bed in a plush room adorned with rich furnishings. Heavy gold curtains covered the large bay windows. A thick carpet covered the floor. All the furniture was polished mahogany.

Where could he be? With a strenuous effort he rose onto his elbows and inspected the bedroom in amazement. The only explanation he could think of was that he must be in St. Louis. If so, he had been unconscious for a long time indeed.

A door opposite from the bed suddenly opened and in stepped the woman who had haunted his conscience ever since he left New York City years ago.

"Adeline!" he blurted out.

She halted, taken aback, then smiled broadly and rushed over to clasp his hand in hers. "Nate! Thank God! You've come around at last!"

Nate was utterly confounded. He didn't know what to say. Although he had expected to meet her when he arrived in St. Louis, the shock of encountering her so unexpectedly left him speechless. Sparked by her exquisite beauty, all of his old feelings for her surged to the surface. He stared into her keen blue eyes and gave rein to memories of the happy times they had shared in New York City.

"Cat got your tongue?" Adeline joked.

All Nate could do was shake his head.

"How do you feel?" she inquired. "Want me to send for Doctor Mangel?"

Finding his voice, Nate croaked, "No. Thank you. I'm fine at the moment."

Adeline scrutinized his face. "You've changed, Nate. You're bigger and broader than I remember. And where did you get all those muscles?" She grinned self-consciously. "You would make any woman proud to call you her husband."

The statement jarred Nate into thinking about his wife and son, and he berated himself for not thinking about them sooner. Feeling a twinge of guilt he nodded at the open door. "Where are Winona and Zachary? For that matter, where am I?"

Sadness lined Adeline's visage. "You're at an estate about twelve miles north of St. Louis. It's owned by an old friend of my father's, Jacques Debussy. When we heard about the trappers who had found you and brought you to the city, I insisted on having you brought here so I could tend you personally."

"Trappers found me?" Nate said, bewildered. Fleeting panic stabbed through him. "What are you talking about? Where is my family? And where is my friend Shakespeare McNair and his wife?"

"I don't know how to tell you," Adeline said, her voice quavering.

"Tell me what?" Nate demanded, sitting up, forgetting all about his wounds and his weakness in his apprehension for those he loved most in the world.

Adeline was a study in sorrow. She wrung her hands and half-turned, her eyes mere slits. When she spoke emotion choked her words. "I would rather that the good doctor or Jacques told you. Anyone other than myself. I don't like being the bearer of terrible tidings."

Nate, scarcely able to breathe, grabbed her wrist. "Don't torture me like this. If you know something, then for God's sake tell me."

"If you insist," Adeline said softly, and stiffened her slender shoulders. She faced him. "The trappers found the bodies of another man, two women, and a young boy near where they found you."

"No!" Nate exclaimed, beset by dizziness. He released her and sank onto his pillow. "I don't believe it."

"I'm so sorry," Adeline said in sympathy, and

put her hand on his shoulder. "Evidently they were attacked by Indians. One of the trappers said something about the Cheyenne. They believed you were spared because the Indians thought you were already dead, killed by a slain panther lying near your body."

"No," Nate said again, with less vehemence. "It couldn't be." Dazed, he shook his head, refusing to accept that Winona and Zach were gone. It was impossible! his heart told him. But his head said something else. Everything Adeline said made sense. It was entirely possible the Cheyennes had somehow tracked them and caught up just after the cat attacked him. Shakespeare and the women would have been preoccupied and easy for the Cheyennes to ambush.

"I wish someone else had told you," Adeline said tenderly. "I can imagine the anguish you must be feeling. I lost both my father and mother two years ago."

"You did?" Nate said absently, the full magnitude of his loss belatedly sinking in. He felt numb in body, mind, and soul.

"Yes," Adeline answered. "But we'll discuss it later. Right now I think you should get more rest. I'll send a servant for the doctor."

"If you want," Nate mumbled, closing his eyes. Her hand lightly caressed his cheek. Then her footsteps drifted to the door and it closed. He rolled onto his side and curled into a fetal posture, unable to achieve a rational thought. Over and over the same two words repeated themselves in his mind: They're dead! They're dead! They're dead!

He had always known all of them ran the risk of death in the wilderness. In a realm where survival of the fittest determined those who lived and those who didn't, anyone could die at any time. But he had always anticipated enjoying a long life with Winona, anticipated seeing their son and other children grow to become mature adults and move away to have families of their own. Eventually he would rock his grandchildren on his knee and tell tall tales of how it was back in the days of his prime.

Now none of that would occur.

Moisture filled his eyes. Tears trickled down his face. He attempted to stop them and he might as well have been trying to stop a flood. Soundlessly he cried, oblivious to his surroundings, feeling acute torment in the depths of his being. An hour later—or was it two?—he cried himself to sleep.

Sunlight on his face awakened him and he sat up, groggy from too much sleep, too little food, and the effects of crying into complete exhaustion. The curtains had been opened and he could see a lush garden outside the window. An elderly man was engaged in trimming rose bushes.

The blanket had slid down to his waist while he slept, and he discovered for the first time he was wearing nothing underneath. He examined the bandages, then pulled the blanket up to his chest.

"You're awake again! How wonderful."

He looked up as Adeline and a stranger entered, a man who wore spectacles, a brown jacket and white shirt, and brown knee-length breeches. In his right hand he held a beaver top hat.

"How fortunate," Adeline said. "Doctor Mangel has just arrived. You can ask him all about your condition."

"Doctor," Nate said.

"Mr. King;" Mangel replied. "You are a very lucky man. I've been informed of your rescue and I can safely say that had those trappers not found you when they did, you wouldn't be with us any longer."

Ghosts of Winona and Zach made Nate scowl. "Luck, like most things in life, is relative, Doctor."

"Eh?" Mangel said, puzzled by the assertion. "I suppose so." He halted at the bed and inspected the bandage on Nate's neck. "Other than being weak and badly malnourished, how are you feeling?"

"Stiff and sore. Otherwise no complaints."

"Excellent. I'll instruct the cook to begin feeding you hot meals. Soups and stews initially, of course, until your stomach adjusts to containing food again. In about a week you should be able to eat solids without any problem."

Nate said nothing.

Doctor Mangel glanced at Adeline. "If you would be so kind as to turn around, I'd like to check the rest of this gentleman's bandages."

"Of course."

Mangel conducted the examination swiftly and expertly. When he was done he hiked the blanket over Nate's chest and stepped back. "There hasn't been any bleeding since my last visit. The worst of your ordeal is over. Given rest and proper nourishment you should be on your feet in a week. In two weeks you should be able to go out for fresh air."

"I can't wait that long," Nate said.

"Why not?" Mangel asked.

"I have something to do. In a week I'll be in the saddle and on my way west."

"You do and you'll kill yourself. Anyone who has lost as much blood as you have must gradually resume normal activities. Stay here and let Miss Van Buren take care of you until I decide you are fit enough to travel."

"I'll do the deciding," Nate insisted.

Doctor Mangel looked at Adeline, who had turned. "Reason with him, will you? It's certain suicide if he doesn't listen to me." He moved to the doorway. "I've said my piece, Mister King. Disobey at your own risk."

When they were alone Adeline fidgeted and clasped her hands at her waist. "I think you offended him."

"Didn't mean to," Nate said with a shrug.

"Why must you leave so soon? Is my company that deplorable?" Adeline asked almost shyly.

"Not at all. But I must see that my wife and son and my friends are buried properly. As it is there might not be anything left of them by the time I get there."

"Oh," Adeline said in surprise. "I should have guessed." She came closer. "If that's all it is, you can rest easy. The trappers who found you buried everyone else." Pausing as if recalling something, she concluded with, "Even a black dog."

Samson too? Nate sagged, feeling utterly empty inside. Everyone and everything that had mattered most to him was gone. All his reasons for living had been stripped from him, torn from his hands by the cruelest of fates. His own life seemed paltry and hardly worth the living.

Adeline, misunderstanding, started to leave. "You need food immediately. I'll have the cook send up a bowl of soup."

"Adeline?"

She stopped and gazed fondly at him. "Yes?"

"Thanks again for everything you've done."

"You can thank me by heeding the advice of your physician and recovering. We have much to talk about, you and I. I would hate to lose you after traveling so far and trying so hard to locate you."

"Why did you come to St. Louis?"

"I'll explain some other time, after you're rested."

He sat and gazed blankly at the window after she was gone. In his mind's eye he beheld the faces of Winona and Zach, floating in the center of the room as it were, both aglow with vitality and contentment. He started to lift a hand, to touch them, then realized his folly and let his hand fall limply onto the blanket.

Their deaths were his fault and his alone. He should never have come to St. Louis. If he had headed home when the Rendezvous concluded, his wife and son would be alive and well, And so would the man who had taken him under his wing and patiently instructed him in the craft of wilderness survival. Poor Shakespeare had been tricked into making the journey, and Nate had to bear the burden of having duped his friend for the rest of his days.

Drowsiness assailed him and he shut his eyes. How accurate hindsight was! If men and women could foresee the consequences of their decisions before those decisions were made, every person would be as wise as Solomon and never make a mistake. Whether by higher design or not, the only way a person learned was through experience, and unfortunately adversity was part and parcel of many of those experiences.

He draped a forearm over his eyes. Even if the trappers had buried his family, he felt compelled to return and erect markers on their graves. He owed them that much. It was the very least he could.

The very, very least.

Chapter Twenty-One

For three days Nate saw no one other than Adeline, Doctor Mangel, and an elderly woman who brought all of his meals, a maid in the employ of Monsieur Jacques Debussy. The maid spoke French fluently but knew little English, which limited their conversations to an exchange of greetings and nothing more.

During those three days Nate saw nothing of the man whose hospitality made his convalescence possible. From Adeline he learned the Debussy family had settled in the St. Louis area back in 1774, ten years after two French fur traders set up a trading post on the site that would later grow to become the city itself. The family prospered, acquired a large estate, and weathered the change in government when St. Louis was acquired by the United States as part of the

Louisiana Purchase in 1804. In succinct response to questions from Nate, Adeline disclosed the Debussy family had widespread business interests, with investments in everything from the fur trade to raising grain and cattle.

On the evening of the third day, feeling much stronger and impatient to be up and about, Nate slid out of bed and padded on naked feet to an open closet. Inside hung his torn buckskins, while in the corner leaned his Hawken. On the floor were his pistols, his butcher knife and tomahawk, and his ammo pouch and powder horn. Everything else had been taken by the Cheyennes. Pegasus, the other mounts, all of the pack animals and all the supplies were gone. He had been surprised to learn the Cheyennes had failed to take his weapons and commented on it to Adeline. She had promptly answered that the trappers came on the scene as the Indians were gathering their booty and the Cheyennes had fled rather than confront six armed whites. In their haste the Cheyennes had neglected to strip his weapons.

Now he donned his britches, grimacing at a series of painful twinges, then shuffled to the window and stood in the warm sunlight. The bedroom fronted to the west and he could see the rosy sun sinking toward the distant horizon. He spotted the gardener digging to the south, and when the man idly glanced in his direction, he waved. Oddly, the gardener put down his shovel and hastened off, disappearing behind a hedge. What was that all about? he wondered.

"You shouldn't be out of bed."

He replied without turning around. "I wasn't expecting you until later."

"Obviously," Adeline said, and came over to stand next to him. "Keep this up and you'll have a relapse. Then you'll be in bed for much longer. Do you want that to happen?"

"I'm recovering nicely," Nate said, smiling at her. He couldn't get over how beautiful she was, even more so than he had recollected, although her face had changed in subtle ways. Thin lines radiated outward from each eye, crow's-feet they were called, and she habitually held her mouth pressed tight, her jaw muscles tense, as if she were under some sort of strain. Her eyes, when not fixed on him, seemed strangely colder than he remembered. But her body was as full and lovely as ever and her voice as smooth as silk.

"Do you still intend to place markers on the graves of your family?"

"I do."

Adeline shook her head reproachfully. "I wish you would reconsider. You said yourself there are no landmarks out on the prairie and you might not be able to find the spot where the panther jumped you. Why risk your life needlessly?"

"It's something I have to do," Nate said.

"You were never this stubborn back in New York."

Nate watched the setting sun.

"You've changed in more ways than I would have imagined," Adeline went on. "You're not the same man who would do whatever I wanted without objecting, who always agreed that I knew best."

"You sound disappointed."

"Not at all," Adeline said quickly. "But it has come as a bit of a shock." She paused. "When I first arrived out here and heard the stories being told, I couldn't believe them. Jacques has many friends who trap for a living, and from them he had learned a lot about you. About how the Indians had taken to calling you Grizzly Killer, and how you were one of the most famous fur men, as well known as Jim Bridger, Joe Meek, or Shakespeare McNair."

The mention of his mentor caused Nate immense grief.

"I'm sorry," Adeline said on seeing his expression. "I shouldn't have brought up his name."

"It will take a while for me to accept the fact Shakespeare is gone. Had you known him you would understand. He possessed a zest for life unmatched by anyone else I know."

They stood in silence for several minutes. A cardinal flitted from bush to bush until with a frantic flapping of wings it darted into the sky. A moment later the reason for its flight became apparent when a man appeared with a pair of large brown dogs on separate long leashes. The man was short and squat, built like the trunk of a tree, wore dirty clothes. He crossed the garden from south to north and vanished around a shed.

Nate's eyes narrowed. There was something about that fellow he hadn't liked, although he couldn't identify what it might have been. "Who was he?" he inquired.

"That was Yancy. He works for Jacques."

"Doing what?"

"Oh, whatever needs doing. He's the foreman of the estate. A more loyal man you couldn't ask for."

"And those dogs?"

"Jacques owns a dozen or so. He uses them to patrol the estate and keep things calm."

Nate looked at her. "How do you mean?"

"The estate encompasses over two thousand acres. As you must know, there are a lot of thieves and other brigands in St. Louis and along the Mississippi River. They give Jacques trouble from time to time by trying to steal some of his cattle and horses. The guards and the dogs usually prevent them from succeeding."

"I see," Nate said' bothered by a vague feeling she wasn't telling him the whole truth. Which was ridiculous. Why would Adeline deceive him? He rubbed his brow and attributed his unwarranted suspicion to being excessively tired and still tremendously upset over the deaths of his family. His mind wasn't functioning as it should. "When will I get to meet Monsieur Debussy?"

"In a few days," Adeline replied. "He's off on a business trip and I expect him back soon."

Nate walked to the bed and sank down in relief. His legs were weaker than he thought and he would have to be careful not to overextend himself for the time being. "You say he was an old friend of your father's?"

"Yes," Adeline said, stepping to a chair. "My father, as you surely remember, oversaw a vast business empire. He was one of the wealthiest men in New York City. In the country, for that matter." She smoothed her dress. "He met

Jacques eight or nine years ago when he visited St. Louis to arrange for grain shipments to points in the East."

"If you don't mind my asking," Nate began, then hesitated, not wanting to upset her by bringing up the subject of her parents.

"How did my father and mother die?" Adeline finished for him.

"If you care to tell me."

Adeline folded her hands on her lap and took a deep breath, her bosom expanding as if inflated. "My father's health started to fail him about three years ago. Somehow I always thought he would live forever, but he never did know how to slow down or how to eat properly or how not to worry over his many financial ventures. Eventually it all caught up with him. One morning my mother found him in his study, slumped over his desk. She contacted his physician right away, but by the time the doctor arrived at our mansion my father had passed on."

"I'm very sorry," Nate said, and meant it. Adeline and her father had been very close and he knew they had both sincerely loved one another. Personally, he had always rated her father as too stern and dictatorial to suit him. But he had to admit Stanley Van Buren had been a devoted parent and always had Adeline's best interests at heart.

"My mother took Father's death extremely hard," Adeline continued in a low, reserved, almost timid voice.

For a few seconds Nate had the illusion that it wasn't a full-grown woman sitting there but a little girl who had been cruelly thrust into the dark by a capricious fate.

"She stopped eating regularly and shut herself in her room for days at a time," Adeline said. "I tried my best to change her attitude. I tried to convince her that she had so much to live for, but she would have none of it. She couldn't bear going on without father. Within a year of his death she took ill and died despite the efforts of two doctors to save her." She stopped and touched a hand to the corner of one eye. "They told me she simply gave up the ghost. She lost the will to live."

Nate was reminded of the story Shakespeare had told about his mother and remorse seized him. He was profoundly sorry he had brought up the subject, undoubtedly disturbing Adeline by stirring memories better left alone. To take her mind off the tragedy he said the first thing that came into his head. "I wonder if Monsieur Debussy would see fit to extend me a loan."

"What?" Adeline said, perplexed by the sudden change in their topic of conversation.

"I sold a great many furs at the Rendezvous this year and kept the money in a pouch in my saddlebags. Since my horse was stolen, I'm penniless. And I'll need money to buy the provisions I'll need for my trip out onto the plains."

"You need not concern yourself about money. What is mine is yours. I will give you whatever you need."

A realization struck Nate and he snapped his fingers. "That's right. You must be wealthy now. As your father's sole surviving heir you stood to inherit the family fortune."

"I inherited every penny he had," Adeline said.

"Then perhaps you would lend me a couple of hundred dollars until next summer. By then I'll have trapped enough beaver to be able to pay you back and pocket a tidy profit besides."

Adeline stared at him as if stunned. "You plan to continue living as a free trapper?"

"Of course. Why?"

"After what happened to your family I had assumed you would be willing to give up living as a savage in the mountains and return to your roots, where you belong."

"I belong in the Rockies. Trapping is all I know. It's in my blood."

"You can't be serious," Adeline said. "You were a fine accountant once, remember? You had a head for figures and complicated calculations. You stood to do well in the business world."

Nate leaned on an elbow and sighed. "Adeline, everything you say is true up to a point. I worked as an accountant at P. Tuttle and Sons, but mainly at the insistence of my father, who convinced old man Tuttle to take me on. And it was *your* father, with a lot of prompting from you, who offered to launch me on a career in the merchant trade."

"And what did you do?" Adeline said, resentment in her tone. "You ran off without a word to anyone to join your uncle in the wilderness." She cocked her head, studying him. "I will never, ever understand how you could throw away a promising future to live as a grubby trapper."

"I like being free."

"Free?" Adeline said, and laughed. "You were just as free in New York City as you are in your precious mountains. Name me one thing you can't do in New York that you can do in the Rockies."

Before Nate could elaborate there arose a shriek of terror from outside. He jumped up and saw a man racing across the twilight-shrouded garden, a lone black man in tattered clothing. Around the shed appeared a pair of bounding brown dogs, perhaps the same pair he seen earlier. They were no longer on their leashes and they bore down on the hapless black in snarling fury. "What is going on?" he demanded.

"I—" Adeline began, and froze as the tableau beyond the window reached its inevitable conclusion.

The dogs rapidly overtook the fleeing black. He spun to confront them, holding his arms up to protect his face, and the superbly trained animals took him low down, each dog tearing into a leg. The man screamed and toppled and there was a swirl of legs and arms and snapping jaws as he fought the dogs.

Nate took a step toward the closet, planning to grab his rifle, throw open the window, and enter the fray, but Yancy and two men raced into view. The men held clubs. They closed on the thrashing figures in the grass, and while Yancy pulled the dogs off to one side the two men beat the bloody black senseless. Then they each grasped an ankle and dragged the man to the north. Yancy and the leashed dogs trailed them.

It had all happened so fast, Nate was flabbergasted. He looked at Adeline and saw her features were flushed. "Do you know what that was all about?"

"No," she responded, shaking her head. "But I assure you I'll get to the bottom of this and let you know." Lifting her hem off the floor she swept out of the room.

Nate had to sit down on the bed again. The excitement had caused minor dizziness and he needed to rest. No one had lit the lamps in his room yet, so he sat there in the gathering darkness and reviewed what he had witnessed. The cruelty of the men with the clubs had greatly impressed him. If they were employed by Jacques Debussy, then there was more to Debussy than Adeline had let on. He gazed through the window at the benighted estate and wondered what in the world he had blundered into.

One way or the other he was going to find out.

Chapter Twenty-Two

Upon awakening the next morning as dawn broke, Nate lay in bed and thought of the incident he had witnessed. Adeline had never returned to offer an explanation, which he regarded as highly peculiar, and he was still determined to discover what had happened to the black man.

He was also hungry enough to eat a bull moose. As he slipped out from under the blanket he felt renewed vitality in his limbs. Stretching, he savored the strength flowing in his arms; he was stronger than he had been since the panther attack, and he craved a heaping portion of solid food, any solid food, not the porridge and soups the doctor had insisted he eat the past few days.

With that in mind, Nate dressed in his buckskins. He strapped on his knife, wedged the tomahawk under his belt, and tucked a flintlock on either side of his belt buckle after reloading each pistol. Feeling like a man renewed, he left the Hawken in the closet and ventured out of the bedroom.

A large hall ran in both directions. His room, as it turned out, was situated at the middle of the corridor. There were other doors on both sides, all closed.

The house was as still as a tomb as he walked down the hall until he reached an enormous dining room opulently adorned with exquisitely crafted furniture and a huge glass cabinet containing gleaming china. Beyond the dining room was an equally spacious living room.

He halted, noting doorways to the right and the left, and speculated on which way to go. At that moment the left-hand door opened and out came the elderly maid bearing a tray of steaming porridge. She stopped in shock on beholding him.

"Good morning," Nate said, and walked over. Through the doorway behind her he could see a large kitchen and a young man hanging pots over a fire. He smiled at the maid and started to bypass her.

"Non, monsieur!"

Nate had to halt when she blocked his path. "Excuse me," he said, and again tried to go around her.

The maid stepped to the side to stay in front of him. *"Non!"* she insisted. *"Oú allez-vous?"*

"I'm sorry," Nate said. "I don't understand." He pointed at the kitchen. "Now if you'll let me by I'd like to get something to eat other than porridge."

"Je ne comprends pas," the maid said, vigorously shaking her head.

"Pardon me," Nate persisted. He put a hand on her shoulder and prevented her from interfering as he started into the kitchen. The delicious aroma of boiling coffee and simmering bacon made his mouth water. "Hello," he stated to announce his presence.

The cook turned, a large spoon in his right hands and gaped. "What are you doing here, sir?"

"You speak English! Excellent," Nate said, moving closer. "My name is King and I've been laid up in bed since my arrival."

"Yes, I know," the cook answered. "Doctor Mangel instructed me on the foods you can eat until you have healed."

"No more porridge and soup. I want solid foods."

"But the doctor—" the cook protested.

"I don't care what Mangel told you," Nate said. He rested a hand on each flintlock and ambled up to the fire. "I want bacon and eggs for breakfast, a mountain of each. And I'd like flapjacks if you have them, six or seven ought to do me."

"I could get into trouble if I do as you wish," the cook declared.

"I'll take full responsibility," Nate assured him. "And if you won't cooperate I'll make the meal myself."

"No one works in my kitchen except me."

Nate grinned. "Then I'd get to work on my order if I were you."

The cook glanced at the pistols, then at the

doorway where the maid stood. He addressed her in French and she nodded and hurried off.

"I'm waiting," Nate said.

Displaying marked reluctance, the young man complied. He fetched eggs from a pail resting on a shelf near a door to the outside, and brought over a bowl containing batter already mixed.

Nate watched eagerly. His stomach rumbled continuously. He couldn't resist plucking a strip of bacon from a pan over the fire and cramming the juicy morsel into his mouth.

"Perhaps Monsieur would care for utensils?" the cook asked, his nose crinkled in obvious repugnance at Nate's lack of manners. "There is an entire drawer of forks, knives, and spoons by his right elbow."

"What's your name?" Nate replied.

"Henri, sir."

"Haven't you ever eaten with your fingers, Henri?"

"Not since I was an infant, sir. We French pride ourselves on behaving as proper gentlemen at all times."

"Do you now?" Nate said, amused by the man's superior airs. "Then don't ever visit any of the Indian tribes west of here or you'll be in for the shock of your life. Why, once I was at a Shoshone village when some warriors brought back a buffalo bull they'd killed. It was the middle of winter and no one in the village had eaten much for weeks. So the braves hacked that old bull into smaller pieces and roasted the meat over a roaring fire." He grabbed another strip of bacon, trying not to laugh at Henri's indignant expression. "But most of the Shoshones were too hungry to wait, so they took to tearing the meat apart with their bare hands and stuffing it into their mouths as fast as they could eat. There was blood and fat and gore smeared all over them by the time they were done. And there wasn't a shred of flesh left on that buffalo."

"You exaggerate, sir. Not even Indians are that barbaric."

"Henri, you have a heap to learn about life," Nate said. "The point I'm trying to make is that behaving like a gentleman isn't all that important in the scheme of things."

"If you say so, sir," Henri said. He cracked four eggs open on the edge of a pan. "But I would no more think of eating bacon without a fork than I would of stepping outdoors without my clothes on."

"The Digger Indians do it all the time. Doesn't seem to hurt them any."

"Indians," Henri sniffed, "can not be held accountable for their actions because they know no better. They're raised as uncouth savages so that is how they live."

Nate's amusement evaporated and he resisted an impulse to dunk Henri in the flapjack batter. He was fed up with hearing whites who had never so much as talked to an Indian insult the Indian way of life. When Winona was alive he had never tolerated such degrading talk, and he would be damned if he'd do so now that she was gone.

From the doorway came Adeline's testy voice. "What are you trying to prove?"

He turned. "So there you are. I figured you must have left St. Louis since you didn't come back last night."

"I went to talk to Yancy, and by the time I got back it was late so I retired," Adeline said, advancing. Today she wore a bright yellow dress that accented the color of her lustrous hair. "I'm sorry if I upset you."

"Are you hungry? Henri is making a breakfast fit for a king," Nate said. He saw the maid in the hallway, still holding the tray and the porridge, and raised his voice. "There's enough for you too, ma'am."

"We do not eat with the hired help," Adeline informed him.

"Why not?"

"The servants have their own quarters, their own dining area. They eat at designated times and the maid has already had her breakfast. So enough of this foolishness and come with me. We'll wait in the dining room while Henri cooks our meals so we can talk in private."

Although disposed to argue the issue, Nate went with Adeline and pulled out a chair for her near the head of the table. She took her seat and he sat down across from her. "I'm surprised you didn't raise a fuss over my eating bacon and eggs instead of porridge."

"I know better now. Why waste my breath when you'll do as you please no matter what I say?"

Nate leaned back and rested his right arm on the table. "You must regret going to such lengths to track me down."

"Not at all. I came for a reason."

"Which you have yet to reveal."

"Only because I didn't want to add to your woes. Since you had just lost your family and friends, I thought it best not to burden you with more bad news."

"What?" Nate said, stiffening. He leaned toward her. "Tell me now."

Adeline's face might have been chiseled from marble for all the emotion she showed. "Very well. I wanted to spare you a while longer. But since you insist, I have the unenviable task of letting you know that both of your parents have died."

For an insane instant Nate told himself she must be joking. Then, with terrible certainty, he knew she was relating a fact, and the full magnitude of the loss hit him with all the force of a runaway wagon. Coming as it did so soon after he had lost his wife and son compounded the severity of the shock. He blinked, stared at the top of the table, and felt his insides twist into excruciating knots.

"I am so sorry," Adeline said. "I've dreaded telling you."

"You did the right thing," Nate muttered, his inner turmoil building and building until it threatened to explode. Not his father and mother! Despite his past differences with them, especially his father, he had always cared for them, always loved them deeply and dutifully. "How—?" he said, and had to swallow in order to continue. "How did it happen?"

"Your mother passed on about six months after you left New York."

Nate rose and gestured angrily. "How can that be? I left New York City over eight years ago!"

"I know," Adeline said.

"I would have heard of her death by now."

"From whom?" Adeline responded. "Your father blamed you for her death and refused to allow your name to be mentioned in his hearing. He told your brothers not to contact you or he wouldn't leave any of them a single cent." She shook her head. "No one wanted anything to do with you."

"Dear Lord," Nate breathed, taking his seat again. He had expected his family to take his departure hard, but not *this* hard! He never imagined them becoming so bitter they would refuse to have anything to do with him. "How could my father blame me?" he asked.

"I was never given all the details, but evidently he took your leaving as a personal betrayal of his love and trust. He had not spoken to your Uncle Zeke in years and wouldn't answer any of Zeke's letters, if you'll recall, and it enraged him that you would take up with Zeke in defiance of his wishes."

"I know he had a feud with Zeke over Zeke's going west, but Zeke was his own brother, after all. I always thought he would change his mind one day and accept Zeke back with open arms."

"If anything he hated Zeke more after you left."

"But what does that have to do with my mother?"

"Your leaving broke her heart, plain and simple. She took to taking long walks in the park across the street from your house, and one day she went for a walk in the rain. The next day she had a fever and the chills, and when she got no better your father contacted a doctor," Adeline detailed. "Your mother, bless her soul, died of pneumonia."

Nate slumped in his chair. Knowing how his father thought, he could understand how the blame for his mother's death would fall on his shoulders. If he hadn't gone away, his mother wouldn't have been pining for him and wouldn't have taken walks in the park. She would still be alive. "How did my father die?" he asked in a whisper.

"Like my father he worked himself to death. Now we're both without parents."

"And my brothers?"

"Sherm never did amount to much. He always drank to excess, and took up a trade in keeping with his habit. He works at a shabby tavern on the waterfront."

"My father must have loved that."

"From my father I learned Sherman was warned to make something of himself or be banished from the family for life."

Nate closed his eyes, his hunger forgotten, wishing he could sink into himself and disappear. Instead of feeling anger at his father, he felt pity. The man had died practically alone in the world, and for no reason other than stubborn pride. What other explanation was there for his father always reacting in the same way when faced with a family member who didn't see eye to eye with him? He had long suspected that his father didn't possess a shred of compassion, and the information imparted by Adeline confirmed it. The man hadn't known how to forgive others, and as a consequence invariably lashed out at those who inadvertently hurt him the most.

"As for Louis," Adeline was saying, "he went into the Army. Plans to make a career of it, I hear."

"Do you have their addresses? I should write them both."

"I'm sorry, no. But I do have something else, important news that has a bearing on the reason I came in search of you."

"What is it?" Nate inquired, not really caring. He was devastated, the fiery inner spark that had sustained him during his travails in the wilderness extinguished by the dreadful loss of both of his parents. First Winona, Zach, Shakespeare, and Blue Water Woman. Now his mother and father. What was left him? His guns and knife and tomahawk. That was all. And Adeline's friendship.

"I've sought you out because of the will," she said. "I know for a fact that your father left over one hundred thousand dollars in the bank, and I have cause to believe he left all of it to you."

Chapter Twenty-Three

Nate snorted and stared at her in incredulous annoyance. "Where did you ever get such hare-brained notions? My father wouldn't give me the time of day, let alone name me as his sole heir." He smiled at her foolishness "Besides, my father never had one hundred thousand dollars in his whole life. I know for a fact that when I left New York he had about five thousand dollars saved up."

"But a lot happened after you left," Adeline said.

"Tell me."

Before she could answer, Henri emerged from the kitchen. He made three trips in all, bringing out their food, a pitcher of milk, a dish of creamy butter for their toast, and maple syrup for the flapjacks.

Nate poked a fork into his heaping portion

of eggs and decided to eat whether he had lost his appetite or not. He needed to regain his full strength so he could bid *adieu* to the Debussy estate and head for—where? Where was he going to go? Back to the mountains? He couldn't see returning to live in the cabin by the lake. The memories would be too painful to bear.

"Bring us a pot of coffee," Adeline directed Henri as he began to leave. "And make certain the coffee is hot."

"Oui, mademoiselle."

Adeline waited until he was gone, then faced Nate. "Now about your father. He entered into a business partnership with my father and three other men a few months after you rode off. They developed a scheme to purchase run-down properties and then restore them to sell at a considerable profit. My father supplied most of the initial capital while your father and the others did most of the repair work that needed to be done."

"I gather they did well?"

"Better than they dared hope. New York City, dear Nate, has grown like a weed since your departure. Thousands of immigrants pour into the city every month and there's not enough good housing to go around. Anyone who owns a building that can be used as a dwelling can sell it at a premium to one of the many landlords who are always in the market."

"And you think my father made a small fortune?"

Adeline rested her elbows on either side of her plate and smiled smugly. "I *know* he did. Papa told me himself."

"Even so, my father would never name me as his heir," Nate noted, and stuck a forkful of tasty scrambled eggs into his mouth.

"I wouldn't have thought so either. But then I spoke with Mister Worthington. He was our family attorney since before I was born, and later, at my father's urging, he became your father's attorney."

"So?"

"So after your father died, Worthington began asking around about you. It seems your father appointed him as executor of his will. He showed up on my doorstep and asked whether I knew your whereabouts. When I wanted to know the reason he became evasive. Said he had something for you and you alone and he wouldn't give me a single clue as to what it might be."

"It could be anything."

Adeline started buttering a thick slice of toast. "I thought so too until I plied Mister Worthington with questions. He flat out told me that neither of your brothers stand to inherit a penny."

"Not even Louis?"

"No."

Nate chewed thoughtfully. If both of his brothers were indeed disinherited, who was left? A few distant cousins his father had hardly known. "I still can't believe it," he said.

"I had my doubts at first, but Worthington assured me your father left you the last thing you would ever expect."

Could it be? Nate wondered, and shook his head.

"Part of the reason I went to so much trouble

to locate you was to let you know Worthington is looking for you," Adeline said.

"I'll have to contact him."

Adeline lowered her fork and her eyes. "I hope you won't be cross with me, but I've taken the liberty of contacting him and informing him he can reach you here at the estate."

"Oh?" Nate said. "When did you do this?"

"The day after the trappers brought you to St. Louis."

Nate picked up a strip of bacon and nibbled on one end. Was there another reason Adeline had gone to such lengths? If so, it eluded him. She certainly didn't stand to gain a cent from his inheritance, if such it really was, and she didn't need it in any event. She was far richer than he would ever be. "You keep hinting at another reason you sought me out. What is it?"

She demurely put down her fork and folded her hands in her lap. "I'd rather not say if you don't mind."

"Why not?"

"Because it is rather embarrassing for a woman to openly discuss matters of the heart."

"I'm afraid I don't understand."

"Don't you?" Adeline asked, her longing gaze boring into him.

Nate sat back, stunned. It had been years since last he had courted her. "I figured you had forgotten all about me," he said.

"I tried," Adeline responded. "Oh, how I tried. I was furious with you for deserting me, and for the longest time I couldn't think about you without throwing things. I would have gladly paid thugs to beat you to a pulp."

"But you didn't."

"No," Adeline said, and blushed. "And as time went by I couldn't stop thinking about you, about the happy times we shared, and how much you meant to me." She paused. "And how much you still do."

There it was. Out on the table, so to speak. Nate feigned interest in his food, his mind awhirl.

"I had no idea you were married until I arrived in St. Louis," Adeline said. "When I heard, I was all set to turn around and go back to New York. But I couldn't bring myself to leave without seeing you at least once. Jacques told me that every trapper shows up at the shop of the Hawken brothers sooner or later, and he was the one who suggested I leave word there. They kindly told Gordon about me, and he came to the hotel where I was staying at the time."

Nate ate more bacon.

"Jacques prevailed on me to move here until we heard from you. He said it might be months before you showed up, and convinced me I would be wasting my money by staying at the hotel any longer."

"I don't know what to say."

"Tell me I haven't come to St. Louis in vain."

He glanced at her. "I can't. Not yet. It's too soon."

Adeline smiled sweetly and nodded. "I understand. And thank you for encouraging me. If I was making a fool of myself you would have told me so."

They ate quietly for the next several minutes.

Nate waged a war with his conscience. On the one hand he was definitely interested in Adeline, and on the other he criticized himself for being a heartless fiend because his darling wife hadn't been dead a month yet and here he was entertaining thoughts about another woman.

Henri provided a brief respite by bringing out a pot of coffee and two cups and saucers. He poured for each of them, bowed, and left.

"I don't want to give the false impression I've retired from society," Adeline said in a whisper. "I've met several intriguing gentlemen, but none of them have meant as much to me as you."

"I had no idea," Nate said, appalled at the torment he must have caused her. For eight years he had convinced himself that she had forgotten all about him, but during all that time she had continued to cherish the memory of their courtship. And now here she was, clearly anxious to renew their relationship, and he didn't know what he wanted to do.

The rest of the meal passed in awkward silence. Nate ate two portions of everything except the flapjacks. Of those he ate three. By constantly eating he hoped to avoid having to talk, and he noticed Adeline was consuming her meal with equal if not more enthusiasm. As he swallowed the last of his bacon he became aware she was scrutinizing him. "What is it?" he asked.

"I can't get over how handsome you are, Far more so than I remember."

"And you're every bit as beautiful," Nate said, and instantly regretted it. He had no right to be flattering another woman with Winona so recently laid to rest. Impulsively, he stood and wiped his mouth on the back of his sleeve. "I think I'll lay down and take a nap. All this food has made me drowsy."

"Want me to walk you to your room?" Adeline offered.

"No, I can find the way. You stay and finish your coffee."

"All right. But I'll be by to see you later."

He whirled and hurried off feeling thoroughly confused and greatly despondent. He owed it to Winona not to take up with another woman so soon, especially Adeline. Winona had always been afraid she would lose him to her. Now here he was proving her right in a sense, and it deeply disturbed him.

Immersed in self-reproach, he retraced his steps to his bedroom, entered, and closed the door. Someone, perhaps the maid, had opened the curtains so he could gaze out over the marvelous garden. He stepped to the window to let the warm sunlight bathe his face and happened to spot a man off to the west.

It was Yancy.

Suddenly he realized he had neglected to press Adeline about the beating of the poor black. Presented with this golden opportunity, he quickly unlatched the window, bent at the waist, and eased over the sill. A cool breeze, laden with moisture as if blowing off of a river or a lake, tingled his skin. He hitched both pistols to make sure they were loose and ready for action, then hastened to intercept the foreman.

As yet Yancy, who was heading to the southwest with his back to the house, had no idea anyone was chasing him. He exhibited the firm, unhurried tread characteristic of a heavy, powerful man who feared nothing or no one.

"Hold on there!" Nate called out, walking as rapidly as he dared. He didn't want to push too hard for fear of bringing on a relapse.

The foreman halted and turned. His stony features betrayed no surprise as he waited for Nate to get closer. "How may I help you, sir?" he asked.

"Do you know who I am?"

"Yes, sir. Nathaniel King, Monsieur Debussy's house guest."

"I would like a minute of your time," Nate said. He halted and deliberately rested both hands on his flintlocks.

"How might I assist you?"

Nate was taken aback by the foreman's polite manner. He'd expected to encounter an uncouth ruffian; instead, here was a proper gentleman. Just like the cook. Were all of the people who worked for Debussy cut from the same cloth? "I need to question you about an incident I witnessed last night," he declared.

"Are you referring to the black man we apprehended while trying to steal a horse?"

"He was a horse thief?"

Yancy nodded. "We caught him in the act of taking one of our best stallions from the stable. He ran and I sent the dogs after him. They're trained to keep a man down but not to kill him."

"I saw him beaten by two men."

"They had to prevent him from fleeing. Both

work for Monsieur Debussy, sir, and they were simply carrying out orders."

"What happened to the horse thief?"

"The usual. This morning he received thirty lashes and was escorted to the south gate," Yancy said, and gestured to the north where the stables were located. "This sort of thing happens all too often, sir. Everyone in the territory knows Monsieur Debussy raises fine horseflesh, and the temptation is more than many cutthroats can resist."

Nate saw a dozen superb horses in a pasture to the northwest. "I didn't know," he said.

"Will that be all, sir?"

"Yes. Certainly."

Yancy smiled and resumed walking to the southwest. He never bothered to look back, and soon went around the corner of a barn.

Feeling decidedly sheepish, Nate turned and made for his room. There was a hedge on his right, and as he took his first step he heard a distinct rustling from the other side. Glancing around, he spied a vague figure running deeper into the hedge rows. Perhaps it had been the secretive gardener, he mused, and didn't stop.

For the first time he could fully appreciate the length and breadth of the estate. Tilled fields and green pastures stretched for as far as the eye could see in all directions. There were scores of hands in the fields, all black workers, which was typical of many large estates in the southern part of the country.

The house was incredible, a mansion of monumental proportions complete with a portico.

There was no way of determining the number of rooms from outside, but if the number of windows was any indication then there were upwards of two dozen. Ancient trees dotted the fertile lawns hemming the house on three sides. On the fourth side the garden boasted more flowers and exotic plants than a jungle.

He paused to survey the estate, and heard someone at the window clear her throat.

"Must we tie you down to insure you get your rest?"

"I needed some air," Nate responded, going over.

Adeline moved back so he could climb inside. Then she closed the window and the curtains. "There. Now you won't have any problem taking that nap."

"You're worse than a mother hen," Nate joked, and sat down on the bed.

"What with everything else we discussed at breakfast I forgot to tell you about the black man," Adeline said.

"There's no need. I just had a talk with Yancy."

"So he explained?"

"Yes."

"Good," Adeline said, moving up to him. She leaned down and gave him a warm kiss on the cheek.

"What was that for?" Nate asked.

"Because I care. Now get your rest."

Nate reclined on his back as she left the room. He touched his fingers to the spot she had kissed, perturbed because he had permitted it. What would Winona say? He reminded himself that

Winona was gone, permanently, and he must give some thought to his future. Young and healthy as he was, sooner or later he would be ready to seek a new wife and rear a new family. And since Adeline had waited eight years she might be inclined to wait a few more.

He could do worse.

Chapter Twenty-Four

Shakespeare heard the door open and turned expectantly, a mug of coffee in his right hand. He took one look at the lean man who had just entered the house, and knew by the man's dour visage that all had not gone well. "Any luck?"

Tricky Dick Harrington morosely shook his head. "No, damn it! I've got every friend I have searching and asking around, and so far there hasn't been any word. It's as if the earth opened up and swallowed him whole."

"Did the earth shoot Winona?"

"No, of course not," Tricky Dick said, moving to the fire. He leaned his rifle against the wall and began pouring himself some coffee. "How is she, anyway?"

Shakespeare glanced at the closed bedroom door. "Sawyer is in with her now. He told me the slug missed her vitals and he took it out without causing infection, so he's optimistic she'll recover."

"Thank God."

McNair gazed at the other bedroom door. "The boy is sleeping at the moment. Your missus is sitting in there with him in case bad dreams wake him up again."

"Ruth has a way with young'uns. She'll comfort him if they do."

Shakespeare took a seat at the kitchen table and placed his mug down. "I'd like to get my hands on the son of a bitch who shot her and abducted Nate."

"Mrs. Flaherty says she saw a man and a woman," Tricky Dick reminded him. "They put Nate in a cart and cut out as if the Devil himself was after them."

"Too bad she didn't pay more attention to them," Shakespeare said, and took another swallow. The slight movement provoked anguish in his right shoulder and he had to set the mug down again. His joints and muscles were much worse than they had been even a week ago, and he dreaded the thought of how badly he would deteriorate over the next couple of months. Alcohol would help deaden the pain, but Blue Water Woman was already suspicious and would interrogate him intently if he took to drinking more and more. And he needed his head clear in this time of crisis. He wasn't going to rest until he had found Nate and paid back the bastards responsible.

He stared at his friend, Dick Harrington, who had trapped in the Rockies for over two decades before giving up the wandering life to marry a fine woman and settle down on the western outskirts of St. Louis in a large cabin. Harrington had acquired the nickname Tricky Dick by once outwitting the fierce Blackfeet. A war party had slain his two friends and taken him captive, then given him his choice of deaths. He could either be skinned alive and staked out in the sun, engage in a trial by combat with their best warrior, or run a gauntlet. Dick had picked the gauntlet, and when the Blackfeet arranged themselves in two long rows and commanded him to run between them, he had whirled and raced in the opposite direction. Always fleet of foot, he had outdistanced the irate braves, and eventually made his way to a friendly village of Crows. Since then the trapping fraternity always referred to him as Tricky Dick, the man who outwitted the Blackfeet.

"St. Louis is a big city," Harrington was saying. "Even if Nate is still here we might never find him. Personally, I figure whoever took him is long gone. Probably went east."

"Perhaps, but I doubt it," Shakespeare said. "Something tells me he's still in the area." He scratched his chin through his beard. "What puzzles me is why he was kidnapped. It defies all reason. The only enemies he has, so far as I know, are back in the Rockies."

"What else can we do?"

"You've done all you can," Shakespeare said. "Passing the word among the taverns was a help.

If any of the trappers hear anything they'll let us know."

"I just hope Nate is still alive," Tricky Dick said.

So do I, Shakespeare reflected, and scowled. Seldom had he felt so helpless. He despised being unable to do anything for two precious people he cared for more than anyone with the singular exception of his wife. Since coming back the other day and discovering Winona on the bedroom floor, he had been unable to get more than a few hours' sleep at a time. Anxiety ate at his innards. He loved Nate as more than a friend; Nate was a son, a replacement for the son he had had many years ago who was taken by the fever.

Who would want to abduct Nate? Why? Why shoot Winona, who had never harmed anyone who didn't deserve to be harmed? And how had the culprits learned Nate was staying at Tricky Dick's cabin?

On second thought he realized that last question was easily answered. The night after bringing Nate to the city, he had gone with Tricky Dick to a tavern. They had imbibed a bit too much and shared the latest news with several acquaintances. Those men, as was the custom in a society where rumors and gossip were of interest to everyone, had spread the word to their friends, who in turn had spread it to theirs, and within twenty-four hours the information had been passed along until there were few souls in the entire city who didn't know that the famous Grizzly Killer had been attacked by a panther and might not pull through.

The bedroom door opened and out walked Doctor Sawyer. Deep in contemplation, he stepped to the fire and helped himself to coffee.

"How's she doing, Doc?" Tricky Dick inquired.

"She's asleep again. Don't wake her up. She needs all the rest she can get," the physician said, joining them at the table.

"Don't worry. None of us will bother her," Tricky Dick promised.

"She would recover faster if she knew her husband was safe," Doctor Sawyer commented. "The worry is weakening her resolve to live."

"We'll find him," Shakespeare said. "It's only a matter of time."

"Which he doesn't have much of unless he's been treated by another doctor," Sawyer said. "He was in no condition to be moved, and I pray the couple who took him exercised care in his transport."

"If they didn't they'll be sorry."

Sawyer looked at the aged mountain man. "I know how you feel. I'd feel the same way if I were you."

For a minute none of them uttered a word. Each sipped his steaming coffee in profound silence.

"I've been doing some thinking about this affair," Sawyer remarked. "It seems to me whoever took Nate didn't want him dead or they wouldn't have bothered to take him alive."

"So?" Tricky Dick said.

"So if they wanted him alive they would do their best to keep him that way. And if they were half as smart as I suspect they are, then they would have called in a physician of their own to take care of Nate."

Shakespeare sat up. "Which means if we questions all the doctors in St. Louis we might learn Nate's whereabouts!" He beamed. "Doc, that's a terrific notion. How many of you medical types are there in this city?"

"Three, counting myself."

"Is that all?" Shakespeare said, and then remembered that doctors were few and far between on the frontier. A city the size of St. Louis would have half a dozen physicians in the more settled sections of the country. But fewer doctors were willing to forgo the chance to make a substantial income by setting up their practice in locales where the majority of the people were dirt poor and would rather pay off a bill with a goat or a pig instead of with coins or hard currency. If there were only three, the job could be accomplished in no time. "What are we waiting for? Let's go visit each and get the one who is treating Nate to 'fess up." He began to rise.

"No so fast, my friend," Doctor Sawyer said, grasping McNair's wrist. "It's not as simple as that."

"Why not? You know them, don't you?"

"Of course. We are all colleagues in the same profession and we frequently share drinks and discuss our cases."

Shakespeare nodded. "Then you know where to find them. Lead the way."

The doctor removed his hand. "Permit me to explain. Only one of them has an office and he is seldom there. The same is true for the rest of us. Speaking from experience I can assure you that our days and most of our nights are spent visiting patients. There are times when I am on the go until near midnight."

"How can we track them down then?"

"I know where each lives. I'll make a point of stopping by and leaving a message. By tomorrow night or the next day I should have an answer for you."

"If that's the best you can do," Shakespeare said, annoyed at the impending delay.

"I'm sorry," Sawyer said, and gave the mountaineer a probing scrutiny. "I have another appointment, but first I'd like to examine you."

"Me?"

"Right now," Sawyer said, standing.

"There's nothing wrong with me," Shakespeare said defensively.

"Then why have I noticed you favoring your right arm on several occasions? Or is it your shoulder?"

"I'm fit as a fiddle, I tell you."

"Let me be the judge of that. Kindly stand and remove your shirt."

Shakespeare hesitated. The last thing he wanted was to have his worst fears confirmed. Not only that, Blue Water Woman had gone out to buy food and would come back at any moment. If she saw the doctor poking and prodding him she would know something was terribly wrong.

"I don't have all day," Sawyer said.

"I'm fine, damn it," Shakespeare groused. "Go tend someone who is really ill." He saw the doctor frown and start to turn, apparently having decided it was useless to argue, and knew he'd won. A grin tugged at the corners of his mouth.

Tricky Dick Harrington looked at Shakespeare. "Why don't you tell Doctor Sawyer the truth?"

"What?"

"Tell him what you told me the other night at the tavern," Tricky Dick said.

"I was drunk. I didn't know what I was saying."

"You weren't that drunk," Tricky Dick said, and faced the physician. "He said his joints have been bothering him something awful and his muscles ache a lot."

"How interesting," Sawyer responded, bestowing a triumphant smile on McNair. "My hunch was right. I can't leave now without examining you."

"Yes, you can."

"Are you familiar with the Hippocratic Oath, Mister McNair?" Sawyer asked.

"Can't say as I am," Shakespeare allowed, wondering what the doctor was getting at and whether to shoot Tricky Dick now or wait until there were no witnesses.

"Hippocrates was a Greek who lived thousands of years ago. He is called the father of modern medicine because he was the first physician to rely entirely on facts and not superstitions."

"What does this have to do with me?"

"Every doctor is required to take the Hippocratic Oath before establishing his practice. Part of it goes like this," Sawyer said, and quoted the section he had in mind. "Into whatever houses I enter I will go into them for the benefit of the sick and abstain from every voluntary art of mischief and corruption." His expression became benign. "So you see I can't leave without ascertaining your problem. And since I don't have all day I would appreciate it if you would behave like a grown man and take off your shirt."

Tricky Dick snickered.

Chagrined, Shakespeare reluctantly stood. Further protests would prove unavailing. His best bet was to get the examination over with quickly, before Blue Water Woman came back. He removed his pistols, his belt, and his buckskin shirt.

"Thank you," Doctor Sawyer said, stepping up to him. He touched the tips of his fingers to Shakespeare's right shoulder, then inspected the left shoulder and both elbows. "Hmmmmm. How long has this condition persisted?"

"Six months, give or take a couple of weeks," Shakespeare admitted.

"And how have you been treating it?"

"Oh, a little of this and a little of that."

"Be specific please."

"Three horn drink."

Sawyer paused in his exam. "I'm not familiar with the phrase."

"He means rum and whiskey, Doc," Tricky Dick translated. "He's been getting whiskey-soaked plumb near every chance he can."

"Ahhh," Sawyer said, and gave Shakespeare a look that implied he expected better behavior from a man of advanced years. He had Shakespeare bend both arms, then carefully felt the swollen areas to satisfy himself as to their extent and severity. Five minutes later he sighed and stepped back. "You may put your shirt back on."

"Give it to me straight," Shakespeare said. He had borne the indignity in stoic resignation, and now that it was over he wanted the truth. "How long do I have to live?"

"Live?" Sawyer repeated quizzically.

"Yep. I've never felt this poorly in all my life so I know it's serious as can be. And it keeps getting worse and worse. I figure by Christmas I'll be wrapped in a dirt overcoat."

"Perhaps you will, but not from the gout."

"Gout?"

"Yes," Sawyer said, smirking. "In your case advanced gouty arthritis, brought on by having too much meat in your diet and not enough fruits and vegetables. The decades of improper eating have taken their toll. I've treated a number of trappers who have shown the same symptoms." He nodded at the right shoulder. "I can't cure you, but if you'll change your diet according to my instructions the swelling will go down and you'll hardly be bothered by it."

"It's just gout?" Shakespeare asked again, amazed and mortified. All this time he'd believed he was going to keel over any day!

"As long as you've been up in those mountains stuffing yourself on buffalo and elk meat, I'm surprised you haven't come down with it sooner. You must have the constitution of an ox."

Tricky Dick Harrington couldn't resist the opening. He cackled, slapped his thigh, and bellowed, "And the brains!" Then he had to duck a punch that would have taken his head off.

Momentarily irate, Shakespeare saw the doctor grin, and started to laugh at his own stupidity. Then he thought of Nate and Winona and promptly sobered. There would be time enough to laugh later. First he had a son to save.

Chapter Twenty-Five

At first Nate had no idea what had awakened him.

He lay still, his body tingling with that pleasant lethargy that was often an aftermath of restful slumber, and listened. How long had he been dozing? From the bright sunlight streaming in the window he gathered it hadn't been very long.

Then it happened. A light tap-tap-tap on the window that was repeated several times, a furtive tapping as if the person responsible was afraid of being detected.

Who could it be? Nate wondered, and sat up. Both flintlocks were still tucked under his belt, and he cautiously wrapped a hand around the smooth butt of the right one as he slid off of the bed and stepped lightly to the window. He saw the hedges, the bushes, the flowers, and the greenest of grass, but not a soul anywhere. Suddenly a hand rose from below the window at the south corner and tapped again.

A slender black hand with long fingernails.

Perplexed, he edged closer and peered down. Lying to one side was a young black woman in clothes that qualified as rags. She was gazing fearfully out over the garden, her top teeth clamped on her lower lip, and as yet had no idea he was standing there.

He checked the grounds, saw no one, and quickly opened the window. "Who are you?" he demanded. "What do you want?"

Instead of replying, she pushed herself off the ground and stepped into the room, brushing past him as she glided to the right, where she pressed her back to the wall. Her breaths issued in fluttering gasps. She was in a state of abject fear, and the gaze she turned on him was like that of a terrified fawn about to be devoured by a ravenous panther. "Please, sir," she pleaded in English that contained a peculiar clipped accent. "Shut window. They see Tatu, they kill her."

Nate hesitated, then glimpsed the gardener moving about at the west end of the garden. He complied with her request and drew the curtains as an added safety measure. She seemed to relax a bit and slumped, her legs quivering from nervous agitation. "Your name is Tatu?" he said.

"Yes, sir. I hear you talk to Master Yancy. You sound like good man. Tatu hope so. You her last hope." Her face became pitiably downcast. "You her only hope."

"I don't quite understand. Can you explain?"

"Tatu hear you talk about Sadiki. You sound like you not like."

Comprehension dawned and Nate nodded. "Oh, yes. The horse thief who was beaten yesterday."

Hatred replaced the sadness on Tatu's face. "Sadiki not horse thief! Him not steal ever. The bad men beat him because Sadiki sneak away from cabin. Him not like being slave."

The very word filled Nate with intense revulsion. Years ago, on his trip west to St. Louis to join his Uncle Zeke, he had encountered several runaway slaves from Mississippi who had been recaptured and were on their way back in shackles. The enlightening experience had embittered him against the institution, and he wasn't alone in his dislike of designating a certain race of human beings as inferior to all others and thus deserving of involuntary servitude. There was a rising tide of sentiment against slavery sweeping the nation, and a number of states, including New York, Rhode Island, Illinois, and Pennsylvania, had banned the practice. In the Southern states, however, slavery flourished. "There are slaves here?"

"Yes, sir. Many, many men and women brought from Africa on big boat. Sadiki and Tatu come one month ago. We told Master Debussy sell us to good man who take care of us, but we not want to stay in this country."

So now Nate could account for Jacques Debussy's fabulous wealth. The slave trade was tremendously lucrative for those daring enough to break the law. Back in 1807 the United States had decreed that further importation of slaves was illegal, but all that had accomplished was to force the slave importers to go underground, to operate a clandestine network all along the Gulf and southern Atlantic coasts. Authorities in the South, most of whom were openly partisan, made no serious effort to stem the trade, nor were they overly helpful to those conscientious Federal officials who were trying to identify and arrest the importers.

"Sadiki very hurt. Sadiki maybe die," Tatu said. "Need doctor. Tatu sneak from field to find someone and hear you." She took a tentative step toward him. "You help us, sir?"

"I'll do what I can," Nate promised. "How many slaves are there on the estate?"

"Tatu not count. A hundred. More, maybe."

"And how many came over on the boat with you?"

"About half, sir. Rest come on other boat two weeks before we do."

Nate pursed his lips. Jacques Debussy would not want to keep such a large number of illegal slaves on the estate longer than necessary, so it was possible Debussy was off somewhere arranging their sale at that very moment. Once he returned the whole lot would be taken away to their new home. Or perhaps they would be divided up and sent to different locations. "How many of you want to escape?" he inquired.

"Sadiki and Tatu, sir."

"That's all?"

"Rest very scared. They know we never see Africa again. No way back."

That was true. But there were a number of antislavery groups who helped runaway slaves build new lives, and most prominent of these were the Quakers. If he could get Tatu and Sadiki to the nearest Quaker congregation they would get all the help they'd need. "How many speak English?"

"Just Tatu, sir. Tatu learn from missionaries in Africa. Learn fine, yes?" she asked, mustering a smile.

"You do right fine," Nate complimented her, and stared thoughtfully at the floor, in a quandary. He would like to free the entire bunch but it would be impossible. There was nowhere he could lead them where they would be safe. Debussy was bound to have influential friends who would rally to his aid and dispatch a large force to suppress any rebellion, as had been done five years ago in Virginia where a slave named Nat Turner led about 40 slaves in revolt and killed some 50 whites. Three thousand armed men hunted the rebel band down, killing almost every last one and hanging Nat Turner.

"You help us, sir?" Tatu anxiously prompted.

"If I do, where would you go? What would you do?" Nate rejoined.

"We go anywhere. We not be *slaves*."

Nate rubbed his chin. Slaves ran away all the time. Not in large groups, as in the Turner revolt, but singly or a few here and there. It was nothing to alarm the average citizen or cause the owners of the slaves to become unduly concerned. Most were brought back by professional slave hunters who tracked the runaways down for a hefty fee. Occasionally runaways managed to elude them and begin new lives in states where slavery had been abolished. If he could sneak Sadiki and Tatu off the estate they might be able to find their way north to freedom. "How many guards does Debussy have?"

"Eighteen. And many dogs."

"Can Sadiki walk?"

"If Sadiki have to."

"You say he snuck away from your cabin?"

"Yes. Him try to find safe way out. Dogs see him, though."

"How did you get away?"

"Guards not watch women as close as they do men. When us women sent into field to work I wait until guards are talking and laughing and crawl into weeds."

"How soon before they notice you're gone?"

Tatu shrugged. "Maybe not until near dark when they take women back to cabins for the night."

"That gives us some time to plan," Nate said. Suddenly shouting broke out in the garden. He stepped to the window and parted the curtain a bit. There were three pairs of guards, each with a dog on a leash, scouring the hedges and flower beds. "They know you're missing already," he announced.

Tatu gasped. "What Tatu do?"

As Nate turned he heard more shouting, but inside the mansion. Would they conduct a search of all the rooms? Turning, he hurried to the closet and opened the door. "Hide in here until it's all clear." He grabbed his rifle and stood back as she obeyed.

"Please protect me," she pleaded, clutching his sleeve. "If they find Tatu they whip her like they whipped Sadiki."

"I won't let them take you," Nate pledged, moved by the eloquent appeal in her frightened eyes.

"You good man," Tatu said.

"It just goes against my grain to see anyone enslaved," Nate responded, and added meaningfully, "I know the value of freedom." He motioned for her to stand in a corner, and closed the door. The shouting was much nearer and he estimated the searchers were in the hall beyond his door. Dashing to the bed he sat down and aligned the Hawken in his lap.

Not five seconds later a heavy fist pounded on the door and a gruff voice called out, "Mister King? This is Yancy, the foreman."

"Come in," Nate said.

The door opened to admit Yancy, a guard armed with a rifle, and one other man, a man Nate hadn't seen before, a thin man with exceptionally pale skin who was wearing black clothes and whose hard features hinted at latent menace and blatant arrogance.

"What is all the yelling about?" Nate asked with just the right air of casual curiosity.

"An accomplice of that horse thief we captured yesterday is on the property," Yancy said.

"You certainly have a lot of problems with intruders," Nate commented. "Don't you have guards posted around the estate?"

"Naturally," Yancy said, his tone flat.

The man in black took a stride forward. "We're going to search your room."

Nate rose, casually holding the Hawken in his left hand, his right free to draw a pistol if necessary. "I don't believe we've been formally introduced."

"The name is Rhey Debussy."

"Are you related to Jacques?"

"Not that it's any of your business, but Jacques and I are brothers," Rhey said. He turned toward the closet and nodded at the guard. "Check in there."

Exercising deceptive nonchalance, Nate rested his right hand on the flintlock and moved a pace to the left where he could better see the actions of all three men. "I'm afraid I can't permit my room to be searched," he said pleasantly.

The trio glanced at him in surprise, the guard freezing in midstride.

"Why the hell not?" Rhey Debussy asked.

"Several reasons," Nate said. "First of all, I don't like your attitude."

Debussy's pale features flushed crimson. His right hand moved the flap of his jacket aside to reveal a pistol. "You dare insult me, *monsieur*?"

"You're the one who has insulted me," Nate replied sternly, and gestured with the rifle at the foreman and the guard. "All of you. You come in here and flat out tell me you're going to search my room without bothering to ask my permission. You treat me like a criminal and imply I have some connection to the horse thief and his accomplice." He straightened, his voice hardening. "And here all this time I thought I was your brother's guest."

"But you are, sir," Yancy said.

"Then why am I not being accorded the respect due a guest?"

Before either of them could answer, into the bedroom bustled Adeline Van Buren. She looked at Debussy, her anger transparent. "What is the meaning of this?"

Yancy bowed. "Your pardon, my lady, but we are hunting for an escaped . . ." he said, and caught himself. "Horse thief," he concluded after a pronounced pause.

"In *here*?" Adeline snapped.

"The gardener thought he saw her come into the house," Rhey Debussy said.

"So you took it on yourselves to disturb Nate?" Adeline said, her eyes blazing.

The man in black refused to be intimidated. "The gardener thought he saw her come in *here*," he elaborated.

Nate deliberately laughed sarcastically. "Your intruder is a woman? Perhaps you should request federal troops to help you track her down!" At the mention of federal troops everyone else visibly tensed. Nate knew he had struck a raw nerve, knew Tatu had told him the truth.

"I find your humor deplorable," Rhey said.

"I find you deplorable," Nate countered.

The pale man flushed even redder and, began to advance, his right hand closing on his gun.

"Rhey!" Adeline declared shrilly. "That will be enough! Leave this instant and take these men with you."

Debussy hesitated, his desire to kill as plain as the hooked nose on his face. His mouth quivered with rage as he abruptly wheeled and stalked into the corridor. The guard followed. Yancy bowed again to Adeline, then exited.

"My apologies," she said to Nate. "Rhey always has had an uncontrollable temper. Jacques, who is eight years older, is the exact opposite. I've never seen him ruffled." She stepped to the doorway. "I must go talk to Rhey. Please excuse me."

He simply nodded as she closed the door, then sighed in profound relief. If they had discovered Tatu there would have been hell to pay! He sat down on the bed and tried to sort out the underlying current between the man in black and his former sweetheart. Rhey Debussy had impressed him as the sort of man who would back down for no one, and yet Rhey had backed down to Adeline. Why? And what would account for Rhey's obvious hatred of him? From the moment Rhey stepped into the room Nate had sensed the man's dislike, like an invisible wave of unbridled emotion washing over him. There must be an explanation but it baffled him.

He shook his head and headed for the closet. For now he must concentrate on helping Tatu and Sadiki. Once that was done he would get to the bottom of the mystery involving Adeline and the Debussy clan. And deep down he sensed he wouldn't like what he would find.

Not one damn bit.

Chapter Twenty-Six

Night cloaked the countryside with an inky mantle when Nate cracked the window and listened intently. A cool breeze fanned his cheek. He heard crickets chirping in the garden, and somewhere to the west a bullfrog croaked. After waiting a suitable interval to satisfy himself there were no guards in the vicinity, he opened the window all the way and slipped outside, where he pressed his back to the wall and held the Hawken ready for use. "Come on," he whispered.

As silently as a ghost Tatu joined him.

Since Nate had already extinguished the lamp in his bedroom, he didn't have to worry about their silhouettes being outlined from within. Now he crept north along the base of the wall, staying low and hugging the darker patches. He stopped shy of a well-lit room and dropped to his knees to scoot under the windowsill. Once out of danger he rose and beckoned for Tatu to do the same.

In his mind's eye Nate reviewed the layout of the estate as detailed by Tatu. The cabins where the slaves were housed were located northwest of the stables, a distance of five hundred yards or more. There was plenty of cover but there were also plenty of guards patrolling the property. He wasn't worried about them so much as he was the dogs. With their keen senses of smell and hearing the dogs would detect scents and sounds the guards would not.

He had to duck under six more windows before he reached the northwest corner of the mansion. Squatting behind a rose bush he glanced at Tatu, and received a kindly smile. He returned the favor, then eased around the bush until he could survey the ground between the house and the shed, then the stretch between the shed and the stables.

Nothing moved.

In a crouch he darted across 20 feet of open space, and knelt in the shelter of a huge tree. Light footsteps to his rear told him Tatu was keeping up. He gazed past the tree, where the grass was dimly illuminated by the glow from a lantern hanging in front of the shed. Earlier he had observed a guard going around to various points where lanterns were hung to light each and every one. Jacques Debussy, apparently, was a thorough man who left little to chance.

He swung to the right, avoiding the circle of light, his moccasins making no noise on the soft carpet of lush grass. Ten yards from the tree was a bush, and he was nearly there when voices arose at the house and a door slammed shut. Instantly he flattened in the shadows rather than risk going on and being spotted. Twisting, he discovered two men had emerged from a side door and were standing under a lantern while one of them lit a pipe. A yard away lay Tatu, as rigid as a log.

The pair began conversing in French.

Nate had no idea what they were talking about. He waited impatiently for them to move, the Hawken on the ground beside him, his right hand gripping the hilt of his butcher knife. If he was spotted he intended to dispatch them swiftly and silently.

The man with the pipe laughed at a remark by his companion, and together they strolled to the east. Eventually they walked around the corner and were gone.

Upright in a flash, Nate ran for the bush and sank to his knees. Tatu's hand touched his shoulder and pointed, and he swiveled to see a pair of guards and a dog crossing the garden from south to north. They hiked past a hedge and were swallowed by the darkness.

Every nerve tingling, Nate continued. Without mishap he passed the shed and gave the stable a wide berth. Beyond reared trees, part of a tract of woodland. When he was crouched among the trunks he felt temporarily safe, and turned to his newfound friend. "Are the cabins in these woods?"

"No, sir. The woods end soon. The cabins are in a field."

Unfortunate, Nate reflected, because it would have made their task so much easier. He rose and stealthily moved to the northwest, moving as an Indian would, testing the ground with the thin sole of each moccasin before placing a foot fully down. With practice a brave could feel twigs and branches underfoot and avoid snapping them, and many of the mountaineers who had lived with the various tribes had developed the same skill.

The woods ended at the border of a well-defined dirt footpath winding like a dust-hued snake in the direction they were going. To take the path would court discovery, so Nate remained in the trees. He traveled over a hundred yards, then drew up short on hearing muted voices and distinguishing vague shapes coming toward him.

Easing to one knee Nate extended the Hawken to Tatu, and after hesitating briefly she gingerly took the gun. He drew his tomahawk and butcher knife and coiled both legs under him.

Soon the shapes materialized into another pair of guards, only these didn't have a dog with them. They were chatting idly, their rifles cradled in the crooks of their arms, at ease and paying no attention whatsoever to the woods.

Nate debated whether to let them go or to ambush them. If he was smart he would kill them simply because they might pose a threat later. But he wasn't a cold-hearted murderer and couldn't bring himself to snuff out another human life unless his own or those of his loved ones were being actively threatened.

His loved ones?

The thought startled him, vividly reminding him that those he had cared for the most were irretrievably gone. Poignant sorrow overwhelmed him, commingled with acute remorse. He had been so busy dwelling on Tatu's dilemma that hours had elapsed since last he thought about Winona and Zachary. What manner of husband and father was he to so readily forget about those who had touched his soul the deepest? Or was it better that he had this situation to deal with since it gave him an excuse to suppress the tormenting memories until the job was done?

The guards narrowed the distance.

He loosened his grips on the knife and tomahawk, his mind made up. Unless they saw him he would let them live. He became aware of Tatu's eyes on his back, although he couldn't say exactly how he knew she was looking at him in anticipation of the moment when he would strike. What would she think when he did nothing? Would she assume the religion she had adopted was a factor?

Tatu had related details of her life in Africa earlier in the day. She had told him about being reared in a large village where her father had been a chief, and how she had been the envy of most of the other women because she lived in the largest hut and her father owned the most goats and cattle. In her tribe the men hunted and defended the village while the women took care of the stock and tended garden plots in a special section of fertile ground known as the "women's land." Pride had entered her tone as she told about the excellent bananas, melons, peppers, and beans she had grown.

For years she enjoyed her tranquil existence, and then the first of two disruptions occurred. On the scene came devout missionaries, men of God who had done their fire-and-brimstone best to convert the natives to Christianity. Some adopted the new religion, which caused rifts in families and between former friends as the two factions treated one another with derision and contempt. The missionaries aggravated the disputes by branding those who failed to convert as vile sinners doomed to a fiery eternity in Hell. Tatu was one of those who adopted Christianity, although as she admitted to Nate, she never stopped praying to the old gods just in case she had made a mistake.

Not a year later fierce raiders swept down on the unsuspecting village one stormy night and wiped it out of existence. Those not taken to be sold on the slave market were ruthlessly slain; old men and women too feeble to make decent slaves, the young children who would make poor workers, and the ill ones were butchered like so many defenseless cattle.

Tatu was taken to a remote cove on the coast where she and many others were hauled aboard a mighty sailing vessel and lowered into a dank hold where they were kept for the duration of the Atlantic crossing. Their rations were meager, barely enough to sustain life. They were denied clothing and heat and compelled to huddle together to keep warm. Fully a third of the captives perished before reaching America.

Nate could readily imagine the sheer horror of her grueling ordeal. He admired her courage and perseverance, and found himself despising the slavers with a heated passion. In his estimation, to treat other human beings like animals was the most vile of practices, and he was determined to do whatever he could to help Tatu and Sadiki.

The two guards strolled on by, talking about a certain woman who worked at a bawdy house in New Orleans who was renowned for her amorous nature and athletic prowess under the sheets.

He waited until they were gone before advancing. The closer he and Tatu drew to where the cabins should be; the more wary he became. There were bound to be more guards near the cabins, and more dogs.

A minute later he spied four points of light up ahead, and slowed. The lights were lanterns hanging from high posts to the north, south, east, and west of a row of squat ramshackle cabins situated in the middle of a wide field.

The layout, probably arranged by Jacques Debussy, was perfect. There was no way the imprisoned blacks could cross the ring of illuminated ground surrounding the cabins without being seen by one of the two pairs of guards, each with a brute of a dog on a leash, who were constantly patrolling the perimeter of the lighted circle.

He padded up to the last of the trees and knelt to study on the problem of reaching those cabins in one piece. If he was to somehow extinguish one of the lanterns, the guards would converge on the run and perhaps unleash the dogs. Yet it would be impossible to get to Sadiki across that ring of light otherwise. A hand fell on his shoulder.

"What do we do, sir?" Tatu whispered, the words barely audible.

"I don't know," Nate admitted. He watched the guards for a while to learn if there was ever a time in their circuit when both pairs were briefly blocked from sight by the cabins. Now and then one of the pairs would momentarily disappear on the far side of one of the buildings, but never both pairs simultaneously. When one pair was to the east of the cabins the second pair was always on the near side. He frowned in frustration. There was simply no way he could do it.

Tatu must have reached the same conclusion. "Tatu could lead them away, sir," she proposed.

"It's too dangerous," Nate responded.

"We must save Sadiki."

"I will think of something," Nate said, and gazed thoughtfully at the structures. He heard the rustle of movement and turned just in time. Tatu was about to dart off into the undergrowth. "No," he whispered harshly, grabbing her wrist.

"We must save him," Tatu reiterated, her voice quavering. "Please. This is the only way."

"The dogs would catch you in no time," Nate told her. "Your sacrifice would be in vain."

"Tatu love Sadiki."

The frank declaration touched Nate deeply, reminding him of his own abiding love for Winona. He would gladly have given his own life to keep her alive, and he sympathized strongly with Tatu. A desperate idea occurred to him and he glanced at the cabins. "Are the slaves chained?" he asked.

"No, sir. But the doors are locked and there are no windows."

"Which cabin is Sadiki in?"

She pointed at the third one.

"All right. Take this to protect yourself." He drew his butcher knife and held it out, hilt first.

"You have a plan?" Tatu asked, gripping the weapon firmly.

"Root hog or die."

"Sir?"

"Never mind," Nate whispered, and took the Hawken. One pair of guards was now to the south of the cabins, one to the north. He lowered himself onto his elbows and knees and crawled toward the illuminated area, directly toward the nearest post. The high grass and weeds concealed him adequately for the time being. He felt Tatu bump his heels as she followed.

Demonstrating the boredom typical of men who had performed the same duty countless times without incident, the guards to the north ambled steadily closer. At the end of the leather leash in the hands of the shortest man stalked a fine muscular mongrel that appeared capable of going head-to-head with a grizzly bear. It was nearly as big as Samson.

Nate parted the grass in front of him with the rifle barrel, never moving the grass more than was absolutely necessary. It would be a fluke if one of the men noticed. And since the breeze was blowing from the northwest to the southeast, unless it abruptly changed the dog would be unable to smell them. As he drew within 15 feet of the post he heard a woman sobbing in one of the cabins, and then he heard the approaching guards speaking in English.

"—fit to be tied, from what Otis said."

"I'm surprised Rhey didn't slap her around some to teach her respect. He'd never let a man talk to him that way."

"Husbands let their wives do things they'd never tolerate from anyone else."

Nate halted, all attention, his mind racing with the implications of their statements. Could they be talking about who he thought they were?

"Not me," said the other guard. "If my wife were to try to boss me around I'd slap her silly."

"Maybe that's why you're not married."

"What do you mean?"

The pair were almost to the post, their soiled clothes and bearded faces clearly revealed in the lantern's glow.

Nate couldn't afford to wait any longer. He pressed the Hawken to his right shoulder, and had started to take aim when the dog suddenly spun directly toward his hiding place and vented a savage snarl.

Chapter Twenty-Seven

Nate fired. The rifle spat smoke and lead and the dog twisted with the impact, then vaulted toward him, but only sailed a few feet before its brain belatedly ceased working, destroyed by the ball that had torn through the center of its forehead.

Taken unawares by the attack, the two guards were slow to react.

Not so Nate. No sooner did he shoot the mongrel than he placed the Hawken down, surged to his feet, and whipped both flintlocks out in a lightning display of ambidextrous ability. One of the guards was trying to bring his rifle into play when Nate thumbed back the hammers and squeezed off two shots that boomed in unison. The balls took the guards in their chests. Both men staggered, and the one who had been holding the leash fell first. A second later the other guard, his face etched in stark shock, toppled.

"Let's go!" Nate urged, beckoning for Tatu. Like an agile doe she was erect and racing toward the cabin containing Sadiki. He jammed the flintlocks under his belt, retrieved his Hawken, and sped on her heels, acutely aware of the shouts arising in different directions. Soon more men and dogs would converge on the cabins, far too many for him to confront alone. Of more immediate concern was the pair on the far side of the field. It would take them all of 30 or 40 seconds to reach the buildings.

Tatu reached the third cabin well ahead of him and began yelling urgently in her native language. Excited voices responded inside.

Dashing up to the locked door, Nate halted and drew back his right leg to deliver a kick. He glanced at Tatu, and was startled to see tears in her eyes.

"We are too late!" she exclaimed in agonized horror.

"What?" Nate replied, hesitating with his leg upraised, listening to furious bellowing coming from near the stable.

"Sadiki is dead!"

A dozen questions rushed through Nate's mind but there wasn't time to ask even one. He lowered his leg and started reloading the Hawken, his fingers flying as he poured black powder into the palm of his hand. He had to roughly gauge the correct amount by feel alone. Then he quickly fed the powder down the barrel. To the east a man shouted.

"Hornung! Dryer! What is all the shooting about!"

Nate tried not to think of the two armed men and the four-legged terror drawing rapidly closer. Yanking a ball from his ammo pouch, he wrapped it in a patch and hastily fed it into the Hawken using the ramrod. As he was replacing the ramrod in its housing he heard pounding footsteps to the right, and whirled to see the guards and the dog appear.

They had no idea he was there. Both men were staring at the bodies sprawled near the lantern post to the west while the guard dog strained at its leash in front of them.

Hardly bothering to sight, Nate shot the beast, the slug ripping into it above the shoulder and knocking it flat. He bounded forward, drawing the Hawken back, and slammed the stock into one of the men as they rotated to face him. The man went to his knees. Nate spun, sweeping the barrel in a tight arc and catching the second man on the tip of the nose. He heard a crunch and blood splattered onto his cheeks and chin, and then he delivered another blow to the man's chin that felled him on the spot. Turning, he saw the first man feebly struggling to stand, and thwarted the attempt by bashing the stock onto the man's head.

Both guards were down.

His blood pounding in his temples, Nate swung around. Tatu was slumped against the cabin, her features shrouded in deep shadow. He darted to her side and clasped her hand. "We have to get away!" he urged.

"Sadiki is dead," Tatu repeated dully. "They beat him some more." She looked up, the tears streaming down her face. "They wanted to know where Tatu was."

Nate jerked on her hand, trying to pull her along. "I'm sorry, Tatu. I truly am. But every guard on the estate will be after us in a minute. We must find someplace to hide."

"Go without me."

"No," Nate said, forcing her to move or be dragged behind him. She balked, too anguished to care about the danger, dragging her feet.

"Please, Nate," she pleaded forlornly. "Tatu has nothing to live for anymore."

"That's nonsense," Nate barked, and succeeded in forcing her into running beside him, although she ran at half the speed she had before. He headed north, away from the mansion, where most of the guards would be coming from, and crossed the ring of light into the veil of night beyond. Trees materialized and he plunged into them, glad for the cover.

A din prevailed to the south, the barking of a dozen dogs mingled with the loud cries of men who were trying to learn what had happened.

Soon the rest would find the bodies and the chase would be on, Nate reflected. He had to put distance behind them, and he wished now he had bothered to learn more about the property from Adeline. Tatu knew the locations of the various buildings and the fields where she had been compelled to work, but she knew nothing of the outlying sections of the Debussy estate. The guards, knowing the area, would have a distinct advantage.

He covered a hundred yards or better at a brisk clip, and halted to catch his breath. Tatu slumped when he released her hand, her shoulders sagged in bitter defeat.

"Tatu wants to die."

"Don't give up now," Nate responded, and set to work reloading the rifle again. He could hear men at the cabins. It was just a matter of time now.

"Tatu never see her home again," she said forlornly. "Tatu is all alone."

"You have me. I'm your friend."

A wan grin exposed her white teeth. "You are a kind man, Nate King. A decent man."

"I'm glad you think so. If you give up, it means everything I've done to help you has been in vain."

For half a minute Tatu said nothing. She finally answered in the small voice of a girl of nine or ten rather than that of a full-grown woman. "Tatu will not let you down, sir."

Replacing the ramrod, he moved northward. While he would have liked to reload the pistols, the task had to wait. At the edge of the trees he spied a tilled field of growing cotton, and he led Tatu between two of the rows.

"They are coming, sir."

"I know," Nate answered, hearing the crackle of underbrush in the strip of trees they had passed through as the guards and their frantically barking dogs pursued them, the dogs following the trail by scent.

He felt exposed in the cotton field, and was relieved when they reached more woodland. As he stepped under an oak tree he glanced over his left shoulder and saw a large group of inky figures at the far end of the field.

"They will catch us, sir," Tatu said.

"Not if I can help it," Nate told her. He increased his speed, threading among the many tree trunks and skirting heavy thickets. Other than a few minor aches his body was holding up well, and he felt like he could go for miles without tiring.

The woodland came to an end after only a few dozen yards. He drew up in consternation on beholding an expanse of lily- and-reed-choked water. There were cattails off to the left and other vegetation that only grew in swampland.

Behind them the raucous chorus of canine barking had become a feral frenzy.

"Is something wrong, sir?" Tatu asked.

"No," Nate replied, and bore to the right, intending to skirt the swamp until he located solid ground.

Tatu swiveled to stare toward the cotton field. "Why do we not go straight ahead?" she wondered.

Nate hesitated before answering. He knew they would lose precious time and ground by trying to go around the swamp, and he knew she realized the same thing. But he had heard stories about swamps, unnerving tales about poisonous snakes, quicksand, and treacherously deep holes a person might stumble on and disappear into in the blink of an eye.

The dogs sounded awful close.

"We go straight," he declared, and took a deep breath as he boldly waded into the chilly water. He held the Hawken at chest height and shoved aside several cattails.

"We must hurry, sir," Tatu urged. "Tatu does not want you harmed on her account."

"Don't worry," Nate said, forging onward. The water rose to his knees, then to several inches below his waist. His buckskin leggins clung to his legs. On all sides frogs croaked, insects buzzed, and things rustled in the night. He thought he saw something long and sinuous swimming nearby and fervently hoped it was his imagination.

The water impeded their progress, compelling them to go slower than they would on dry land. To compound their problem, in spots the bottom was a sticky muck into which their feet sank up to the ankles. Occasionally what felt like underwater vines tugged at their legs.

Chafing at the delay and dreading an encounter with a cottonmouth or a massasauga, Nate bypassed a stand of high reeds. He repeatedly checked his pistols to make certain the water had not risen high enough to cover them. Although neither was loaded and he didn't have to worry about the powder being rendered useless, he would still have to thoroughly dry and clean each piece if they became submerged to prevent future fouling.

He looked at Tatu, who was sticking close to him as if for protection. The poor woman. When he thought of the vile injustice she had suffered and the grueling hardships she had endured, it made his blood boil. What he wouldn't give to have Jacques Debussy in his sights for a few seconds! Slaying the slaver, though, would be certain suicide since there were bound to be relatives such as Rhey or friends who would seek revenge.

"Listen, sir," Tatu said.

Nate slowed and cocked his head, puzzled by her request. Most of the frogs and insects had fallen silent, and he could hear the dogs still barking wildly. Then he noticed the difference. The dogs were barking, all right, but the sound was coming from the east, and not to their rear as before.

Mystified, he continued northward. Was it possible the dogs had lost the scent and were being taken around the swamp rather than through it? If so, Tatu and he would easily reach the far side first and escape.

Another 20 yards went by, and then Nate made a startling discovery. The dogs weren't *behind* them. The dogs were almost abreast of their position, approximately 30 yards to the east, which meant the guards and their canine helpers were on a parallel course but moving far more swiftly than the two of them could hope to do.

How was this possible?

He concluded his foes were taking a trail through the swamp, perhaps nothing more than a narrow game trail but a dry route nonetheless, a trail he might have found if he had kept skirting the swamp instead of listening to Tatu. Now the guards would get out in front of him and be able to cut him off. "Damn," he swore, and hastened northward.

Less than 15 yards away trees appeared, and where there were trees there was usually solid ground. He pumped his legs, making a loud splashing noise that couldn't be helped. Tatu churned the water beside him. With any luck the noise would frighten off every snake within a mile.

At last he spied the dark outline of a small island. Eager to get on firm footing once again, he pulled out well in front of Tatu and reached the bank well before her. Breathing heavily from his exertions, he clambered onto the bank and sank to his knees, grateful for the momentary respite. To the east the dogs barked on.

Or most of them did.

The patter of onrushing paws alerted him to the fact he wasn't alone on the island, and he glanced up in alarm to see a pair of large dogs bearing down on him with their lips curled back and their razor teeth exposed. Instantly he lifted the Hawken, pointed the muzzle at the bigger of the two, and got off a shot. His target twisted and fell, but the other dog never missed a beat as it ran in close and sprang.

Nate barely got the rifle up in time to deflect the brute's snapping jaws. He was bowled over onto his back, the dog growling viciously and trying to bite into his neck. To dislodge the dog he rolled to the right, but the beast clung to him as if endowed with talons rather than claws. Those flashing teeth narrowly missed his throat again, and he was about to make a desperate bid for his tomahawk when a shadowy form loomed overhead and a knife streaked through the air.

He heard a thud as the blade hit home.

The dog vented a howl, tried to pull free, and died on its feet, saliva and blood dripping from its bottom jaw.

Drops spattered onto Nate's face as he shoved the beast to one side and stood. Tatu was holding the dripping knife, her chest heaving.

"I thought it had you, sir," she said breathlessly.

"It almost did," Nate responded, and took her arm to lead her northward again. Undergrowth snapped and cracked to the east and he spun, horror creeping over him on spying nine or ten figures charging toward them. Some were guards, some were dogs. "Run!" he shouted, and gave Tatu a shove to get her started. She took only a few strides when a steely voice yelled a warning.

"Stop where you are!"

Tatu ignored the command and took another step, and suddenly the night blossomed with flashes of light and clouds of gray smoke.

As long as Nate lived he would never forget the ghastly sound of the two balls smacking into her flesh, one right after the other. Another buzzed past his head, but he ignored it and dashed to Tatu's side as her legs buckled. He got an arm around her waist, then heard a low snarl and had to let go and whirl to meet yet another dog head-on. The dog went for his left wrist and clamped down hard before he could evade it. Backing away, he tried to shake the heavy brute off, but the dog clung tenaciously, digging its teeth ever deeper. He awkwardly attempted to club it with the Hawken using only his right arm, and swung twice, gathering strength with each blow. As he lifted the rifle for another swing something slammed into the back of his head, and he saw the earth rushing up to meet his face a moment before his consciousness faded and died.

Chapter Twenty-Eight

Voices brought him around, angry voices in heated conversation, and he listened to them while struggling to fully revive, handicapped by a splitting pain in his head and terrible agony in both shoulders. Try as he might he couldn't get his mind to function properly. He seemed to be floating in a bizarre nether realm somewhere between dreams and reality.

"—told you it would never work! Now we've gone to all this trouble for nothing. When will you learn that sometimes I know what I am talking about?"

That was the voice of Rhey Debussy.

"I've never said otherwise, have I? And my plan would have worked perfectly if those bumbling guards hadn't let that African escape. Until then I had Nate eating out of the palm of my hand."

That had been none other than Adeline Van Buren.

"Don't be so sure," Rhey responded nastily. "King isn't the same gullible boy you courted in New York City, as I've tried to tell you many times. He's a mountain man, damn it, and one of the best. You can't play your little games with a man like him."

"Games?" Adeline hissed. "I'm doing this for us, you fool. And if you hadn't gambled away what little money I had left, I wouldn't be doing this at all." She paused. "What I ever saw in you I will never know."

Nate heard a slap, then Adeline uttered a mocking laugh.

"That's it! Beat me silly! Violence is your answer to everything, isn't it? Why couldn't you be more like your brother? Jacques knows how to treat a lady."

Rhey's retort was laced with venom. "Show me a lady and I will treat her as such. All I see before me is a conniving tart who was so spoiled by her precious papa when she was a girl that she has yet to grow up and become a mature woman."

"I am not a tart!" Adeline snapped.

"What else would you call someone who uses her considerable physical charms to lure a former lover into marriage just so she can have him murdered and claim his money as her own?"

Adeline sputtered. "Nate was never a lover. He was too kind, too decent to even think of taking me to bed. All he ever did was hold my hand and kiss me now and then."

"How charming," Rhey said in disgust.

"And as for the rest of your allegation, how else are we going to raise that much money? From your gambling? You, the perennial loser? Or perhaps from your brother, who has rarely spoken to you in a decade and who only let us stay here because I talked him into it?"

Rhey Debussy made no comment.

"What? No more blistering insults? Could it be I'm right after all. Taking Nate's money is our best hope."

"You don't even know for certain if his father really bequeathed it to him," Rhey said lamely.

"Like hell I don't. I never told Nate, but Worthington confided in me that Nate is the sole heir. So all I have to do is lead Nate on until he's begging for my hand in marriage and we're fixed for life."

"Conveniently forgetting to inform him, of course, that you are already married to me."

"He'll never know. We were married in New York, and there is no way he can find out about it here in St. Louis. My plan is perfect."

"It's too late now," Rhey said. "He must be disposed of."

"It's *not* too late. I'll concoct some story, blame everything on Jacques or Yancy. I'll say I had no idea Jacques is a slaver. Nate'll blame them and I'll be in the clear," Adeline said. "Then we'll move him to a hotel and take adjoining rooms. It will work perfectly."

"Too risky," Rhey replied. "Sooner or later someone he knows will see him."

"Then we'll convince him to go to New Orleans. As far as I know he's never been there so we should be safe."

"I don't know. . . ."

The voices drifted away, and Nate waged a silent war with a great black cloud threatening to engulf his mind. So now he knew! Not everything, but enough to understand the real reason Adeline had traveled to St. Louis and gone to such lengths to find him. The revelation stunned him. How could demure, sweet Adeline have been transformed into such a cold-hearted temptress and potential murderer? And here he thought he had known her inside and out. Apparently he hadn't known her true nature at all, and had only admired her for her beauty.

He tried to open his eyes and his eyelids fluttered.

Vaguely, he discerned a mound of hay and several stalls, but then the cloud overwhelmed him and oblivion claimed him once more.

The acrid scent of horse urine tingling his nostrils awakened him the second time, and he opened his eyes immediately. The pain in his head had diminished to a tolerable level but the agony in his shoulders was worse. He found out the reason why when he glanced to his right and left.

Rhey Debussy, or some of the guards, had secured his wrists with a stout rope and tossed the other end of the rope over a high beam in the stable, then hoisted him into the air until his moccasins were 20 feet above the earthen floor.

His shoulders hurt so badly because he had been dangling for hours and they had been bearing his weight all that time.

He hung in a back corner of the stable, to one side of the wide center aisle. By twisting his neck he could see that the great door hung open revealing a portion of the sunlit sky. He couldn't be sure, but from the angle of the sun on the door he calculated it was early or mid-afternoon, which meant he had been out for many hours.

Where was Tatu?

The question jarred him. He hadn't thought about her earlier, preoccupied as he had been with the discussion he overheard. Was she still alive? He recalled her being shot and shuddered. Within him an intense rage flared and smoldered, and he craned his neck back to study the beam 15 feet overhead. Reaching it would be impossible.

He turned to his left and spied a hayloft. Maybe, just maybe, he could get there. He swung his legs to one side, then swept them toward the loft, and repeated the motion until his body began swinging like a pendulum. Each swing took him a little closer to the loft and also worsened the misery in his shoulders. He gritted his teeth to keep from crying out and kept swinging.

Gradually he neared his goal. The tips of his moccasins were no more than a yard from the loft when he heard voices approaching the stable. Instantly he stopped swinging, but his momentum carried him back and forth in ever-decreasing arcs. Would he stop in time?

The voices grew louder and louder. There were two or three men joking and laughing.

Nate guessed they were at the great door. He was still swinging, but not much, and he held his body rigid to slow himself down even more. With luck they wouldn't be able to see him until they advanced down the aisle a dozen feet or so. He closed his eyes, feigning unconsciousness.

"—didn't like it at all. I thought he would shoot Rhey then and there."

"Do you blame him? Rhey never told Jacques about this Nate King. Jacques has too much at stake, and he's worried what will happen if friends of this King fellow come looking for him. Rhey never should have brought him here."

"You know Rhey. He probably figured he could do whatever he wanted before Jacques came back. Too bad for him Jacques came back a month early."

The rope continued to sway as Nate scarcely dared breathe. He cracked his eyelids enough to see the aisle and saw three guards standing 15 yards off. None were paying any attention to him. Slowly the rope ceased swinging entirely, and finally he was hanging limp.

"Let's get this over with," one of the guards was saying. "We'll carry him to the quicksand east of here, slit his throat, and dump him in. No one will ever find the body."

"What about his weapons?"

"Jacques said we could divide them as we see fit. They're in the tack room."

Nate tensed as the trio strolled toward him. One of them moved to undo the rope while the other two waited below to catch him as he was eased to the floor. Only one of the men below was armed, with a large knife on his right hip. Nate had to remember to stay limp as he was enfolded in strong arms, the rope around his wrists was removed, and he was slung over the left shoulder of the biggest guard as if he was no more than a sack of potatoes.

"I want to get back by dark," the big one commented. "Promised Marie I'd see her tonight."

"You've been seeing a lot of her, Vern," said the man with the knife as he came toward them.

"So?" the big one retorted. "What business is it of yours?"

Nate's mind raced. Should he make a bid for freedom now or wait? If he waited, he might be tied again or more guards might join these three and he would be so outnumbered he couldn't possibly escape. As near as he could tell no one else was in the stable at the moment. If he moved fast he would take them totally by surprise. The one with the knife had fallen in behind Vern. To his right walked the third guard.

He uncoiled with the speed of a striking rattlesnake, swinging his right fist around and up. The guard on the right started to turn, having detected movement out of the corner of his eye, and Nate slammed his fist into the man's nose, crunching cartilage and causing the man to stagger backwards with blood gushing from his broken nose. Never slowing for an instant, Nate straightened and boxed Vern on the ears with all his might. Vern bellowed and let go to clasp his ears, which was what Nate wanted. He swiftly gouged his thumbs into Vern's eyes, then pushed off from Vern's shoulders and alighted on the balls of his feet in the center of the aisle.

Two of the guards were hurt and momentarily distracted. But the third man had already drawn his knife, and now he began to step past Vern and attack Nate. Vern, who was rubbing his eyes in a frantic effort to clear them, stumbled and collided with the knife-wielder, throwing his companion off stride.

Nate sprang, his flowing form as lithe as a panther's, his hands clamping on the wrist of the arm bearing the knife at the same moment he pivoted, bending the arm down as his knee rose to ram into the guard's elbow. There was a loud snap and the guard screeched and dropped the knife.

There was no mercy in Nate's heart, no compassion in his soul. These men had helped consign countless blacks to a bitter life of hard toil. They had hunted him down the night before, and for all he knew it was one of them who had shot Tatu. In his heart was a craving for revenge, and so it was he scooped up the knife in a fluid move and rammed it to the hilt into the stomach of the man with the broken elbow. The man doubled over, wheezing pathetically. Nate kept moving, knowing another loud cry would draw more guards if the fight hadn't already attracted attention, yanking the blade loose and swinging his right arm in a wide arc. The blood-covered blade bit deep into the throat of the man with the shattered nose as the man's mouth widened to yell. Then Nate shifted, spearing the knife at Vern.

Only Vern was ready for him. Blinking rapidly as tears streamed down his face, Vern had recovered sufficiently to see the knife aimed at his chest and to step to the side with agility surprising in one so large. He rumbled deep in his chest like an enraged bear and swung a ponderous fist.

Nate ducked, slid in closer, and lanced the knife into Vern's midriff. Vern grunted and grabbed at his abdomen, his fingers closing on an empty hole because Nate had the knife out and was sweeping it up and in, straight into Vern's neck, puncturing the jugular. He pulled the knife free and stepped back, prepared to stab again.

It wasn't necessary.

Vern collapsed on the floor beside his fellows. All three thrashed and convulsed violently. The guard with the broken nose became still first, then Vern, and lastly the man who had been stabbed in the stomach. This last one still breathed shallowly.

Nate spun, fearing additional guards would pour into the stable at any second, but all was quiet. Several of the horses regarded him nervously although none whinnied. He ran toward the great door, remembering the statement about the tack room. Near the entrance, to the left, was a partially open door, and he sprinted to it and threw it wide.

He smiled in relief on spying his Hawken, both pistols, and his tomahawk and knife lying on a work table. Taking a stride, he reached out to grab the rifle as his foot bumped into something on the floor. He looked down, thinking it might be a saddle since their were many others in the room, plus all the tack typically found in a stable of such size. His smile evaporated, replaced by commingled horror and sorrow.

Tatu lay on her back, the front of her tattered clothes tinged crimson from dried blood, her eyes locked open in death, her lips parted as if about to deliver a kiss.

"No," he said softly, and crouched. He gently touched her cheek, feeling constricted in his chest. She had been a kind, decent woman, and she had not deserved such an unjust fate. He swallowed hard, then rose and quickly reloaded all three of his guns. In under two minutes he once again possessed all of his weapons, and he cast a final look of misery at Tatu before stepping into the middle aisle.

Outside the sun shone. Outside birds chirped and somewhere someone laughed. In Nate a storm raged, a storm so intense he wanted to scream with sheer fury. He thought of rushing to the mansion and slaying Jacques and Rhey and as many as he could take with him. But it would be certain suicide. Better to get his vengeance in another way, and he had just the way to do it, a way to close down the slave plantation once and for all.

He brought a blanket, saddle, and bridle out of the tack room and placed them near a fine bay in a nearby stall. Saddling took but another minute, and he swung up and turned the horse toward the great door as two armed guards appeared.

Chapter Twenty-Nine

"What in the hell!" one of the pair exclaimed.

Nate goaded the horse into a trot and deliberately rode between the two men, lashing out with both legs as they tried to leap aside. He sent the man on the right flying and caused the other guard to stumble and fall. Then he was in the open and bringing his mount to a gallop, his body flush with the back of the horse, riding as an Indian would.

Shouts broke out and to his rear a gun blasted. Whoever had fired missed, and soon he was in the garden among the hedges. At the mansion someone yelled instructions. Guards were being directed to cut him off.

He turned a corner and nearly rode down the gardener, who was trimming a bush. The man leaped out of the way almost at the last moment and shook an angry fist in his wake. There were two more shots, from the east, neither scoring.

Beyond the garden lay fields, and in some of them blacks were laboring diligently under the hot sun. In the distance beckoned a fence and a large gate toward which he angled his steed. Once off the Debussy estate he could easily elude his pursuers. He would be safe!

Or would he? Not only would Rhey and possibly Adeline want him dead so he couldn't spread the word about their nefarious scheme, but Jacques himself wouldn't care to let him live since he knew too much about the slave-smuggling. It was likely men would be sent to dispatch him. He would be all alone in a city of strangers and enemies.

Well, not quite. He had a few friends who lived in St. Louis, a few former trappers who had forsaken the wild and free life of the mountains for the settled security of a job in St. Louis. There was Tricky Dick Harrington for one, and Santa Fe Bill for another. He was unsure of where exactly Harrington lived, but he did know that Sante Fe Bill spent a lot of time at the Flint and Power, a tavern popular with those in the trapping trade.

Off to the left a guard ran to intercept him. He saw the man lift a rifle, and immediately swung to the off side of his horse, using the heel of his left foot and his tenuous grip on the saddle horn to keep him on the animal. Peering under the bay's neck he saw the man hesitate, then deliberately aim at his mount's head. The intent was obvious. Kill the horse and the guards could slay or catch him without too much trouble.

Still hanging precariously, Nate jerked on the reins. The horse cut to the right as the gun cracked, and the ball missed by a wide margin. He rose into the saddle and galloped straight for the gate. Many of the blacks in the field had stopped working to witness the tableau.

He put more distance behind him. Glancing back once he spied a couple of riders dashing from the stable, but he enjoyed a substantial lead and wasn't worried.

At the gate stood a lone guard who didn't seem to know what was happening. The gate hung open, yet he made no attempt to close it. Instead he stepped to the middle of the opening, a rifle in his left hand, and held aloft his right to get Nate to stop. "What's all the ruckus about?" he yelled.

Nate slowed, grateful the man hadn't recognized him. "We must close the gate," he declared. "One of the slaves has escaped."

"*Another* nigger has flown the coop?" the guard responded, and shook his head. "At the rate they're getting away I don't see why the boss bothers smuggling them into the country." Turning, he began to walk toward the gate. He suddenly halted and shot a quizzical look at Nate. "Wait a minute here. You're not one of the guards. Haven't I seen you somewhere before?"

By now Nate was close enough. Again he rammed his heels into the bay, and as he galloped up to the unsuspecting guard he leaned down and swung his Hawken. The heavy stock struck the man full on the right ear and the guard sprawled onto his face, his rifle falling in the dust.

Nate almost whooped for joy when the gate was behind him. A road, a narrow dirt track, meandered in the general direction of St. Louis, but he didn't take it. There were hills covered with dense forest to the southwest and it was into these he raced. The undergrowth closed around him and he changed direction once more, riding due south.

Now he was in his element, the wilderness. He deliberately turned the chase into an obstacle endurance race, forcing the bay through heavy thickets, jumping logs, and sticking to the driest, hardest ground he could find. He left tracks but not many. Unless the guards were skilled trackers they would be drastically slowed.

Ten minutes elapsed without a trace of his enemies. He rode to the crest of a hill, keeping to the brush, and studied his back trail. Oddly, there were no horsemen anywhere. This disturbed him. Did they suspect he would head for St. Louis? Did they know of a shortcut and were they at that moment on their way to intercept him? To be safe he must act on the assumption they did.

So rather than head directly for the city he swung in a wide loop to the west. He avoided isolated farms and small hamlets in case Jacques Debussy had sent riders out to request help in tracking down another "horse thief," which in a sense he certainly had become. The day waned, twilight fell, and night had crowned the countryside when he finally spied lights of the city ahead.

He sighed in relief, confident he could lose himself in St. Louis.

At the outskirts, along an isolated road, he drew up and dismounted. A tree provided an ideal spot to tie the bay. As much as he would have liked to keep it, he had to consider that agents of Debussy were already scouring the city for him and undoubtedly had been provided with an accurate description of the horse. He would do better on foot.

It felt strange to be among a lot of people again. For the first few minutes he glanced suspiciously at everyone who walked past, certain one of them would shout, "Here he is!" and a swarm of Debussy's men would swoop down on him with guns blasting. But hardly anyone paid any attention to him. A few nodded. Several said, "Good evening." None behaved in other than a normal manner.

He began to relax. Debussy's men couldn't be everywhere. And the more he pondered the matter the more he realized that Jacques Debussy wouldn't want to draw a lot of attention to the situation at the estate by dispatching a small army of guards into the city after him. Someone was bound to ask questions, and while there were many in St. Louis who believed slavery should flourish, there were also many who wanted the practice eliminated. One slip and someone might contact the federal authorities, who would have little sympathy for the slaver. Debussy could well wind up in leg irons.

Nate wondered if Debussy might not be involved in other smuggling operations besides blacks from Africa. Debussy undoubtedly had a sophisticated organization that would enable him to bring anything he wanted into the country, with his seafaring ships probably transferring their illicit cargoes to smaller boats that then carried the slaves or whatever up the wide Mississippi River to St. Louis.

He decided that Debussy's wisest choice would be to have him slain quietly by paid assassins. So he must be on his guard always and trust no one at all. After what he had learned about Adeline, he wouldn't even trust women.

How could someone have changed so drastically? he asked himself. She was nothing like the woman he remembered. Where before she had been a pampered princess, spoiled rotten by her doting parents, she was now shrewdly manipulative, even downright dangerous. How she ever could have married a man like Rhey Debussy eluded him.

Nate suddenly halted, amused by his reflection. Why should he marvel at the changes in Adeline when he had changed as much if not more, only in a different manner? He was no longer the gullible aspiring accountant who had lived a life of quiet desperation, chained to the routine of a daily job while dreaming of living the adventurous life of a Jim Bowie or a Daniel Boone. Now he was living as he had always wanted.

But alone.

The thought brought a chill to his spine. He missed Winona and Zach more than words could express, and he wished he could relive the events that had compelled him to travel to St. Louis so he could alter the fabric of destiny and spare them their terrible fate.

He gritted his teeth in rage at himself and hurried on, trying to recollect where the Flint and Powder was located. St. Louis was much different than he remembered it. The city had grown tremendously. There were many more people, many more streets and avenues, and even whole sections that had not been there when last he visited.

Over half an hour was spent comparing landmarks as he vaguely remembered them, and he was about ready to give up and try to find somewhere he could lodge for the night when he stumbled on a wide thoroughfare he recognized. Taking a right at the next block brought him into the narrow street on which the Flint and Powder was located.

The front door had been propped wide with a broom to admit fresh air, and from within arose the boisterous sounds of drunken singing, hearty laughter, and lusty swearing. He hurried inside, and was immediately enveloped in a crowd consisting of rowdy trappers in buckskins who were in all likelihood fresh in from the mountains, rough rivermen who were more than willing to fight anyone at the drop of a hat, and equally tough wagoners who brought in tons of freight every month in their heavy wagons.

Most of the interior was dim and thick with pipe smoke. The few lit lanterns did little to alleviate the gloom. Not one customer seemed unduly interested in his arrival as he threaded among them and up to the long bar. Only then did he realize he had no money.

Or did he? He opened his ammo pouch and rummaged in the bottom. At the Rendezvous he had purchased sweets for Zach and seemed to recollect placing the change in the ammo pouch, as was his custom when he didn't want to burden his pockets with a lot of coins that would jingle when he walked. As every mountaineer was well aware, the quieter a man walked in grizzly country, the longer he lived. Sure enough he found a few coins, slightly more than enough for an ale, and placed his order.

The beefy man behind the bar brought the mug over, and Nate moved toward the rear of the establishment. He didn't think he would find a place where he could sit and think, but in one corner was an empty table. Fatigue coursed through him as he sat down and sagged in forlorn dejection.

Now what?

He sipped at the delicious, tangy ale and contemplated his options. Unless he could find Sante Fe Bill or Tricky Dick Harrington his prospects were bleak. He had no job and practically no money, which meant he couldn't return to the Rockies even if he wanted to. Horses and supplies didn't grow on trees.

Not that he would leave until his score with Rhey Debussy and Adeline was settled. He was in debt to them for taking care of him after he was brought to St. Louis, but all the time they had entertained an ulterior motive. They were desperate for the money they believed he would inherit, and in cold deliberation had plotted how to steal the funds and dispose of him. Somehow he must get even with them.

Then there was the problem of Jacques Debussy. Contacting the proper federal authorities should be adequate. He didn't have a personal grudge against the elder brother, but as matter of principle he would do all in his power to stop the influx of slaves.

He took another sip, then stiffened. Off to one side were two men, trappers by their attire, who were studying him and whispering excitedly. Why? He lowered the mug and stared at them, expecting them to come over and announce themselves. To his chagrin one of them turned and hastily exited the tavern while the second man blended into the merrymakers and was lost in the press of customers.

Damn it all! he fumed. What did it mean? He started to rise, acting on the assumption it could only be more trouble and intending to depart. Then it hit him. Why should he? He was sick and tired of running. Anger replaced his concern and he took his seat again. If those men were going to contact Debussy, let Debussy's assassins come. He had met every challenge in the wilderness head-on and he would do the same here and now.

Another swallow of ale tingled his throat. He set the mug down and reclaimed the Hawken, which he had leaned on the back of his chair, and aligned the rifle on the top of the table with the muzzle pointing straight ahead. Next he loosened both pistols under his belt and the tomahawk and his butcher knife.

There. He was ready. If they came the fight would be the big story in the next day's newspaper. Settling back, he slowly drank while scanning the patrons for anyone who might be observing him.

Minutes went by. After 20 he had finished his ale but refused to leave. He would make his stand right there and hang the consequences. After 40 he began to consider that he might have been mistaken. And at the end of an hour he braced his chin in his palm and gloomily stared at the Hawken. If Debussy had men in the city they should have arrived by then.

In a way he was disappointed. Confronting them when he was ready was preferable to having them pick the time and location. Perhaps they wanted to shoot him in the back as he walked along a deserted street. Or maybe they were—

"Well look at this, boys. Who do we have here? As I live and breathe, it's the great Grizzly Killer!"

Nate's head snapped up at the first word and he recoiled in amazement. He became speechless with shock. For standing near his table were the very last people he would have expected to encounter in St. Louis, the very last people he wanted to encounter *anywhere*.

Standing in postures of haughty contempt, grinning in smug satisfaction as their eyes glowed with evil purpose, were the Ruxton brothers and Robert Campbell.

Chapter Thirty

Nate slowly recovered his composure. The three men made no move to attack him; they merely stood and grinned. He placed his right hand next to the Hawken while under the table he gripped his left flintlock. "I sure am having a run of bad luck lately," he commented.

"Ours has just changed," Campbell declared. "We've been searching for you for days. I was beginning to think I'd have to head back to the mountains and try to find your cabin."

"Why have you been looking for me?" Nate asked.

Campbell ignored the question. "We left the Rendezvous three days after you did, although I wanted to leave the same day." His humor evaporated. "But Niles Thompson and other friends of yours were watching us like hawks. They didn't leave us alone for a minute. Finally, in the middle of the night, we slipped away."

"Why?" Nate persisted.

"I'd hoped to overtake you with the caravan, but couldn't. When we caught up with the caravan, you'd just left. So we tracked you across the prairie, but lost the trail when your tracks were wiped out by a buffalo herd," Campbell related. "So I figured we'd come on to St. Louis and hope for the best." He encompassed the interior of the tavern in a sweeping gesture. "Every trapper who visits the city stops at the Flint and Powder sooner or later. I knew we'd cross paths again."

"Why, damn your hide!" Nate angrily bellowed, drawing the attention of many of the nearby customers. He had started to rise when, to his astonishment, Campbell and the Ruxtons simply turned and made their way to the entrance. Before going out Campbell paused and gave a cheery wave. Then they were gone.

Bewildered, Nate tried to make sense of the encounter. The only reason he could see for the three cutthroats to travel all the way to St. Louis after him was to get revenge for the incidents at the rendezvous. Knowing Campbell as he did, Nate was certain the man hated him with an abiding passion. And now that they had found him they would be certain to spring whatever surprise they had in mind at the earliest opportunity.

Why had they left so soon? He glanced at the front door, his forehead creased in deep thought. It was doubtful they would try anything in the crowded tavern. Even in St. Louis the citizenry wouldn't stand still for callous murder. Duels were another matter. They were honorable clashes conducted almost daily on Bloody Island, but he.couldn't see Robert Campbell or the laconic Ruxtons challenging him to one because the contest would be fair, carried out according to the established rules for such affairs. No, they would strike when it suited them best, when there would be no witnesses who might later inform his friends, and when they were certain to have an advantage.

What if they were waiting outside at that very moment?

The longer he pondered, the more convinced he became that they would lie in wait in a nearby alley and pick him off after he emerged. Because of the tavern's rowdy patrons, St. Louis residents tended to give the streets nearest to the Flint and Powder a wide berth, especially at night.

And if he tried to avoid the inevitable by staying until the tavern closed, he would be playing right into their hands. There would be even fewer people on the streets, making their chore that much easier. Perhaps, if he departed immediately, he could evade them.

Rising, Nate grabbed the Hawken and made for the right-hand corner at the rear of the establishment. If he recollected correctly there was a back exit into an alley that would bring him out on a well-lit avenue where his enemies would be reluctant to ambush him. He didn't know if they knew of the alley, but was inclined to think they did not. None of them, so far as he was aware, had spent much time in St. Louis, although all three had probably heard many stories from those who did make the trip on a regular basis.

He smiled when he spied the door in the shadows. There were a few men at the table closest to it but they paid him no mind whatsoever. Chuckling at his cleverness, he raised the latch and stepped out into the narrow, dark alley, then closed the door behind him. A repugnant odor assailed his nostrils and he realized countless tavern patrons had used the alley to relieve themselves.

Nate hurried toward the avenue some 25 yards off. The grimy walls of buildings hemmed him in on both sides and he didn't like the feeling of being penned in, as it were. Other than a few inches of filth underfoot, and what appeared to be a couple of stacks of wooden crates, the alley was empty.

He started to go past those crates when a shadow swooped down and slammed into him, knocking him against the right-hand wall, the impact causing him to lose his grip on the Hawken. Harsh laughter in his ear told him the nature of the shadow, and he twisted and clawed for his butcher knife. A sharp object cut through his buckskin shirt, slicing into the flesh over his ribs, and with a mighty effort he shoved his assailant off.

"Now, bastard, we have you!"

Despite the lack of light Nate recognized one of the Ruxtons. He never had bothered to learn their first names and couldn't tell them apart. But he was all too familiar with their reputation, and had no doubt the knife held in the right hand of the brother he now faced could be used savagely and efficiently. He whipped out his own and began to move in the direction of the avenue.

"No, you don't," the Ruxton brother hissed, skipping in front of him and jabbing to force him to stop.

Nate halted and crouched, emptying his mind of all thoughts as he had been taught to do in a knife fight. His survival depended on relying exclusively on his finely honed instincts and reflexes. Any distraction at a crucial juncture, even a fleeting thought, might result in his death.

"I will carve you into little pieces and have them sent to your family," the Ruxton taunted.

Being reminded of Winona and Zach added fuel to Nate's growing rage and he suddenly lunged, slashing at the man's neck, and came within half an inch of ending the fight then and there. The Ruxton brother leaped back just in time, then instantly countered with a swipe of his own.

Nate parried, their blades ringing loudly in the confines of the alley. He stabbed at the man's chest but missed. The dull glint of Ruxton's knife gave him enough warning to dart to the left and spare his midsection. He sprang again and nicked Ruxton's shoulder.

Undaunted, the lean man tried to spear the tip of his knife into Nate's throat, but was a shade too slow. He pressed his attack, swinging again and again, coming at Nate from different angles with each attempt, trying to break through Nate's guard. He seemed to become increasingly frustrated as every blow was blocked or dodged with uncanny speed.

Although Nate was pleased at his performance, he was becoming winded sooner than he would have expected. After all he had been through in the past 24 hours, compounded by not having eaten a solid meal in all that time, and coming as it did on the heels of his extended recuperation, he was in no shape for a prolonged fight. Somehow, he must prevail quickly. He tried to entice Ruxton into making a reckless mistake by deliberately holding his knife a little farther from his body than was ordinarily safe, but his foe was too experienced to fall for such an obvious ploy.

He was tempted to draw a flintlock, but doing so would leave his left side exposed. Not for long, true, but it might be all Ruxton needed to penetrate his guard and stab him. No, there must be another way of defeating his adversary.

Although he had willed himself not to think, he wasn't being very successful. Another thought occurred to him, spurring him on even more. What if the other Ruxton brother or Campbell or both should show up? They were probably watching the front of the tavern, but he couldn't be certain they would stay there forever. It was very likely the other brother would come back soon to check on his sibling. They rarely did anything apart.

He lashed out and Ruxton backed up, then countered. The blade flashed past his eyes and he twisted sideways to expose less of his body. As he did his left hand brushed against the tomahawk. In a burst of inspiration he saw a means to vanquish the killer and put the idea into operation.

Nate ducked a swing that would have partially scalped him and intentionally retreated. Not much, only a yard or so, but it gave Ruxton the impression that he was tiring and wasn't as confident as he should be. All the while he presented just his right side to Ruxton while his left hand gradually strayed to the handle of the tomahawk.

Perhaps anticipating victory, Ruxton renewed his attack with fierce vigor, demonstrating why the Ruxton brothers were widely feared by whites and Indians alike.

Nate again retreated, feigning fatigue. Warding off an underhanded cut that would have severed his genitals, he swung halfheartedly. Ruxton adroitly blocked the move with his knife and their blades rang together once more. Then, while their arms were briefly locked stiff and motionless, he yanked the tomahawk out, raised it on high, and brought the razor edge hurtling downward.

Ruxton tried to evade the blow. In desperation he hauled his arm back but he was too late. The tomahawk sank into his yielding flesh an inch shy of the joint, biting deep, severing major veins because immediately a geyser of blood spurted forth. He threw back his head and screamed.

Stepping in close, Nate reduced the scream to a gurgling whine by slashing his knife across Ruxton's throat. Pivoting, he buried the tomahawk in the side of Ruxton's neck, and when Ruxton staggered backwards he wielded the tomahawk again with all the strength he could muster.

The tomahawk, which had already cleaved a gash inches deep, practically beheaded the man. Ruxton's head flopped over and he crashed into a wall and slid to the ground, his eyes locked wide open in amazement at his own demise.

Losing no time and heedless of the blood on both weapons, Nate stuck the tomahawk under his belt, jammed the knife in its sheath, and anxiously searched for the Hawken. He found the rifle moments later, scooped it into his hands, and raced for the end of the alley. Campbell and the brother were bound to have heard the scream. They would be on his heels in a flash.

He was almost to the avenue when a rifle boomed and the ball buzzed past his ear. Rounding the corner on the right, he poured on the speed. There were dozens of people in the street, including many couples strolling arm in arm. They all gave him a wide berth or moved out of the way, a few of the men shouting questions, demanding to know what all the commotion was about.

If they only knew.

Nate glanced over his shoulder and saw a thin figure dash out of the alley and sprint in pursuit. Potential witnesses wouldn't deter the other Ruxton now. Knowing the Ruxtons as he did, Nate guessed the surviving brother was mad with rage and craved revenge. The second Ruxton would stop at nothing until he was dead and buried.

"Look out, you fool!"

He faced front, startled to see a stunned couple mere yards away, and threw himself to the right to avoid a collision. As it was his shoulder slammed into the shoulder of the man and nearly knocked the irate citizen off his feet. He kept on running, a string of curses in his wake. He heard angry shouting farther behind caused by the bull-headed Ruxton, who was considerably less considerate of the pedestrians and bowled over any in his path.

An intersection appeared, and on a whim Nate sped across the avenue, narrowly avoiding a passing carriage, and down a side street. Had he taken a right he would have wound up near the tavern, and he suspected that Campbell would be coming from that direction to head him off.

Lining the street were stately older residences. It was one of the affluent sections of the city where the rich lived in luxury every bit the equal of that enjoyed by their counterparts in New York City or Paris. There were high hedges and lush yards and tall trees on either side.

He stuck to the street and repeatedly looked back, expecting to see the avenging Ruxton brother appear at any second. Oddly, he didn't. Forty yards from the intersection he came to what appeared to be a city park and halted. Cocking the Hawken, he waited. Where was Ruxton? he wondered.

A full minute went by and Ruxton didn't appear. Nate realized he was standing in the dim glow from a lantern suspended next to a gate across the street, and promptly moved into deep shadow under a spreading willow tree where he couldn't be seen. When another minute elapsed he concluded the brother had indeed given up, if only temporarily.

He waited five more minutes to be sure, though. Then he cautiously started back toward the avenue. Somehow he must locate Tricky Dick Harrington or Sante Fe Bill soon or be forced to spend the night on the streets, a distinctly unappealing prospect given all the footpads and worse loose in the city between dusk and dawn.

The snap of a twig saved his life.

Nate pivoted to see the second Ruxton brother hurtling over a low hedge on his right. Knife out, teeth exposed in a savage snarl, Ruxton swooped down like a lean bird of prey. Nate barely got the rifle high enough to deflect the knife before the brother smashed into him and they both tumbled to the ground.

Again Nate lost the rifle. He rolled, grimacing as pain racked his shoulder. He surged to his knees, drawing both pistols as he rose and extending both arms, his thumbs pulling back the hammers. Like a panther Ruxton had leaped erect and now charged, his knife aloft, livid with stark fury.

Nate fired both pistols simultaneously. A cloud of smoke enveloped both muzzles and for a few anxious seconds he couldn't see Ruxton. Then the breeze cleared the smoke and he saw the brother lying flat and lifeless not a yard away. Elated, he started to lower the pistols when a heavy hand fell on his shoulder and he spun, just knowing all his effort had been in vain, that it would be Robert Campbell with a flintlock aimed at his head.

Instead, to his profound and thorough consternation, it was Shakespeare McNair.

Chapter Thirty-One

"Shakespeare." Nate shouted, rising and impulsively hugging his mentor. Indescribable waves of pure joy washed over him. He was stunned, confused, disoriented. "How—?" he blurted out. "You can't be!"

"Not now," Shakespeare said, looking at the dead Ruxton. "Those shots will draw folks from all over. We have to get out of here." He took hold of Nate's arm and started to hasten off.

"Wait!" Nate said. "My rifle." He wedged the flintlocks under his belt, retrieved the Hawken, and excitedly followed on McNair's heels as the ancient mountain man dashed into the night faster than most men half his age were capable of doing. They ran to the corner and turned left while all around them there were loud cries as people tried to find out who had done the shooting.

After going a hundred yards Shakespeare slowed and walked along the side of the street. "We're in the clear."

Nate noticed that his friend kept glancing around as if expecting to be attacked at any moment. "Don't worry. I think I lost Campbell."

Shakespeare glanced at him. "Robert Campbell is in St. Louis?"

"He showed up at the Flint and Powder with the Ruxtons," Nate explained, savoring the sweet elation of having been reunited with the man he esteemed more than any other. "But forget about him! How did you find me? Better yet, what are you doing alive? Adeline told me you had been killed by the same Indians who killed Winona and Zach. And how—"

"Nate, your wife is alive," Shakespeare said, cutting him off. "So is your son."

"What?" Nate said, and halted. It felt as if his entire body had suddenly gone completely numb. He tingled from head to toe and had the greatest difficulty in forming coherent thoughts.

"Winona and Zach are alive," Shakespeare reiterated. "Zach is fine, but Winona was shot and she's still weak from the loss of blood. Doc Sawyer says she'll be fit as a fiddle in another week or two."

"Shot?" Nate repeated, utterly confounded. He tried to take a step and couldn't. For some reason his limbs were locked in place. "I don't understand," he said weakly.

Shakespeare tugged on Nate's arm. "I'll explain on the way. We can't stay here. Not only is there Campbell to worry about, but you know better than I do that Adeline and her husband will stop at nothing to have you killed now that you've escaped their clutches."

"You know about them?"

"We learned about them only today. Now come along," Shakespeare directed, and practically dragged Nate after him. "I won't feel safe until we're at Tricky Dick's."

Dumbly, obediently, like a long-lost puppy following its newly found master, Nate followed Shakespeare along a winding maze of streets, avenues, and alleys. He lost all track of time. He lost all track of distance. His sense of direction was completely askew. When he was finally led into a house he barely paid attention to what kind or where it was located. Seated at a table were Blue Water Woman, Tricky Dick Harrington, and another woman who must be Dick's wife. They were beaming happily.

"You found him at last!" Tricky Dick exclaimed, coming over and clapping Nate on the shoulders.

"Pierre and Logan were right," Shakespeare said. "They did see him at the Flint and Powder. By the time I got there he had left and the tavern was in an uproar. It seemed a man had just been killed in the alley out back, and when I went out I saw it was one of the Ruxton brothers. So I began asking every person I could find if they had seen anyone leave the alley. Thank God there were plenty who remembered seeing two men run by. I caught up with him just after he killed the other Ruxton."

"Good riddance to trash," Tricky Dick said,

and looked into Nate's eyes. "Are you all right? Would you like to sit down?"
"No," Nate said softly. "My wife and son. Where are they?"
"In the bedroom there," Tricky Dick said. "They're both asleep. But neither of them have slept much at all since you were kidnapped by that"—he caught himself and glanced at his wife—"woman."
Nate shuffled toward the door, but stopped when Shakespeare addressed him.
"There are a few things you should know before you go in there. I'll let Winona tell you who shot her. She was trying to stop your former sweetheart and her husband from carting you off. We've been hunting for you ever since. Doc Sawyer had to pressure one of his colleagues, a Doctor Mangel, into telling him where you were being held. Apparently Mangel was paid a hefty sum to keep it secret."
"That's right," Tricky Dick confirmed. "McNair and I had put the word out among all the trappers in the city to be on the lookout for a man answering your description. It was two of them who spotted you at the tavern. They might not have recognized you if it wasn't for those stitches in your forehead."
Nate recalled the two men who had stared at him and then hurried out of the Flint and Powder. "Thank you," he mumbled.
"We still don't know what Adeline and Rhey Debussy were up to," Shakespeare mentioned. "Care to tell us later?"
"I will," Nate promised, and stepped to the

closed door. He leaned the Hawken against the wall, then entered. A lantern on a table, turned low, cast enough light to enable him to clearly see Winona slumbering in a bed and Zach lying on a quilt on the floor. Beside the boy lay Samson. The huge dog lifted its massive head, uttered a low whine, and padded over, its tail bobbing crazily.

"Hello, big fellow," Nate said softly, and nearly choked on the words. Tears filled both eyes. He blinked, swallowed, and bent to stroke Samson's neck and chin. "Never thought I'd be glad to see your ugly face."

Straightening, Nate stepped to a chair and carried it closer to the bed, to a spot where he could sit and see both his wife and son. He slumped into the chair, feeling weak, his temples throbbing. Zach snored lightly while Winona's lips quivered every now and then. He stared at them, overwhelmed by his exquisite good fortune.

They were alive!

They were alive!!!

More tears flowed. He tried to hold them back and couldn't. They poured out of his eyes and down over his cheeks and chin and he simply sat there and let them. His nose ran but he didn't care. There was a constriction in his throat but he didn't mind. All that mattered was seeing his loved ones again and knowing he would once again hold them in his arms and care for them as a devoted husband and father. Nothing else seemed important.

Zach tossed in his sleep, rolling onto his back, and Samson walked over and licked the boy's forehead. Zach mumbled and swatted at the air as if at a fly.

It was too much for Nate. He buried his head in his hands and let the tears gush in earnest. A bottomless well had been tapped and there was no end to the geyser. Low sobs were torn from his throat and his chest heaved with the mere effort of breathing. He doubled over, racked with misery, and cried uncontrollably.

Suddenly he stiffened. Two sets of arms, one big and one small, had encircled his shoulders, and he lifted his head to gaze tenderly into the tear-filled eyes of Winona and Zach. His wife bent down to tenderly kiss him on the brow while his son tried to hug the life out of him. How long they embraced he could not say, but at long last he forced himself to stand and escorted Winona to the bed. She slid against the wall and he lifted Zach up beside her. Then he sank down on the outside, on his side, and draped an arm over both of them. None of them bothered to speak since no words were necessary. Nate looked from one to the other until his eyelids became heavy from fatigue and he drifted asleep, the happiest man alive.

An elbow in the ribs abruptly awakened Nate and his eyes snapped open in alarm. For a fleeting instant he had imagined himself back in Adeline's clutches, but the sight of his wife and son calmed him and he smiled contentedly. Zach, whose tossing and turning had been responsible for rousing him, was still sleeping. Winona, however, must have been awake for some time. She was lying still, affectionately staring at him. "Good morning, dearest," he whispered.

"Good morning, husband," Winona said softly, and reached out to stroke his cheek. "We have missed you."

"How do you feel? Shakespeare told me that you were shot."

"I am weak but I live," Winona said, tracing the outline of his ear with her forefinger. "And now that you have returned to us safe and well I will heal quickly."

"Who shot you?"

"I only knew his first name at the time. He came here with Adeline Van Buren while I was watching over you and they took you away, Since then I have learned from Shakespeare that the man's full name is Rhey Debussy and he is Adeline's husband."

"I know," Nate said, scarcely able to contain the flaming hatred that coursed through his being. Rhey Debussy! He never had liked the man, and now his feelings were justified. Was it possible that somehow, deep down, he had sensed what the murdering swine had done to Winona? Did that explain his immediate dislike?

"We did not learn the identity of the man with Adeline until yesterday morning when Doctor Sawyer paid us a visit. For some time he had suspected another doctor named Mangel knew where you were being held, but Mangel would not tell him at first," Winona related, and tears rimmed her eyes. "All we knew was that Adeline, a man named Rhey, and another named Yancy were involved. But we did not know the last names of the men and had no—"

"Yancy?" Nate said suddenly.

"Yes. He works for a man named Jacques Debussy. On the day you were taken by Adeline and Rhey, this Yancy came up to Shakespeare, Tricky Dick, and Ruth while they were out shopping and asked them for directions to a hotel in the middle of the city. They had to draw a map in the dirt before he understood and went away."

"He was deliberately stalling them," Nate deduced, his features hardening. So the foreman had played him for a fool too!

"That is what Shakespeare guessed," Winona said. "But he didn't know for certain until yesterday evening when Doctor Sawyer pointed Jacques Debussy and Yancy out to him at the Devil Tavern. Then Shakespeare figured everything out."

Nate placed a hand on her neck and gently stroked her soft skin. "I'm sorry," he whispered.

"For what?"

"For all you've been through because of my stupidity."

"It was Adeline Van Buren and her husband who have caused us all this harm, not you."

Filled with guilt and remorse, Nate shook his head. "I should never have come to St. Louis. I should have put Adeline from my mind the minute that trapper told me that she wanted to see me."

"Why *did* she send for you?" Winona inquired.

Nate told her everything, about how Adeline and Rhey needed money and had schemed to obtain his inheritance. About how they had spirited him to the estate of Rhey's brother, Jacques. About the lies concerning Winona and Zach being dead. About his encounter with the black woman from Africa, the subsequent tragedy, and his narrow escape. About his fight with the Ruxtons and being found by Shakespeare.

Winona listened attentively. When he concluded she averted her eyes and sniffled. "Now it is I who should apologize."

"What are you talking about?"

"I failed you as a wife. I did not have the faith in you every wife should have in her husband."

"I don't understand," Nate said, puzzled.

She looked at him, her eyes haunted by self-reproach. "I was not certain you would come back to me. I thought you might prefer Adeline over me."

"Never!" Nate said vehemently, and was stunned when she began weeping. He caressed her hair and squeezed her arm and assured her again and again that he loved her, but she cried continuously for over ten minutes. When the tears ceased he offered a comforting smile. "When will you get it into your pretty head that the only woman I love is you? I wouldn't have married you if I cared for someone else, and now that I have you I'm never letting you go. You're stuck with me until we're both in our graves, and even longer if you take the Good Book into account. I have known more joy with you, Winona, than I ever believed it was possible to experience. So get used to me. I'm yours forever." He smiled again, pleased with himself, positive his kind words would make her exceedingly glad. So he was all the more astounded when she started crying again, only worse than before.

He lay there and waited for her to calm down, wishing he understood her better. What had he said to upset her again? Sometimes he wondered if men and women were ever meant to have a complete understanding of each other. They were so different, and not just physically. Men and women were as emotionally and mentally different as two sides of a coin, yet together they complemented one another as if meant to do so by a higher power.

"I will never doubt you again, husband," Winona said at length. "If I ever do you may send me back to my people."

"Didn't you hear me? You're staying with me forever," Nate told her, and had started to lean forward to give her a kiss when he accidentally bumped into Zach and woke the boy up.

"Pa!" Zach squealed, and gave Nate a ferocious hug. "You are back! I thought I was dreaming. Are you back for good?"

"I'm back for good," Nate promised. "Although there are a few things I have to do over the next couple of days, so I'll be gone for just a little while now and then."

"What do you have to do?" Zach asked.

"I plan to make the people who hurt your mother wish they were never born."

Chapter Thirty-Two

Yancy was in a foul mood as he hiked along the narrow path that cut through the center of the woods between the stable and the cabins housing the blacks. In his right hand he held a whip, in his left a club. On both sides reared tall trees that blocked off much of the early morning sunlight and he walked in deep shadows. There was a crisp, invigorating nip to the air that he hardly noticed and little appreciated.

Inwardly, Yancy simmered. His day had gotten off to a rotten start when Jacques Debussy called him in and reprimanded him severely for his part in the deception Rhey and that damn woman had played on Nate King. And here he thought he had been doing the right thing. Rhey, after all, was Jacques's brother, and Jacques had told him to do whatever he could to make Rhey's stay pleasant. So when Rhey had asked for help he had naturally volunteered.

Those two fools!

Now that Jacques had told him everything and made him aware of the gravity of the situation, he more fully understood how Rhey and the bitch had jeopardized the entire operation. Unless King could be found and eliminated, they were all in danger of being arrested, tried, and imprisoned. And all because of those two!

He should have known, though. Rhey had always been the black sheep of the family, and he obviously hadn't changed. Even when Jacques and Rhey were young, it had always been Jacques who was the sensible one, who attended to the family enterprises and worked at increasing the family wealth. Rhey, on the other hand, had no head for business. His sole knack was for spending money, not making it. Small wonder that their father left the property to Jacques and a pittance to Rhey. And it had come as no surprise when Rhey spent all of his on women, wine, and gambling in a span of mere months. Ever since, Rhey had lived by his wits and his luck. Twice Rhey married wealthy women and squandered their riches recklessly. One of the women shot herself, the other became a hopeless drunkard. Then Rhey went to New York for a high-stakes card game and somehow met Adeline Van Buren. Once again his mysterious charm served him in good stead, and he wound up taking her as his third wife. Of course he spent her money.

And now, thanks to those two idiots and their devious scheme to steal King's inheritance, Jacques Debussy was in danger, the man Yancy had served faithfully for decades, the man he respected more than any other, the man who had given him a small house of his own and who paid him handsomely to manage the estate and act as overseer of the blacks.

Thinking of the dumb Africans only incensed him further. Ever since that buck nigger had been beaten to death and that woman had died, the rest of the latest shipment had been restless and surprisingly uncooperative—surprisingly because whips and clubs usually sufficed to bring the blacks into line. In five minutes he would be at the cabins. Then he would teach them to obey. They would learn, or else!

Yancy rounded a curve, immersed in thought, his head bowed, his knuckles white from clenching the whip and the club so hard his hands hurt. He took several strides, then suddenly realized there was someone on the path in front of him and glanced up, expecting it would be one of the guards. Recognition shocked him to his core and he drew up short in consternation. "You!" he blurted out.

"Hello, Yancy," Nate said.

Startled, Yancy took a half step backwards. There was another man with King, a grizzled mountain man in buckskins who stood to one side with a Hawken pointed at Yancy's midriff. And on the other side of the path sat a huge black dog, almost a bear, its tongue hanging out as it panted quietly. "How did you get onto the estate?"

"It was easy," Nate responded. "We've fought the Blackfeet and the Utes. Compared to them your guards are incompetent dolts."

"One yell from me and those incompetent dolts will fill you and your friend here full of lead," Yancy promised.

The white-haired mountain man chuckled. "One yell from you will be your last, friend. And we'll make our escape the same way we snuck in. So go ahead and yell. My trigger finger is itching and I need to scratch it."

Yancy couldn't understand how both of these men could be so unconcerned. Didn't they realize they wouldn't get out alive? "What is it you want? Why are you here?"

"I came to see you," Nate said.

"Me?"

Nate nodded. "I came to kill you."

The blunt assertion shocked Yancy. He stared at the rifle in the crook of King's arm, then licked his lips. "Me? What did I do?"

"You stalled Shakespeare and Tricky Dick Harrington the day Rhey and Adeline kidnapped me," Nate said. His features hardened. "The day my wife was shot."

"They shot her? I didn't know that. Rhey just told me they were going to take you, was all."

Nate turned and handed his rifle to Shakespeare. "Remember, if he wins you're not to harm him."

"I remember," Shakespeare replied testily. "And I still think I should shoot the varmint no matter what the outcome."

"No."

Puzzled, Yancy looked from one to the other. "What are you talking about? If you win what?"

"The fight between you and me," Nate said, facing him and moving slowly forward. "We'll settle this man to man. Just the two of us." He halted. "Unless, of course, you try to attract the attention of your men. Then my friend will put a ball right between your eyes."

"Let me see if I understand this. You're issuing a personal challenge and when I win I can just walk away?"

"*If* you win. That's the deal."

"Weapons?"

"You can use your club and whip. I'll use my knife and tomahawk."

Yancy looked at the pistols under King's belt. "What about those flintlocks?"

For an answer Nate pulled out both guns and deposited them at Shakespeare's feet. Stepping to the middle of the path he folded his arms across his chest and nodded. "I am ready when you are."

"You're a fool, do you know that?" Yancy taunted, and lifted his immensely powerful arms. "No one has ever beaten me, King. Not at wrestling or boxing or with any type of weapon. Why, half the men in St. Louis fear me and the rest fear the mention of my name. I've killed nine men in my time, not counting blacks." He hefted the whip and the club. "You should forget this folly and leave now while you still have life in your limbs."

"You're not the only one who has a reputation," Nate mentioned, unruffled by the boasts. "Among the Indian tribes of the Rockies and the plains I'm called Grizzly Killer because I've slain more grizzlies than any other white man."

"Grizzlies are strong but they're dumb brutes. Fighting a man is a whole different proposition."

"I've fought my share," Nate said, lowering his arms. "Now shall we begin or will you try to talk me to death?"

"You're even a bigger fool than I thought," Yancy said, shaking his head. "Since you're insisting on a fair fight, I'll be fair to you. I must kill you, you see, in order to prevent you from causing trouble for my employer, Jacques Debussy. But I will allow your friend to leave unmolested if you give your word that he will not tell the federal authorities about our slaver operation."

"Shakespeare does as he wants. The only promise I can give you is that your death will be swift and as painless as possible."

"You charitable bastard," Yancy said in a deceptively sweet tone, and then struck with all the might in his right arm, flicking the whip back behind his head and forward again so that it arced toward Nate King's face.

Had Nate been a shade slower he would have lost an eye. He ducked, or tried to, and the lash bit into his forehead instead, adding to the wounds previously inflicted there by the panther. Sliding to the right enabled him to evade a second swing, and as he straightened he drew both his butcher knife and his tomahawk simultaneously.

"You're a fast devil," Yancy snapped, and worked the whip with skilled precision, his arm ceaselessly in motion, never pausing for an instant so that he could keep King constantly at bay.

Nate winced when the lash tore into the flesh of his left arm, but he successfully prevented the whip from inflicting more serious injuries by the deft use of his tomahawk and his knife to block most of the blows. He tried several times to slice the whip in half, but each time Yancy jerked the lash back with a lightning move of the wrist.

Yancy was taking his time. He had whipped scores of blacks since becoming overseer, and he knew how to shred a man's flesh piece by bloody piece until his victim was in acute torment and pleading to be spared. After all the trouble King had caused, he desired to do the same to this upstart mountain man who didn't know enough not to meddle in the affairs of his betters. A confident grin curled his lips as he swung again and again.

Nate began to wonder if he had made a grave mistake. The whip's long reach prevented him from getting any closer to the foreman. Every time he tried, Yancy would snap the whip and make him jump aside or be torn open. He must get in close, though, in order to prevail. His weapons were designed for close-in fighting; beyond arm's length they were useless unless thrown, and he wasn't ready to risk losing one just yet by having it batted down by Yancy's club before it could strike a vital organ. So he stepped back and dodged and weaved in a wide circle around his enemy.

Gradually Yancy became concerned. He noticed with alarm that very few of his blows were landing and those that did had little effect. And despite his prodigious strength, his right arm was slowly but surely becoming fatigued. Swinging a heavy whip strained anyone. And despite all his experience, he had rarely wielded his whip for more than five minutes at one time. Normally, that was all it took to win or convince an arrogant black to fall into line. Not this time. Nate King danced effortlessly around him and he became increasingly frustrated by his failure.

Nate tried to cut the lash again, but missed. Out of the corner of his eye he noticed Shakespeare was holding Samson by the collar, as they had previously agreed he should do. Otherwise the dog might pounce on the foreman and rip his throat open before either of them could prevent it. Suddenly something wrapped tightly around his right ankle, and he realized he had committed a grave blunder by allowing himself to be distracted at such a critical moment. The next instant his leg was roughly yanked out from under him and he crashed down onto his back.

"Meet your Maker!" Yancy bellowed triumphantly, and sprang with his wicked club upraised even as he kept the whip taut by pulling back on the handle so Nate wouldn't be able to rise.

In desperation Nate lifted the tomahawk barely in time and deflected the club. The impact jarred his arm to the bone. Twisting and bending forward, he slashed his knife at Yancy's ankles, and the foreman jerked his legs back to spare them. In a smooth continuation of the same movement, Nate angled the edge of the knife into the whip and chopped off the last three feet.

Yancy stumbled rearward. For such a broad man he was surprisingly light on his feet and he swiftly regained his balance. He glared at the severed whip, then at Nate. "I've underestimated you, King. You're better than most. Perhaps the best I've ever tangled with."

Without uttering a word, Nate charged, flailing away with the knife and the tomahawk.

Taken aback, Yancy darted to the right. Even without the lash the whip was still a deadly weapon and he worked it once more, aiming at King's head.

Nate deliberately hunched his shoulders and took the brunt of the blow there rather than in the face even as he kept charging. He swung the tomahawk but was countered by the club, then pivoted and stabbed the knife up and in.

Shock etched Yancy's blunt features as the keen blade parted his skin and scraped against a rib. Incredible agony exploded in his body and he almost cried out. Frantically he wrenched to the left and felt the blade slide out of his body, a sickening sensation that caused him to double over and gasp.

Pressing his advantage, Nate stepped in and slashed once more, aiming at the foreman's thick neck. Had the knife connected it would have partially decapitated Yancy, but he, by ducking low, preserved his neck at the expense of his scalp. The tip of the blade tore his head from back to front and blood gushed forth.

Yancy's anxiety was transformed into a blinding rage by the thought of being beaten by a simpleton trapper from the high mountains. Never had he been bested and never would he be! Venting a bestial cry, he dropped the useless whip and employed the club like a madman, delivering ferocious swipes that could cave in a human skull as if it were a mere eggshell.

Nate adroitly warded off the initial blows with his tomahawk, but inevitably a swing penetrated his guard and he felt a tremendous concussion on the side of his head that dropped him to his knees. Dimly he heard Yancy laugh, and glanced up to see the club being lifted for the killing blow. Almost as if his arm had a mind of its own, up went the tomahawk, straight into Yancy's groin. Yancy's eyes became white saucers and he froze, gurgling and sputtering. Gritting his teeth, Nate surged upright and swung the tomahawk one final time, ripping Yancy's throat from one side to the other. A crimson spray struck him in the face and chin, and then the foreman's eyes fluttered and he sank slowly to the ground as if lying down peacefully to sleep. For a minute Yancy's limbs twitched and his body convulsed. Nate stared grimly at the corpse and let his body relax.

"You did it," Shakespeare said softly at his elbow.

"Not quite," Nate responded. "Not yet."

Chapter Thirty-Three

The Devil Tavern had been built five years before by an Englishman who patterned it after a famous tavern by that name in his native country. The decor and furnishings were those that would be found in any British tavern or pub, and many a visiting Englishman had expressed delight and satisfaction at finding an oasis of genuine British culture in the midst of a wasteland of barbarians and barbaric customs. The prices, as a result of the expenses the owner bore in maintaining the proper atmosphere by relying on certain imported articles, were higher than those at most other taverns. As a consequence the Devil Tavern attracted customers who were more well-to-do than most of the patrons who frequented establishments of lesser repute.

At taverns throughout the country and in Europe it was quite common for social clubs to be formed, and the Devil Tavern was no exception. Some of its more affluent customers had organized the Apollo Club, one of the most exclusive in the entire city. Only the wealthiest could afford to join. The club boasted a membership of 17 prominent men, and foremost among them was Jacques Debussy.

Tricky Dick Harrington provided Nate with the commonly known history of the tavern and the club while they waited, along with Shakespeare, at the mouth of an alley half a block north of the Devil Tavern. "They have a man posted at the door to keep out any rowdy types," he concluded. "I'd never been in there until Doc Sawyer took Shakespeare and me in the other day."

"And we wouldn't have been permitted inside if not for Sawyer," Shakespeare threw in. "He goes to the tavern often and the man at the door knew him."

Nate, leaning on the corner of a general store, glanced at his mentor. "How did Sawyer persuade Mangel to tell him my whereabouts?"

"From what I can gather, those two never have been very friendly. Sawyer threatened to report Mangel if he didn't cooperate," Shakespeare said. "You owe Doc Sawyer a lot. He was the one who figured out Mangel must have been consulted about you and took it from there."

"I'll thank him again the next time he comes to see Winona," Nate said, and stared at the entrance to the Devil Tavern.

"How much longer are we going to keep a

watch?" Tricky Dick asked. He squinted up at the afternoon sun. "We've been here pretty near four hours already."

"You can leave whenever you want," Nate told him. "I'm staying until Jacques Debussy shows up."

"Sawyer claims he comes here daily," Shakespeare said.

"Maybe Jacques has left the . . ." Tricky Dick began, and happened to gaze toward the tavern. "Look there!"

Nate had already spied the three people walking up the busy avenue. He placed a hand on a flintlock as Rhey Debussy, arm in arm with Adeline, strolled casually along beside another man who must have been Rhey's brother. There was a family resemblance, although Jacques had gray hair, broader shoulders, and a neat mustache and beard. All three of them were dressed in the height of current fashion.

"Didn't expect the others," Shakespeare commented.

"Me either," Nate said. "But it works out for the best this way. Now we don't have to force Jacques to tell us where to find Rhey. And I can present my challenge in public among plenty of witnesses. Jacques will be surrounded by his friends so he won't dare interfere."

Tricky Dick cocked his head and regarded Nate critically. "I still think you'd be better off jumping Rhey some night with your knife. Why go to all this bother?"

"I want it done properly," Nate answered. "And I don't want any of his friends to track me down later to get revenge. This way everyone will know the fight was fair."

"But you've never done it before and Rhey has," Shakespeare said. "He'll have an edge."

Nate watched the trio enter the tavern. "We'll give them time to get comfortable, then we'll go in."

"You didn't answer me," Shakespeare said.

"You didn't ask a question."

"What if Rhey kills you?" Tricky Dick inquired.

"Then I'll die knowing I did the right thing. A man who would let someone hurt his wife and not do anything about it is as yellow as they come and doesn't deserve the woman's love." He took his hand off the flintlock and spoke vehemently. "Rhey Debussy will rue the day he harmed Winona."

Shakespeare and Tricky Dick exchanged looks, but neither made any reply.

Fuming with impatience, Nate allowed about five minutes to elapse before he headed for the Devil Tavern. There was something about his expression that caused a number of passersby to stop and stare, but he paid no attention to them. All he could think of was Rhey and Adeline and the suffering they had put Winona through. At the fancy door containing a glass pane he paused to take a breath, then jerked the door wide and strode into the cool interior.

Immediately a husky man in a suit detached himself from a stool by a bar on the right and came over, all smiles. "Pardon me, mate, but I think you want one of the taverns down the street."

"I want this one," Nate said. There were few customers at the bar due to the early time of day. At a table sat four men playing cards. Ahead was a narrow, dark corridor leading to other rooms. Since the Debussys and Adeline weren't near the bar, they must be back there.

"No, you don't," the man said, still smiling as he placed a firm hand on Nate's arm. "Now why don't you be a good fellow and leave?" He glanced around as the door opened and Shakespeare and Tricky Dick came in. "What is this, a party?"

Nate hit him. His right fist swept up from below his waist and landed solidly on the man's jaw. Teeth crunched, the man's head snapped back, and then Nate had to catch him to keep him from crashing to the floor. He slowly eased the unconscious man into a chair and looked at the server behind the bar, who was gawking in amazement. "The Debussy brothers," he demanded.

"Who?" the server blurted out. Then he said, "Oh. Them. They're in the third private room on the left."

"Thanks," Nate said, and stalked down the corridor until he reached the indicated door, which was closed. Not bothering to knock, he flung the door open and stepped into a plush dining room that would have suited the queen of England. Seated at a round table were Jacques, Rhey and Adeline, and three other men. They glanced up at his unannounced entrance, Jacques and the other men in surprise, Rhey and Adeline in bewilderment.

"I beg your pardon, *monsieur,*" Jacques said,

rising with a napkin in his hand. "What is the meaning of this intrusion?"

"I'm here to extend an invitation," Nate said coldly, never taking his eyes off Rhey. He knew the bastard carried a derringer, and held his right hand near his flintlock in case Rhey became reckless.

"An invitation?" repeated a portly man with a wine glass. "I don't understand, young man. Explain yourself."

"This son of a bitch," Nate said, pointing at Rhey, "shot my wife. I demand satisfaction, and I demand it today." So saying, he strode over to the table and before any of them could deduce his intent, he slapped Rhey Debussy full across the mouth.

Rhey recoiled at the blow, then snarled like a rabid wolf and went to reach under his jacket.

"You do and you're dead," Nate assured him. "If you're not a coward, meet me on Bloody Island in two hours to settle our differences."

Silent until that moment, Adeline shot out of her chair and clasped a hand to her throat. "Bloody Island? Are you insane? You won't leave it alive."

"That remains to be seen," Nate responded, his eyes locked on Rhey. "What will it be, Debussy? Do you have a shred of honor left in your soul?"

Livid with rage, Rhey stood and shook a fist. "You should have left St. Louis while you had the chance. I accept your challenge!" He angrily pulled a gold watch from his vest pocket. "My seconds and I will be on Bloody Island at six P.M. Show up if you dare."

"I'll be there," Nate vowed.

Rhey stormed out of the dining room, brushing past Shakespeare and Tricky Dick.

"I'll make sure he leaves," McNair volunteered. "Wouldn't want him to hide and shoot you in the back on your way out." Turning, he hastened off.

The portly man set down his wine glass and folded his arms on the tabletop. "Young man, perhaps you would care to offer an explanation? My name is Thaddeus Hamilton and I have considerable influence in this city. Maybe you have heard of me?"

"No," Nate replied.

"I have," Tricky Dick interjected. "Hamilton is the richest man in St. Louis, even richer than Jacques Debussy."

Jacques Debussy's face betrayed his anxious state. He dropped his napkin and took a step forward. "Thaddeus, I assure you this mountain man's grievance is of no consequence. It is a personal thing between Rhey and him."

Nate faced Hamilton. "Were you aware Jacques Debussy is a smuggler and that he deals in slaves from Africa?"

"I was not," Hamilton said sincerely. "All of us here have always been under the impression Jacques makes his money in land and by selling crops and stock." He appraised Nate carefully. "Do you have proof of this allegation?"

"I saw the operation with my own eyes," Nate said.

Jacques placed his hands on his hips. "Don't listen to him, Thaddeus. He's spreading falsehoods to get his petty revenge on my brother." Turning to Nate, he said, "May I speak to you alone?"

"Lead the way."

The older Debussy stepped to a corner of the room and put his back to the wall. Lowering his voice, he declared, "Why are you doing this to me? It was Rhey and that woman who abducted you, Rhey who shot your wife. I've forced them to tell me everything, and I must say I do not agree with the manner in which they conducted themselves." He ran a hand over his slick hair. "I was not even home when all this occurred. You have no reason to cause me trouble."

"You're a slaver," Nate said. "That's reason enough."

"*Think,* man!" Jacques said. "It would be worth your while to forget this whole thing and return to your mountains. I will give you enough money to live comfortably the rest of your days. Or I will buy you a house here in St. Louis. All you must do is agree not to spread any more stories about me. Is it a deal?"

"No," Nate said.

In exasperation Jacques hissed like an aroused cottonmouth. "Why not? What can you possibly gain by opposing me? Thaddeus isn't the only one with influence. I'll crush you like I would a fly."

"You'll be too busy hiding from the federal authorities to pay any attention to me," Nate predicted.

"You contacted them?" Jacques asked in horror.

"I sent a letter over an hour ago. Within a week the military should pay your estate a visit."

Jacques's face was beet red from his chin to his hairline. His lips moved but no words came out. He leaned on the wall for support and sagged. "Do you have any idea what you have done? I will be arrested and imprisoned."

"Only if they catch you."

A minute went by and Jacques was silent. At last he seemed to get a grip on himself and straightened. "I should be angry at you, but I'm not," he said gloomily, looking into Nate's eyes. "Rhey and Adeline are to blame for this, not you. And I am partly at fault for being stupid enough to allow them to live at my mansion while I was gone." His mouth became a thin slit. "If you don't kill my idiot brother I may do so myself." A thought seemed to strike him. "Was it you who killed Yancy?"

Nate nodded. "It was a fair fight."

"Because of the part he played in Rhey's plot?"

"Can you think of a better reason?"

Jacques Debussy's features were pallid. "No," he said, so low the word was barely audible. "In your shoes I would have done the same." He smoothed his jacket and coughed lightly. "I trust you will excuse me. There is much I must attend to."

Nate stood aside and allowed Jacques to leave unmolested. Inwardly a conflict raged. Had he done the right thing? After all, Jacques had not been involved with the scheme to steal his inheritance. Why bring the man's criminal empire crashing down? The answer was easy, supplied by the memory of a frightened African woman named Tatu. He returned to the table.

"Might I inquire as to what transpired between Jacques and you?" Thaddeus Hamilton asked. "He looked as if he had seen a ghost."

"I imagine you'll find out soon enough," Nate responded, and bestowed a smile on Hamilton and the others. "I'm sorry, gentlemen, for barging in. Now if you'll excuse me, I must prepare for my duel." With a nod he headed for the door but Adeline barred his path.

"Nate, I need to talk to you."

"No."

"But it's important. Please."

"If you need someone to talk to, find your husband," Nate snapped, and walked around her. Where once he had cared for her with all his heart and would have done anything to please her, now it required all of his self-control not to punch her in the face. Simply being close to her filled him with bitter, choking fury. He hurried outside and found Shakespeare waiting.

"Rhey walked off in a huff."

"Then let's go to Tricky Dick's," Nate said. He took a few paces, then turned and rested a hand on each man's shoulder. "I'd be honored if the two of you would be my seconds."

"I ain't never been a second before," Tricky Dick said. "What do we do?"

It was Shakespeare who answered. "That's simple. We insure the rules are followed."

"That's all?" Tricky Dick asked.

"And we cart Nate home if he gets his fool head blown off."

Chapter Thirty-Four

Bloody Island was situated in the middle of the Mississippi River. The only way on or off was by boat unless a person was foolish enough to try to swim and contend with the sometimes swift currents that swept past the narrow island on both sides. No one lived there. Birds made their homes in the few trees and occasional snakes and frogs paid the place a visit, but otherwise a shroud of deathly stillness normally blanketed the island from one end to the other.

Decades ago, shortly after the turn of the century, the island had been the site of a duel between two prominent St. Louis residents in which one of the participants received a ball through the heart and bled copiously before dying. Ever since, the nickname Bloody Island had stuck.

Over the decades scores of duels were held there. The island was isolated and afforded privacy. More importantly, the duelists need not worry about accidentally hitting innocent bystanders since only the aggrieved parties and their seconds would be present. The field of honor had claimed the lives of seven of the city's most distinguished citizens, not to mention all those who barely rated a mention in the newspaper.

Nate had viewed the island from a distance several times, but he had never been as close as now. The rowboat in which he sat was making slow progress from the riverbank to the island as the oarsman labored strenuously. He sat in the stern, facing forward. In the middle seat was a local boatman, who added to his meager income by ferrying duelists. Near the bow sat Shakespeare and Tricky Dick, the latter fidgeting nervously and frequently licking his lips.

Nate could see another rowboat already on the shore of Bloody Island. Close by were three men and a woman with radiant blond hair. Adeline! What was she doing there? Women, as a matter of decorum, were rarely present at duels. He wondered if Rhey had brought her deliberately, knowing full well her presence would distract him.

The current jostled the rowboat and the oarsman grunted as he struggled to keep the boat steady.

Nate glanced down at his flintlocks and swallowed. Although he had been the challenger, he couldn't quite believe he was actually going to take part in a duel. He knew a lot about them, as did most everyone else in the country. Duels were the accepted way of resolving otherwise irreconcilable disputes, and many famous men had fought a duel at one time or another.

President Andrew Jackson himself was a noted duelist. Before assuming the presidency he had nearly lost his life when his opponent struck him in the chest a second prior to his own fatal shot. The heavy coat Jackson often wore had saved his life by stopping the ball before it could reach his heart.

Then there had been the relatively recent duel between Secretary of State Henry Clay and Senator John Randolph of Virginia. Both had emerged unscathed, but the fact that such notable political figures routinely engaged in duels testified to the widespread practice by both the high and the low.

And here he was about to do the same, Nate reflected. They were almost to the island now, the boatman making for a strip of shore near the other rowboat. He remembered how fiercely Winona had clung to him before he left Tricky Dick Harrington's and the worried look in Zachary's eyes, and hoped he wouldn't let them down.

A tall man in a beaver hat approached as the boatman beached his small craft. "Greetings, gentlemen," he welcomed them. "I'm Abner Collins, one of Rhey Debussy's seconds."

Nate had to wait until Shakespeare, Tricky Dick, and the boatman stepped out before he could do the same. He walked over to Collins. "This is Shakespeare McNair and Dick

Harrington," he introduced his friends. "They will serve as my witnesses."

Debussy's party walked up, Rhey Debussy standing rigid and stern.

"May I introduce Maurice Evans," Collins said, indicating a short man sporting tremendous sideburns.

There were nods all around.

"Since Monsieur Debussy has been challenged, he has the choice of weapons," Collins mentioned.

"I know," Nate said, dreading a miscalculation on his part. According to the stories making the rounds, Rhey had slain four men in duels, each time with a pistol. Rhey was neither an accomplished swordsman nor very skilled with a knife. As Nate was a competent marksman, he was counting on Rhey selecting pistols as the weapon of choice. "Has he decided?"

"He has," Collins confirmed. "He has selected flintlocks and graciously allows you to use your own if you wish."

"Thank you," Nate said, relieved. By the strict code of conduct all duelists adhered to, Debussy had the right not only to pick the type of weapons used but the actual weapons themselves. Frequently the challenged party would arrive at the prearranged site bearing a set of pistols or swords with which he was intimately familiar but which his opponent had never so much as touched; the opponent was thus at a distinct disadvantage. Since Rhey was an accomplished duelist and aware of the edge he would have by supplying the arms, Nate wondered why Debussy was allowing him to use his own gun. It didn't quite make sense.

"If you have no objections, I will do the counting," Collins proposed.

"It's fine with me."

"Excellent. I will do a standard ten-count, at which time you both will wheel and fire. As Monsieur Debussy demands satisfaction, you realize that if by some chance both of you should miss, you must reload and duel again."

"I understand," Nate said. To demand satisfaction at a duel meant that it must be waged until one of the combatants died. There were duels, like the one between Randolph and Clay, in which both parties walked away unhurt because neither insisted on the ultimate sacrifice.

"Shall we?" Collins said, and motioned at a field bordering the shoreline.

They walked to the field, Nate and his friends bearing to the right, Debussy and his party to the left. Nate saw Adeline staring intently at him, but refused to meet her gaze. He halted after going 15 yards and handed one of his flintlocks to Shakespeare. "I'll want this back in a bit," he said, grinning.

McNair hefted the pistol and frowned. "Remember to turn as soon as you hear the count of ten. Don't rush your shot, but don't take forever to aim either."

"I know what to do," Nate said.

"Oh?" Shakespeare said, and poked Tricky Dick with an elbow. "He's never fought a duel in his life yet he acts like an expert."

"I could never do this," Tricky Dick said. "I'd rather tangle with a grizzly."

Nate smiled.

"Gentlemen!" Abner Collins called. He had moved farther into the field and was standing between the two groups. "Shall we begin?"

Grasping the remaining flintlock in his right hand, Nate walked to where Collins stood. Rhey approached and stopped, glaring his spite.

"You both know the code," Collins said. "Stand back-to-back and wait until I begin my count. At each number take a step. On ten turn and fire. Do either of you have any questions?"

Rhey impatiently shook his head. Nate responded, "No."

"If you are both ready, assume the position," Collins directed them.

Nate positioned himself in front of Collins and pivoted on his heel, then felt Rhey's back bump his as Debussy complied. He held the pistol with the barrel pointed skyward, as was traditional. Memories of the only duel he had personally witnessed flitted through his mind, a contest between two gamblers that had left one man dead, the other seriously wounded. Would he wind up a corpse? he wondered, and shook his head in annoyance to clear his thoughts. Now was not the time to indulge in such speculation.

"Are you ready?" Collins inquired.

"I am," Rhey replied.

"Yes," Nate said.

"Then we shall begin," Collins said, and cleared his throat. "One."

Nate took a measured stride and felt his mout abruptly go dry. He also felt oddly flushed.

"Two," Collins stated loudly, the sound of hi hurried footsteps clear as he rapidly backed awa from their line of fire.

Again Nate took a pace. His palm had becom moist with sweat and he tightened his grip o the flintlock. He began to think that Tricky Dic had been right. He should have jumped Rhey o a darkened street somewhere.

"Three!"

Nate noticed that Collins was calling out eac number louder than the one before. He wa tempted to look at Shakespeare and Tricky Dick to be reassured by their presence, but he stare straight ahead as the unwritten rules dictated.

"Four!"

An appalling weakness crept into Nate's limb and he managed the step with an effort. What wa happening? Was fear taking over? He couldn' permit that to happen.

"Five!"

The next stride was even harder. He bit hi lower lip until it hurt, using pain to force hi mind to focus. Slowly the weakness dissipated.

"Six!"

Nate saw a crow wing past the north end of th island and was reminded of the ancient supersti- tion that crows and ravens were harbingers o disaster.

"Seven!"

In 15 seconds he could be dead. The though sobered Nate like no other could. Fleeting panic welled up within him, but he suppressed it. He had chosen this course of action; he must see it through to the end.

"Eight."

Nate caressed the trigger with his finger and swore he could hear his heart pounding in his chest.

"Nine!"

He used his thumb to cock the piece and tensed his arm muscles for the motion to follow. Strangely, he seemed to have developed extraordinary hearing. The sounds of chirping birds, the lapping of the Mississippi on the shore, and even the buzz of a passing bee were as clear as could be.

"TEN!"

Nate whirled as fast as he could, a lightning spin on the soles of his feet. Then, eerily, he had the illusion that everything was transpiring slowly. He saw Rhey Debussy had also turned, saw Rhey extend his pistol, and remembered to stand sideways to make himself a smaller target as he extended his own flintlock. The birds still chirped, the Mississippi still lapped, yet the sounds were different, impossibly pronounced and melodious. He heard the blast of Debussy's pistol at the same instant smoke blossomed from the end of the muzzle, and he twisted in pain as an intense stinging sensation lanced his left shoulder. Sighting along the barrel, he saw Debussy's eyes enlarge in terror a heartbeat before he squeezed the trigger and his gun boomed and kicked ever so slightly in his hand. Nothing happened, though, and he thought he must have missed. Rhey stood there, staring blankly, until suddenly his arms went limp, his knees buckled, and he fell, pitching onto his face.

Just like that it was over.

He slowly lowered his pistol as Collins and Maurice Evans ran to Rhey. Evans rolled Debussy over and both men examined him. Adeline, curiously, stayed where she was, wringing her hands, appearing every inch a frightened little girl rather than the woman she was. He heard someone running toward him and hands clapped him on the back.

"Congratulations, son!" Shakespeare said happily.

"You won!" Tricky Dick added. "I never would have believed it if I hadn't seen it with my own eyes."

Nate felt nothing. He had expected to feel elated if victory was his, but instead he felt a bizarre emptiness deep within. His palm tingled where it touched the flintlock. He wedged the gun under his belt and opened and closed his fingers until the tingling disappeared.

Abner Collins and Evans were walking toward him.

"You have won, *monsieur*," Collins announced gravely. "Monsieur Debussy took a ball in the chest that from all indications pierced his heart. We will let everyone know the duel was fair and honorable."

"Thank you," Nate said.

"We shall take care of the body," Collins said. "There is no need for you to remain if you care to leave."

Nodding absently, Nate headed for the rowboats. His limbs were sluggish and he experienced a desire to lie down on the spot and sleep. Shrugging it off, he gained strength with every step. He was halfway to the river when a shout brought him to a halt.

"Nate! Wait! Please!"

He faced her. His friends continued to the boats without comment. Her golden hair sparkled in the sun and her features were as fresh as the morning dew. She filled out her dress as few women could and swayed suggestively as she walked.

"Spare me a minute of your time," Adeline entreated, halting and placing a tender hand on his wrist. "It's all I ask, and after all we once meant to each other it's the least you can do."

"What do you want?"

"I want to say how glad I am that you won. I knew you would," Adeline said, and grinned. "I convinced Rhey to let you use your own pistol. Told him it wouldn't be fair otherwise and I'd never speak to him again if he didn't."

Nate gazed at the body and saw a splash of crimson on Rhey's chest.

"Now I'm a free woman," Adeline declared, beaming. "Free to live as I want. To go where I please." She paused. "And to see whomever I want."

"That's nice," Nate said lamely, and started to leave, but Adeline held onto his wrist, restraining him.

"Hear me out, please," she said. "I know you must not think very highly of me after all that has happened, and I don't blame you. You shouldn't be angry at me, however, because I was as much a pawn in this affair as you were." She sidled in next to him. "Rhey used me as badly as he used you. It was his idea to try and obtain your inheritance. He made me go along with him and beat me when I objected." A trace of moisture rimmed her eyes. "Rhey was the one who shot your squaw, not me. He's the one who should bear all the blame."

Nate slowly began prying her fingers off his arm.

"I'm not finished yet," Adeline objected. "Listen, Nate. You and I meant a lot to each other once. Now we can be just like we were. All you have to do is give up your childish notions of living like some grubby Indian and come with me. Think of it! You and I together again! What do you say?"

"No."

Adeline started as if struck. "But I'm all alone! I have no one besides you! And I have no money. Rhey used the last of our funds to pay a doctor the money we owed him." Tears poured down her cheeks. "What will I do without you? What will become of me?"

"Who gives a damn?" Nate responded, and walked out of her life forever.

Chapter Thirty-Five

Nate was eager to reach Tricky Dick's and let his family know he was alive and well. He chafed at the slow crossing of the Mississippi River, and once out of the rowboat took off at a rapid clip, his long legs eating up the distance. Shakespeare effortlessly stayed by his side, but Tricky Dick had a difficult time trying to keep up and protested mildly several times.

At last they came to the tree-lined lane on which the Harrington house was located and Nate took the lead, making for the front door with a broad smile on his face. Winona and Zach would be overjoyed! And in a few weeks, after Doctor Sawyer judged Winona fit for travel, they would return to their rustic cabin in the majestic Rocky Mountains and never, ever visit so-called civilization again.

He burst into the house and opened his mouth to announce his arrival. But the sight of Winona, Zach, Blue Water Woman, and Ruth all seated at the kitchen table with their wrists tied behind their backs caused him to stop so abruptly he almost tripped over his own feet. "What in—?" he blurted out, and a hard object jammed into his spine.

"We meet again, Grizzly Killer."

Nate held himself perfectly still, chilled by the malice in the familiar voice. Behind him arose a startled exclamation from Tricky Dick, and then a warning from the intruder.

"Make one move, either of you, and I will blow this son of a bitch in half! Put your weapons on the floor and go over by the table."

Everyone knew the threat would be carried out. Nate heard scraping noises as the rifles and pistols were deposited, then watched as his friends came past him. Tricky Dick appeared apprehensive. Shakespeare was clearly furious.

"Now turn around, bastard!"

Nate obliged, keeping his hands out from his sides, and calmly returned the malevolent stare of Robert Campbell. "I should have expected you to show up here."

"It took me a while to learn where you were staying," Campbell replied, smirking. "I was spying on this house when you left earlier, and figured I'd prepare a proper welcome for you when you returned."

"What do you plan to do?" Nate asked. He noticed Campbell had previously cocked the rifle now aimed at his stomach, and all it would take was a slight tug on the trigger to send him into eternity.

"That should be obvious. I've come to kill you."

"Then let the others go. They're not part of this."

"I have no intention of laying a finger on the women and your brat," Campbell said scornfully. "But McNair and Harrington are another matter. They might try to get revenge later. I can't let them live."

"What if they pledge their word not to come after you?" Nate proposed, trying to stall, to give himself time to devise a plan. His life hung in the balance. Unless he could trick Campbell into lowering his guard for an instant, his wife and son would see him slain in cold blood.

"Not good enough," Campbell said. "Harrington might keep his promise, but not McNair. He'll agree to anything just so he can hunt me down later."

Nate had an urge to swat the rifle aside and pounce, but common sense dictated he hold still for the time being. Even if he deflected the barrel, Campbell would still get off a shot, and at such short range he was bound to be seriously wounded or worse.

"So you first," Campbell said, and tapped the butt of his rifle against one of the two flintlocks tucked under his belt. "Then your good friends." He smiled. "You have no idea how much I've anticipated getting even, how I've longed to look you in the face as you die."

"You should have left well enough alone."

Campbell took a step backwards, nearer the open door, and angrily wagged the rifle. "What? And continue to have everyone laugh at me behind my back because I could never get the best of the high and mighty Grizzly Killer?"

"No one ever made fun of you," Shakespeare spoke up.

"I know better!" Campbell snarled. "I could see the laughter in their eyes when they walked by and hear them whispering when my back was turned. I was the laughingstock of the Rendezvous and I knew it!" An enraged gleam animated his eyes and he seemed on the verge of firing.

Nate girded himself to spring. They wouldn't be able to keep Campbell talking indefinitely, and if he took the first shot it would leave Shakespeare and Tricky Dick free to jump on Campbell before the man could pull a pistol. He judged the sacrifice worthwhile if it spared the lives of his companions.

"With you out of the way," Campbell was saying, "next year I'll be the big man at the Rendezvous. I'll beat everyone at wrestling and horse racing and I'll win a bundle of money."

"All this trouble because you lost a few wrestling matches and a horse race," Nate remarked bitterly.

"It's more than that, you fool. In the mountains a man is only as good as his reputation, and you ruined mine by beating me."

"You're wrong. All we engaged in were friendly contests, nothing more. No one cared much one way or the other who won."

"I cared!" Campbell practically roared.

Nate was ready. He had tensed to leap when from behind Robert Campbell a fierce growl filled the doorway. Instinctively, Campbell glanced over his shoulder, and in that brief interval Nate lunged and plowed into his nemesis, wrapping his brawny arms around Campbell's waist and bearing both of them to the floor near the door. He glimpsed Samson, who must have come back from rabbit-hunting again in the tract of woods near the Harrington house. Then an elbow caught him on the jaw and bright stars swirled before his eyes.

He lashed out in pure reflex and struck Campbell on the chin. A knee hit his inner thigh and he began to push up off the floor; unexpectedly Campbell let go of the rifle and a knife materialized in its place. With a flick of his right hand Nate seized Campbell's wrist and held the knife at bay even as Campbell grasped his other arm. They became locked in a death struggle, each exerting himself to the utmost. As he already knew, Campbell was incredibly strong and applied inexorable pressure, slowly but surely driving the gleaming tip of the blade toward Nate's exposed throat.

Nate strained as never before. Every muscle was employed. His face became bright red and his veins bulged. But he was unable to stop the knife from edging closer. Eight inches separated his jugular from the blade, then six and four and two. In a bold gamble he suddenly slid his hand higher on Campbell's wrist, giving himself better leverage, and wrenched sharply, twisting

Campbell's arm and the knife toward Campbell as he shoved downward with all of the power in his physique.

Caught by surprise, Robert Campbell failed to counter the move. He screeched as the blade sank to the hilt into his chest, then roared with rage as he shoved Nate from him and tried to rise to his feet.

Nate drew his tomahawk. He crouched, set to attack, but Campbell was in no shape to continue the fight. Sputtering, Campbell rolled onto his side and succeeded in rising to his knees in a costly effort that brought a spurt of blood from his nostrils and mouth.

"No!" Campbell cried.

No one else spoke.

"I won't die now!" Campbell bellowed, and attempted to stand. His knife fell from his weakened fingers and he swayed as if dizzy. "No!" he cried once more, and turned a mask of vile abhorrence on Nate. "You!" he said, jabbing a finger. "You so—"

Nate saw Campbell stiffen, heard him gurgle, and straightened as Campbell collapsed, exhaled, and died. He stepped up to the body and nudged it twice to be certain before drawing the knife out of Campbell's chest and wiping the blade clean on his foe's shirt.

Tricky Dick Harrington came over, gaping first at Campbell and then at Nate. He mustered a feeble smile and said, "Don't take me wrong, Nate, but I sure am glad you don't visit all that often. You have a born knack for getting into more trouble than any man I've ever met."

"I know," Nate said, and emphasized softly. "Believe me, I know."

Weeks passed.

During that time Nate ministered to Winona as if she were a little girl instead of his wife, always there to fetch her a drink or food or whatever she might need. When not tending her he sat around and chatted with Shakespeare and Tricky Dick, and it was during one of these discussions he learned about Shakespeare's gout. Other than a few jests, he let his mentor off easy.

Finally came the day when Doctor Sawyer announced that Winona was fit to handle the long ride across the plains to the mountains. It was a sunny Wednesday afternoon and Nate walked Sawyer to the lane.

"I can't ever properly thank you for all you've done for us. You should have let me pay you more."

The doctor laughed. "How refreshing! A lot of my patients are always complaining they can't pay because of all their debts. Perhaps they'll follow your example."

Nate held out his hand. "We'll never forget your kindness." They shook, and he stood and watched the physician depart. As Sawyer reached the corner another man appeared and stopped the doctor, apparently to ask a question. Sawyer turned and pointed at Nate.

The man smiled and hurried forward. A stocky fellow with white hair and a gray mustache, he wore fine but rumpled clothes and had a brown leather satchel slung over his right shoulder. As he neared Nate he doffed his hat and pulled a handkerchief from his pocket to mop his perspiring brow. "Pardon me, sir. But are you Nathaniel King?"

"I am."

"My name is Howard Worthington. I don't know if you're aware of it, but I was your father's attorney at the time he passed on."

"Adeline told me," Nate said, shaking.

"Good. How is she, by the way? It was her letter that brought me to St. Louis, and when I went to the Debussy estate where she was supposed to be staying, I found the federal authorities had taken it over and arrested a goodly number of people. Some horrid business about importing slaves, I believe. Anyway, through an officer I learned that Adeline frequented an establishment called the Devil Tavern, and there I learned from a gentleman named Hamilton that you were staying at Richard Harrington's." He paused long enough to take a breath and glance at the house. "And here I am. That fine man back there indicated who you were. I hope you don't mind my informal manner, but I feel as if I know you after all your father told me about your upbringing."

Nate was amused by the attorney's rapid-fire style of speech. He realized that Worthington hadn't bothered to wait for an answer about Adeline, and wondered if the man was really interested in her welfare.

"It has been extremely difficult tracing your whereabouts," Worthington briskly went on. "You have no idea how hard I have been working on this case. If I'd known it was going to be so taxing, I might have refused to represent your father." He replaced his hat. "Dear man that he was, he entrusted me with executing his last will and testament, but I can't collect my full fee until the estate has finally been settled."

The attorney took another breath and Nate took advantage to get a word in edgewise. "Is it true he left a substantial inheritance?"

"What? Oh, yes. Adeline tell you that, did she? Between the money your father made investing and the sale of the house as stipulated in his will, whoever receives the inheritance stands to collect one hundred and four thousand dollars."

Nate whistled.

"Yes, sir. Your father was much wiser than Adeline's father in my opinion."

"How so?"

"Didn't she tell you? Perhaps not, given the circumstances. But her father speculated heavily after reaping hefty profits from real estate enterprises involving your father. He lost practically every penny," Worthington disclosed. He leaned forward to whisper in confidence, "Which explains why Adeline took up with that Rhey Debussy character. Rumor has it she thought he was rich and would restore her family's fortune."

So Adeline had married Rhey for his presumed wealth even as he had married her for the same reason. Nate grinned at the irony.

"But I digress," Worthington said, unslinging the satchel. "I'm sure you're more interested in the will. The money is yours provided you meet one stipulation." He opened the flap top and took out a folded sheet of paper. "It's all explained in this letter your father wrote."

Feeling unaccountably nervous, Nate took the paper and stepped to one side. He unfolded it, read the heading, and felt conflicting emotions tear at his heart. Then he plunged ahead, reading quickly:

Dearest Son:

I write this on my deathbed, the first communication we have had in years. The fault, however, is not mine. Had you been a dutiful son and stayed at home we would never have suffered so bitter an estrangement.

Here is your chance to redeem yourself. I've always cared for you the most of all my sons, and I prove this now by the offer I'm making.

Every cent I've made is yours provided you meet one small condition. You must forsake living in the wilderness like a simple savage and return to New York City. Prove your mettle by making something of yourself. Erase the dark blot put on our family name by yourself and my misguided brother Zeke.

None of my sons have turned out as I had hoped. You have all let me down with your stubbornness and stupidity. Prove that you, at least, have some sense. Accept my offer. Go into business for yourself. Justify my selfless love. Be a man for once.

Your devoted father

Nate stared at the scrawled signature for the longest while, swept up in a whirlpool of memories and feelings and thoughts. Only when the attorney coughed did he look up.

"Well?" Worthington prompted eagerly. "What is your decision?"

"Just this," Nate said, and methodically tore the letter into tiny pieces that drifted to the ground around his feet.

Worthington conveyed sincere shock. "Do you realize what you have done? Now your brothers stand to inherit the money."

"Thank you for traveling so far to see me," Nate said, and headed toward the house where Winona was waiting in the entrance.

"Do you realize what you have done?" Worthington called after him.

Nate paid no attention. He inhaled deeply, savoring the scent of the grass and the trees and a hint of moisture wafting from the Mississippi River. At the doorway he halted and put his hands on Winona's waist. "I love you," he said.

"What was that all about?"

"Nothing," Nate said. "Nothing at all." He gave her a kiss to stifle further questions, then stood back and smiled. "I'm ready to go home. How about you?"

"I was waiting for you to ask."